KILLER UNKNOWN

Lyle was found inside Death by Java. He'd gotten in because someone with a key had let him in; I was sure of it. That meant the killer had to be Valerie, Mickey, or one of her employees, which consisted of a bunch of women in pink dresses and white bows. I knew women could be killers, just like men, but it was hard to imagine someone like Farrah murdering Lyle, even as small as he was, while she was wearing a pink dress.

And there'd been no blood. Could one of the women have strangled him? Bludgeoned him to death? If so, with what? I needed to know the cause of death to even know what to think.

"Someone had to have had a good reason to kill him," Dad said, cutting into my thoughts. "I doubt it had to do with some minor health violation. He might have seen something he wasn't supposed to see. Or perhaps he had enemies beyond Valerie . . ."

Books by Alex Erickson

Bookstore Café Mysteries
DEATH BY COFFEE
DEATH BY TEA
DEATH BY PUMPKIN SPICE
DEATH BY VANILLA LATTE
DEATH BY EGGNOG
DEATH BY ESPRESSO
DEATH BY CAFÉ MOCHA
DEATH BY FRENCH ROAST
DEATH BY HOT APPLE CIDER
DEATH BY SPICED CHAI
DEATH BY ICED COFFEE
DEATH BY PEPPERMINT CAPPUCCINO
DEATH BY CARAMEL MACCHIATO
DEATH BY JAVA
CHRISTMAS COCOA MURDER
(with Carlene O'Connor and Maddie Day)

Furever Pets Mysteries
THE POMERANIAN ALWAYS BARKS TWICE
DIAL 'M' FOR MAINE COON

Cat Yoga Mysteries
A POSE BEFORE DYING
A PURRFECT DATE

Published by Kensington Publishing Corp.

Death By Java

ALEX ERICKSON

Kensington Publishing Corp.
kensingtonbooks.com

KENSINGTON BOOKS are published by

Kensington Publishing Corp.
900 Third Avenue
New York, NY 10022

All Kensington titles, imprints, and distributed lines are available at special quantity discounts for bulk purchases for sales promotion, premiums, fund-raising, educational, or institutional use. Special book excerpts or customized printings can also be created to fit specific needs. For details, write or phone the office of the Kensington Sales Manager: Attn.: Sales Department. Kensington Publishing Corp., 900 Third Avenue, New York, NY 10022. Phone: 1-800-221-2647.

KENSINGTON and the KENSINGTON COZIES teapot logo Reg US Pat. & TM Off.

First Kensington Mass MarketPrinting: November 2025

ISBN: 978-1-4967-4554-5
ISBN: 978-1-4967-4555-2 (ebook)

10 9 8 7 6 5 4 3 2 1

Printed in the United States of America

The authorized representative in the EU for product safety and compliance is eucomply OU, Parnu mnt 139b-14, Apt 123
Tallinn, Berlin 11317, hello@eucompliancepartner.com

Death By Java

1

Warm sunlight streamed in through the car's window, and I basked in a glow that was both familiar, and yet, strangely foreign. I closed my eyes against it, letting the busy world vanish as I leaned against the glass in the back seat. Yes, I knew the sun was the same one that gave light to Pine Hills, Ohio, where I lived, yet it felt somehow more special here in Redwood Village, California, where I'd grown up.

A buzz of conversation filled the car, yet I'd tuned it out ever since I'd climbed in, just wanting to enjoy a few moments of quiet now that I was no longer trapped on a plane. The stress of the last few days was slowly bleeding away, though I knew the peace would be short-lived. Concerns about fluctuating power at my bookstore café, Death by Coffee, along with the fact that I was going to be staying with my dad and his girlfriend in my childhood home with my boyfriend, Paul Dalton, at my side would soon have my anxiety skyrocketing.

But right then . . . peace.

"What do you think, Krissy?"

"Hmm?" I reluctantly opened my eyes. Paul was regarding me from where he sat buckled in, deep blue eyes sparkling in the sun.

"Were you asleep?" he asked.

"No." I stifled a yawn. "Just relaxing."

"She'll sleep like the dead for about eight hours once we're at the house," my dad, James Hancock, said from the passenger's seat up front. I couldn't see his eyes to know if they were sparkling, but his bald head sure was.

Next to him, his girlfriend, Laura Dresden, nodded. I couldn't see her face since I was sitting directly behind her, but I could *feel* her grin. "The last time she was here, we were afraid she might sleep through the entire weekend."

"Ha-ha." I stuck out my tongue, though nobody could see it. "I'm not that bad. Travel wears me out."

Paul took my hand and squeezed. There was a nervousness in his smile. While he knew Dad and Laura from their visits to Pine Hills, this was the first time he'd traveled with me to my hometown. It was a part of my life he'd only heard stories about.

Redwood Village—simply called the Village by those of us who lived there—seemed massive compared to a small town like Pine Hills, but it was still just a cozy little town, sitting just outside of the much bigger Los Angeles. In the years I'd been gone, the Village had grown by leaps and bounds, filling up with small businesses and more and more housing developments so that I was beginning to worry they'd have to change the name to something that reflected the growth. Redwood City just didn't have the same ring to it.

My phone buzzed in my lap. I glanced at the screen, then turned it back over again without answering.

"Rita?" Paul asked.

I nodded. "She wants me to call her as soon as I get to the house."

"That's, what now? Twelve texts?"

"Since we've arrived." Another ten had awaited me when we'd landed. To say Rita Jablonski wasn't happy about me leaving her behind was an understatement. She was a self-proclaimed James Hancock number-one fan, and I wouldn't be surprised if it was the truth. Dad wrote mystery and thriller novels for a living, and Rita had read every last one of them at least five times. She'd wanted to come along so she could pick Dad's brain about his latest book, but I'd refused. These next two weeks were for me, Paul, Dad, and Laura. I'd let nothing else get in the way of that.

Anxiety tried to bubble up, and I squeezed my phone to suppress it. Thinking of Rita made me think of Death by Coffee and the problems we'd been having with the electricity in the building. It had started only a few days ago, and nothing we did seemed to help. I desperately wanted to call my co-owner and best friend, Vicki Lawyer, to check in, but she'd made me promise that I'd enjoy my vacation and would let her handle it.

I gave it another hour, maybe two, before I broke down and called.

"We're supposed to have great weather," Dad said. "We should plan on hitting the beach at least a couple of times over the next two weeks to take advantage of it." He craned around the best he could to see Paul, who was sitting directly behind him. "You ever been to an ocean beach before?"

Paul shook his head. "I've never had the pleasure."

"You're going to love it." Dad turned back in his seat with a groan and a popping of his back. "I was also thinking we could check out some of the sites around the Village. We have an interesting history. Some people think it's called Redwood Village because of the redwood tree, but as you can see, there are no redwoods here. It's actually a flower . . ."

I let Dad's voice fade as I turned my attention back out my window. We'd just entered the downtown portion of the Village. Traffic wasn't too bad at this time of day, but I knew it could get hectic, especially around shift changes. There was a ton of foot traffic along wide, well-maintained sidewalks, which were decorated with various flowers, including redwood sorrels when they were in season. Even with so many people packing the walkways, the Village held that cozy vibe I'd always loved.

A contented smile started to spread across my face, but it froze when my gaze landed on a business I'd only heard about up until that very moment.

The building was situated on a popular street on a busy corner, making it a prime location for foot traffic. A sign above the door featured a cup of coffee with steam spilling from it, spelling out the words *Death by Java*. A sprinkling of beans lay around the base, next to a pair of stacked books.

"You've got to be kidding me," I muttered. I'd known my high school bully, Valerie Kemp, was opening a bookstore café, and that she was using my own shop as inspiration, but seeing it in person was something else.

I couldn't see inside the café, but I did note that most people walked past it without paying it much more than a glance. Curiosity warred with annoyance. I desperately wanted to know what it looked like inside to see if Valerie had copied the exact layout of Death by Coffee, or if she'd come up with something original. Death by Java was bigger than my own place, but it was also in a bigger town, so the increased size was understandable.

"Do you want to go in, Buttercup?" Dad asked, using the pet name he'd had for me since I was little.

I bit my lip. Did I? If Valerie was there, she'd make a scene. I just *knew* she would proudly explain how her place was *so* much better than mine, all while acting like she was paying me compliments.

"Let's stop," Paul said, squeezing my hand. "It's better to get it over with now than to let it eat at you."

I hated to admit it, but he was right. If I didn't stop in and have a look, I'd obsess over it until I did, which would ruin the trip for everyone. "Okay. Let's do it."

It took Laura five minutes to find us a place to park. Another two just to squeeze us into the space between two much larger vehicles. On-street parking could be bad in Pine Hills, but here in the Village, it was always a nightmare.

We climbed out of the car with my entire body groaning at the movement. After a good stretch, Paul took my hand, gave me a reassuring smile, and then the four of us walked the short distance to Death by Java.

"You ready for this?" Dad asked, hand on the door.

"No. But let's do it anyway."

He gave me a reassuring smile, then he opened the door.

"You know exactly what you're doing!"

The shout met us the moment we were inside. Valerie Kemp, with her spritzed, bottle-blond hair, her long, shapely legs, and insultingly trim body, was standing, her hands—manicured nails and all—pressed firmly to her hips as she faced off against a short man in a ball cap whose back was to us. She was wearing heels and a too-tight blue dress that left little to the imagination. She looked like she was ready to head out for a night on the town.

"I'm going to hit the restroom," Dad said, eyeing the confrontation with mild interest. "My bladder isn't what it used to be."

"I think I'll join you," Paul said. "That was a long flight, and I feel like I'm going to float away."

"Count me in." Laura turned to me. "You want to come along and scope out the stalls?"

"No," I said, still watching as Valerie and the guy in the hat continued to argue. "I'm okay."

Dad and Laura headed toward the back, where the restrooms were marked with large letters declaring one for men and the other for women, and below each, in smaller, yet readable print, NO EXCEPTIONS.

Paul hesitated.

"Go," I told him. "I'll be fine. I'd rather talk to Valerie without you all watching over my shoulder anyway."

Another beat, and then he leaned forward to kiss me on the cheek before half-waddling to the restroom.

"I'm only doing my job," the man in the ball cap said. He was holding a tablet with one of those rubberized cases on it that looked as if it had been dropped numerous times. "If you would just—"

"I can't believe this!" Valerie spun, took two angry steps away, then stormed right back over, heels *clack*ing on the hard floor. "You're trying to run me out of business. You're jealous of my success!"

"Success" might have been a strong word, I thought, looking around. The tables were clean*ish*, as was the floor. The trash bins weren't quite overflowing, but I think that had to do with a decided lack of customers more than them having been emptied recently. There were no stairs leading to the bookstore portion of the bookstore café like there were at Death by Coffee, but the design was similar. The bookshelves were nice, but the books themselves appeared to have been shoved haphazardly into place with no rhyme or reason. Some were practically hanging off the shelves, as if someone had tossed them back without bothering to stand them upright.

Casually, hoping not to be noticed, I slinked around the side so I could get a look at the menu board behind the counter. A pair of young women, both dressed in pink dresses with white bows at the waist, stood watching the exchange between Valerie and the man. One was snapping and popping her gum in interest, while the other appeared bored, as if this was something that happened on a daily basis.

"Jealous? Have you looked at this place?" the man said. "I'm being generous if anything!"

"Generous! I ought to—"

"Val." Another man stepped forward and put a meaty hand on Valerie's wrist, stopping her from saying whatever it was she'd had to say. He was tall and muscular, with that bronzed look about him that spoke of a lot of time spent under the sun.

"Now, listen here, Mickey—"

"No, *you* listen, you pipsqueak," the man, Mickey, said. He flexed biceps that were clearly gym-made and rolled his head, causing his neck to crack and pop. "I've had just about enough of you coming in here and harassing my Val."

My Val? I kept my gaze glued to the menu board, though I had yet to read it. Last I'd heard, Valerie was dating a guy named Hugh.

"I'm not harassing anyone!" the man with the tablet said. "I'm telling you, the condition of the—"

"You'd better be more concerned about *your* condition, egghead." Mickey advanced a step.

The man in the cap backed up a step, toward the door. "You can't keep me out of here like this. I have a right to inspect the machines."

"You have a right to leave." Mickey grinned, clearly thinking himself a genius for his high school–quality comebacks.

The man looked from Mickey to Valerie, then decided to cut his losses as he turned and walked out of Death by Java. I half-expected Mickey to shout, *"And stay out!"* after him, but all he did was clap his hands together as if knocking away dust before turning and walking back behind the counter and through a door, into the back room.

Which left me as the only other person, other than Valerie and her employees, in the dining area.

"Krissy Hancock?" Valerie said, gaze zeroing in on me. "Is that really you?"

A denial was on my lips, but instead, I smiled. "It is. Hi, Valerie."

Heels *clack*ing, Valerie crossed the distance between us and surprised me by giving me a hug that consisted of all arms and a lot of air between us.

"It's good to see you!" she said before turning to her two employees. "Dee. Nadia. This is Krissy. She's the one with that basic little coffee shop I told you about."

Both Dee and Nadia gave me a tight smile before going back to staring vacantly around the room.

I somehow kept my own smile in place, despite the jab at Death by Coffee. With Valerie, that sort of thing was expected. She'd never been good at compliment-ing anyone, other than herself. As a kid, she was the poster child for the snooty, popular girl, who only cared about herself, and she'd apparently never grown out of it.

"Who was that?" I asked, nodding toward the exit.

"Him?" Valerie made a face. "Lyle Carrigan. He's no one. Just some health inspector who's been doing his best to make my life miserable for the last month or so."

A health inspector. Quite suddenly, I wasn't too keen on buying a coffee, despite needing a jolt of caffeine after my long flight.

"What brings you to California?" Valerie asked, taking a step back to look me up and down. "You don't look like you're here for anything too special, not dressed like that. Did you hear about us all the way back in Michigan?"

"Ohio," I corrected. "Pine Hills."

Valerie waved a dismissive hand in front of her face. "Whatever. Same difference."

Her tone was really rubbing me the wrong way, which was why I let my annoyance get the better of me when I said, "It seems dead in here. Is it always like this?"

I expected Valerie to come off with some smart remark about how her place was so much better than mine, but she surprised me by saying, "I don't know what's going on. I've done everything right. I looked at what you did and improved on it in every way, yet I can't seem to draw in customers!"

Perhaps it has something to do with your attitude. My lips puckered, ready to deliver the verbal jab, but thankfully, Dad, Laura, and Paul chose that moment to return, keeping me from saying it.

"I feel better," Dad said, joining us. "Valerie. It's good to see you."

She gave him one of those brief, not-quite-a-smile expressions that was just this side of impolite.

"Are you getting anything?" Paul asked as he took my hand. "I could go for a coffee."

Valerie's gaze latched on to our hands and, oddly, she stiffened. "You saw Mickey, right? He and I just recently started dating. He's a dear. He helps out around the place quite a bit. Aaron and Hugh stop in when

they can, too. I can't seem to keep them away." A titter-
ing laugh followed.

Aaron was her ex-husband, and as I mentioned before, Hugh was her ex, so I found it hard to believe either man would come around. Then again, it wasn't
like Valerie chose boyfriends based on intelligence, so
who knew?

"That's nice," I said, tugging on Paul's hand as I
eased toward the door. "We really should get going. It
was nice to see you, Valerie."

Panic flashed across Valerie's face. "You know, I
wouldn't mind if you stopped in again soon. Perhaps
you could give me some pointers on how you manage
to lure people into your place? I tried to advertise, gave
out samples, but it didn't help. I'm not sure how people
are overlooking us, and maybe you'd be able to, I don't
know, help."

I glanced around at the café, at the emptiness of the
place, and felt a brief flare of guilt and compassion.
Valerie and I had never gotten along, but I wasn't one
to hold a grudge. "I'll think about it," I said. "But the
next couple of weeks are for family. If I get a chance,
I'll—"

"Thank you!" Valerie grabbed my free hand and
squeezed. "I don't know what I'll do if I'm forced to
close because people around here don't know a good
thing when they see it."

I extracted my hand from Valerie's grip, fought
down a massive eye roll. "Good luck. I'll see you around,
Valerie."

I led the way out the door. Relief flooded me as I

was back out under the sun and away from Valerie's desperation. I felt bad for her, I really did. But I had a feeling the problems with her bookstore café had a lot more to do with how she treated her customers than a problem with visibility or their awareness of Death by Java's existence.

"That was fun," Dad said as the door closed behind us.

"Shush, you." Laura nudged him with her elbow, though she was smiling as she did.

"Get out! Now!"

I jumped at the shout coming from next door. A bald man with a sweaty scalp, wearing a mustard-stained apron, was physically shoving Lyle the health inspector out the door of a place called Tito's Deli. A name tag hanging from the apron declared the bald man to be Tito himself.

"I have a right to—"

"I don't have time for you or your rights," Tito said with a final shove. "Come back when I'm not so busy." A pause. "And when you're not being paid to harass hardworking folk!"

With that, he spun and slammed the door in Lyle's face.

The health inspector stood there a long moment, as if debating on whether he should go back in, before he tapped something into his tablet. That done, he walked quickly away, muttering to himself.

"Let's get out of here," I said.

Dad nodded. "Agreed."

I leaned in close to Paul. "I promise the Village isn't like this all of the time."

He laughed. "It's kind of charming."

That was one word for it, I supposed.

"If you want to see charming, there's this park on the south end of town you just have to experience," Dad said as we started back to the car. "Krissy used to go there all the time and . . ."

I groaned inwardly, but let him rattle on. I had a feeling that by the end of this trip, Paul was going to know everything about my childhood, whether I wanted him to or not.

2

"So . . ." Paul made a slow circuit around the room. "This is where you grew up, huh?"

I flopped onto the bed, arms spread. The mattress was slightly too cushy, causing me to sink down farther into it than I liked. It wasn't my childhood bed, yet a contented groan escaped my lips, and I considered just closing my eyes and drifting off for a well-deserved nap. Though, as late as it was, the nap would likely end up turning into a nightlong sleep, but right then, I was okay with that.

"It seems kind of bland for you," he went on. "Are you sure this was your bedroom as a kid?"

I cracked open an eye to find Paul examining a plain brown dresser with a white doily atop it. "Yes, this was my room. Still is, I suppose. But if you haven't noticed, I've grown up."

The room was admittedly lacking in the decorations department. When I'd moved out for college, Dad had kept the room as I'd left it. But once I'd made the trek to Pine Hills to open Death by Coffee with Vicki, he'd begun the process of turning it into a guest room. I'd taken most of my things with me, and those that I'd left behind were likely stored away in a box somewhere. Knowing Dad, he wouldn't have thrown anything out.

"It's nice," Paul said. "My childhood bedroom was the size of a shoebox. I could roll from my bed, right out the door." He said it fondly, with a wistful smile. "You have enough room in here for a whole gaggle of teenage girls."

"Yeah, well, the gaggle consisted of Vicki and only a couple of others." I wondered where those other high school friends might be, how their lives were going. As far as I knew, they were still living in the Village, though I couldn't be sure. I'd gone to the same college as Vicki, so we'd kept in touch, but my other friends had chosen different paths. Back then, without the fancy cell phones and social media we had today, it wasn't as easy to keep in contact, so we'd slowly drifted apart.

"I imagine Valerie wasn't one of those friends."

I snorted, closed my eye again. "Hardly. I think she was in the house once. Maybe twice. We were part-nered in my high school Spanish class and had to make chili for some silly competition. She showed up and watched me do all the work, criticizing me all the while."

"Did you win?"

"No. The winning chili wasn't edible. They used the hottest peppers they could find, which meant it got all the votes because it made Mr. Salazar sick."

"Figures." He chuckled, then sobered. "So, what's the sleeping arrangements?"

I patted the bed without looking at him. "It's big enough to share."

A beat. "You don't think I should sleep on the floor? Or in another room, perhaps? I don't mind the couch."

"Dad wouldn't hear of it. If you don't want to sleep beside me . . ."

"Oh no, I do. It's just . . ."

"I get it. It's weird for me too." Though I was old enough that it shouldn't have been. It's what I got for never having a real boyfriend while living here. It made something as simple as sleeping next to someone a new experience, one I was strangely nervous about.

"Where's the bathroom?" Paul asked. "I think I need to splash some water on my face."

"First door on your right," I said, making a vague gesture in that direction before propping up and looking at him. "Are you okay? This isn't too much for you, is it?"

"I'm fine." His smile had an uncertain edge to it. "Just nervous."

"Don't be. You know Dad and Laura love you."

"I know. I just don't want to rock any boats."

"You won't."

"I'll get over it after a good night's sleep." He leaned over and kissed my forehead. "I'll be right back." With that, he slipped out the door, closing it softly behind him.

As soon as he was gone, I fished out my phone and put in a call.

"Hey, Krissy," Vicki said, sounding out of breath. "I take it that you made it okay?"

"Safe and sound. How are things at Death by Coffee?"

A pause, and then, "Good. Mason had a look—"

I couldn't help it; I groaned.

"Don't groan at me. He can be handy when he wants to be."

"Sorry." I grunted as I rolled to my feet. "That wasn't a groan because I didn't think Mason was incapable of fixing anything. My bed was trying to eat me."

"There's a joke in there somewhere that I'm going to let slide," Vicki said. "Just be glad Mason didn't hear you."

"Oh, I am." A beat, and then I asked, "What did he find?"

"It's more like what he *didn't* find. The lights went out again, and since Mason was here at the time and he had his tools with him, he went ahead and had a look. He couldn't find anything wrong. All the stuff that was supposed to light up lit up, and everything else checked out, whatever that means. I called the electrician again and got the same runaround, so who knows when they'll show up."

"If ever."

"I know. It's been three days, and it seems to be getting worse. Something's not right, and I'm afraid there's a short somewhere that will end up starting a fire if it isn't taken care of." She made a frustrated sound. "I don't even know if that's possible. I talked to a few other business owners on the street, and none of them are having any issues, so it appears as if it's isolated to just our place."

"Do you think we should shut down?" I asked, dreading the answer. Shutting down meant no business. And no business meant it would be hard to pay the bills, especially if the electrician, a man known to be on the glacial side of slow, kept dragging his feet about fitting us onto the schedule.

"Not yet. I'm keeping a close eye on things. Besides, you're in California. You shouldn't be worrying about this."

"I know, but—"

"No buts. Have fun. If you want to punish yourself, go say hi to my parents. I'm sure they'll have a lot to talk to you about."

I laughed. "I'll bet." Vicki's parents, Gina and Frederick Patterson, blamed me for Vicki not choosing to follow in their footsteps by acting in low-budget films, and they weren't afraid to let me know it. "I guess I should go." Down the hall, the bathroom door squeaked open. "I'll check back in a day or so."

"You do that. Hopefully, I'll have news by then."

I clicked off just as Paul returned. Laura was right behind him, dressed in running shorts and a tank top, with her hair pulled back out of her face in a loose ponytail.

"Sorry to bother you two," she said, "but I was about to head out for a walk and was wondering if either of you wanted to come with me. James is staying here, so if you want to hang out with him, I understand."

I looked over at Paul. "Well . . ."

"If you want to go, go," he said. "I could use a little downtime myself." He stifled a yawn as he sat on the edge of the bed. His eyes briefly widened and his legs splayed outward as the mattress gave way and tried to swallow him.

"You don't have to if you don't want to," Laura said. "I like the company, but I have earbuds for that too."

"No, I want to go," I said. "Just because I'm here, doesn't mean I should skimp on my exercise." I'd been trying to stay active over the last few months and had been seeing results. I wasn't back to my college-age weight, but I was getting there. Slowly. "Give me a few minutes to get changed, and I'll meet you in the living room."

Laura shot me a thumbs-up, then headed back down the hall.

Paul shifted onto the bed so that he was lying across it, hand supporting his chin. "Mind if I watch?" he asked.

I closed the door by way of answer. Then I dug out my running clothes and made a show of getting changed. I left him grinning a few minutes later.

"Ready?" Laura asked from the dining room, where Dad was sitting at the table with his tablet, which, unlike Lyle Carrigan's, didn't have a protective case over it. He was squinting at the screen in a way that made me think he was looking over a publishing contract and was struggling to make sense of the legalese.

"Ready."

A quick peck from each of us on Dad's cheek, and then Laura and I headed out into the California evening.

Dad's house was situated in a residential district populated by wealthier, but not filthy-rich, residents of the Village. It wasn't too far from downtown, and that was the direction Laura headed when we started our walk. A surreal feeling washed over me as we began. Memories of running down this very street as a kid, of trick-or-treating at these very houses, warred with the here and now. Families I'd once known had moved. Additions were added to houses. New siding, new roofs, new lives. I knew the area, and yet, at the same time, I didn't.

"You okay?" Laura asked after a few minutes of silence.

"Yeah. Just thinking." We passed by Valerie's old house. Her parents still lived there, as was indicated by the KEMP in big, block letters by the door. They, like Valerie, always had a certain air about them, one I'd much rather steer clear of. "I've been back to the Village often over the last few years, yet this time feels different."

"Is it because Paul is here?"

I shrugged. "Maybe? I don't know. It's the same as I remembered, and yet . . ."

"I get it," she said. "You might need some time to settle in. You just got here a few hours ago, and it's"—she glanced at her watch—"nearly ten in Ohio. Your entire system probably needs time to adjust."

I didn't think that was it, but I let it go. Talking about it was only making me feel melancholy, like I'd left and the Village had moved on without me. *Which is the natural state of the world.* Weird how you never think about it like that until you're confronted with it. "How're things going with you and Dad?" I asked.

Laura's smile lit up her entire face. "Great, actually. There was a bit of a bumpy stretch when I moved into the house, but that was more because I felt self-conscious about it. He's lived there for years, and here I was coming in, feeling as if I was trying to replace your mom." She shook her head as her smile faded. "I know no one else saw it that way, but I couldn't help it."

"Mom would be happy for him," I said, and I meant it. "She wouldn't have wanted Dad to be alone. She would have loved you."

Laura blinked rapidly and coughed into her hand, clearly overcome. It took her a moment before she could speak again. "We've talked about moving." She glanced at me askance. "You know? Finding a place to start over that's just ours? He's the one who broached the subject, though I can tell he doesn't really want to move."

My heart hiccupped. I hadn't lived in that house for more years than I cared to admit, yet the thought of it no longer being Dad's house made me feel as if I was about to lose my own home. Him moving meant that when I came back, I'd be staying somewhere else, somewhere unfamiliar. It wouldn't be like coming home anymore.

"And?" I asked.

"And I don't think a move would be good for him. There're too many good memories for him there. And even if there weren't, it's a good house, in a good location. I feel at home there, and I know he does too."

Up ahead, downtown Redwood came into view. Most of the businesses were closed, or near closing, so traffic was minimal. There were still a decent number of pedestrians walking down the sidewalk, enjoying the pleasant night air, but most of them were out for ventures other than shopping. The bars and restaurants were all likely packed, and they would be until late in the evening, despite it being a weekday.

Laura and I fell into a comfortable rhythm, legs and arms pumping. We weren't power walking, but it wasn't a casual stroll anymore either. I was handling it pretty well, thanks to my recent exercise routine, though my body was a little confused about the timing since back home in Ohio, I would be settling in with my orange long-haired cat, Misfit, for the night.

"There's a light on."

I looked toward where Laura was pointing.

Death by Java did, indeed, have a light on inside, though it was faint. No one was outside the bookstore café other than a couple people walking by. Tito's Deli was closed and completely dark next door, making the soft glow coming from inside Valerie's place of business seem all the more curious.

"Strange," I said. "Maybe she's fixing whatever it is that the health inspector was complaining about."

"Do you think you're going to help her?" Laura paused at a crosswalk, then we crossed, putting us on the path to Death by Java. "She seemed pretty desperate when we left earlier."

"I'm not sure." And I'd tried not to think too much about it.

Since we were already headed that way, we continued toward Death by Java. There was no harm in having a little look, and it didn't mean I planned on helping Valerie. I was, to put it bluntly, curious. A light on after closing wasn't really all that strange. I'd been in Death by Coffee after hours countless times. And, really, it was still early, with darkness yet to fully fall.

The door was locked, and a sign on the door proclaimed the bookstore café to be closed, as expected. The light was coming from the back room, its door propped open by something I couldn't see from outside. The glow held steady for a couple of seconds before it shifted, causing the light to dim. A beat later, and it steadied once more.

"That was odd," Laura said.

I made a noncommittal sound. I was getting weird vibes from the place. The movement of the light had reminded me of a flashlight, not an overhead bulb, though it was hard to tell since the back-room door was only open partway, and I couldn't see anything beyond. As far as I knew, there was a desk lamp back there, and Valerie, or one of her employees, had walked in front of it.

"I come by here on my walks all the time, and I've never seen a light on inside this late before." Laura cupped her hands around her eyes and peered through the glass.

"We should probably go before someone thinks we're trying to break in." No one was paying us any mind, yet I was getting creeped out.

Laura nodded, and we turned back the way we'd come.

The walk back to Dad's was uneventful and full of

light chatter about plans for the next two weeks. Shopping and beach trips were heavy on the agenda, and I couldn't say I was unhappy about that. Though, after our nighttime visit to Death by Java, I was thinking I might at least talk to Valerie and see what I could learn about her troubles.

And to make sure it really was her back there and not a thief. Though why anyone would steal anything from a struggling bookstore café, I wouldn't know.

By the time we were back to the house, I was ready to call it a night and head for bed. The time difference between California and Ohio always got to me, and I was sure Paul was struggling as well.

"Oh, my Lordy Lou! You can't be serious!"

Rita Jablonski's voice hit me like a slap in the face. It had come from the dining room, of which I could see little from the front door. Indignation warred with frustration as I marched across the living room and toward the dining room, where Dad had just chuckled and asked, "Would I lie to you?"

"Well, now, how would I know?" Rita said. "You've bamboozled me in your stories more than once. Who's to say you couldn't do the same to my face!"

"Stories are different," Dad said. "Honesty with one's readers is paramount to keeping a good relationship with them, especially with such an important reader as yourself."

"Oh my!" Rita sounded breathless.

I entered the dining room, already talking, and with Laura right behind me. "What do you think you're doing here—" I cut off in surprise when I saw what awaited me.

Dad was sitting at the table, a steaming mug of coffee next to his tablet, which was propped up in front of him. Rita's smile filled the screen, so close that she had to be holding her own device inches from her face.

"Why, there she is," Rita said, pulling back slightly so that I could see the pillow behind her head. "I was beginning to wonder if you'd make an appearance tonight."

"Hey, Buttercup," Dad said, glancing back. "Have a nice walk?"

"I . . . What . . . ? How . . . ?" I sputtered.

"It's video chat, dear." Rita gave an exaggerated roll of her eyes. "I realized that I could talk with James without leaving the comforts of my own bed, so I sent him a message, asking if he'd like to have a little pow-wow, and he agreed!"

"I couldn't look at that contract any longer," Dad said. "Rita gave me the perfect excuse to set it aside for a little while."

"I . . ." Was speechless.

"It's better than the alternative." Laura spoke low enough that only I could hear.

"I think I'm going to bed," I said. It took my brain a moment to realize that Paul was nowhere in sight. "Paul?"

"He hasn't come out since you left," Dad said with a chuckle. "I think he crashed the moment you were out the door."

I nodded. Lucky him.

"Goodnight, Buttercup," Dad said. "I'll see you in the morning."

"Goodnight, Dad." And then, because she was there, "Rita."

"Goodnight, dear. Remember, you're not at home, so you and Paul had better be on your best behavior. You wouldn't want your father to know what you two get up to at night."

Laura's sudden snort of laughter had her turning and fleeing into the living room. Dad, for his part, turned a deep shade of crimson, which likely matched my own sudden flush.

Thoroughly embarrassed, I fled, determined to keep my bedroom door wide open and a light on, not just for tonight, but for the entire two weeks ahead.

3

I stifled a yawn as I waited for the coffee to finish percolating. I was out of bed at first light and had quietly taken my morning shower before I'd headed to the kitchen to get the coffee started. Paul was still soundly asleep, mummified in a blanket he'd wrapped around himself, as if making sure there was no chance we'd accidentally touch during the night. It was kind of cute—and appreciated, considering Rita's comments.

Down the hall, a door opened. A few moments later, Laura appeared, wrapped in a blue robe that was cinched at the waist. Her hair was only slightly mussed from sleep. When she saw me at the counter, she smiled and came over to join me.

"Did you sleep okay?" she asked as she leaned against the counter.

I made a so-so gesture with my hand. "Let's just say Rita's parting shot had me wishing for bunk beds."

Laura laughed. "You're not the only one it got to. Your dad spent most of the night at the edge of the bed, like he was afraid you might walk in on us at any moment. I swear, he nearly fell out of it at least twice."

"I think Paul was about to go sleep on the couch."

"Maybe we should arrange a little living room campout for the boys. I'm sure they'd love it. It might send them right back to their childhoods."

"Send who, where?" Dad spoke through a yawn as he entered the kitchen.

Laura winked at me before pushing away from the counter. "Pancakes? I'm cooking."

By the time the pancakes were done and coffee served, Paul had joined us, looking as rough as I felt. We sat around the small, circular table, like a real family. No one was married here, and Dad and I were the only two who were related, but there was definitely a sense of *right* as we dug in.

And yet . . .

I poked at my pancakes, barely tasting them. They were good, don't get me wrong, but my mind was elsewhere, and I couldn't seem to get it focused on the here and now.

"What's wrong, Buttercup?" Dad asked, setting aside his fork.

"It's nothing."

A shared look around the table.

"That doesn't sound like nothing," Paul said while the other two nodded.

"It's just . . ." I sighed. "It's Valerie. I know I don't owe her anything, yet I feel guilty for not helping her when she asked. I'm pretty sure we could all tell that Death by Java was struggling."

"I'm not sure there's much you can do to save that

place," Laura said. "I hate to say it, but it's true. There's a negative vibe that I think the customers can feel."

"I know." I stabbed at a square of pancake with my fork and let it hang there, uneaten. "But if she is forced to close and I didn't at least *try* to give her a few pointers, I'd feel terrible. I mean, it's not like I'm some great businesswoman or anything. Vicki takes care of a lot of the business side of things, but some of the basics . . ." I shoved the bite into my mouth, talked through it. "I could do that."

"Why don't you talk to her?" Dad asked. "Stop in, take her on a tour of her own place. You could point out any problem areas you see, tell her what you think she should do to fix them. You could talk to her employees, show them how you do things, and if they take your advice, great. If not . . ." He shrugged. "That's on them."

"Your dad and I can show Paul around town while you do that," Laura said.

"Take him to that park I mentioned yesterday," Dad added.

I mulled it over, made a face. "I'm here for you," I said. "Not Valerie. I'd feel bad skipping out on you for this."

"You're here for two weeks," Dad said. "I'm pretty sure we could spare you for a few hours. It's not like I'm saying you should spend all day there. Go in, have your say, and then be done with it. It'll make you feel better."

"Otherwise, you'll obsess over it all week," Paul added.

He was right, but I didn't want him to be. I mock-pouted and muttered, "I don't obsess."

Another shared look around the table. Thankfully,

no one contradicted me, or else I'd have obsessed over *that* all day.

"We can drop you off once we're done here," Dad said. "We'll take Paul to that park, show him around." He grinned. "I have a few stories I can tell him about some of the trouble you got into as a kid. Do you remember that time you saw the squirrel go into that hole and you—"

"*Not* another word!" I pointed my fork threateningly at him.

Dad raised his hands in surrender, though the mischievous grin told me that *that* little tale wouldn't be our secret for long.

"Are you sure you don't want me to come along?" I asked, aiming the question at Paul. "I don't want you to feel abandoned. We're here together."

He pulled me into a one-armed hug and kissed my temple. "I'll be fine. Go. Help Valerie. Clear your mind. It'll make the rest of the trip go by that much smoother."

With the plan decided upon, Paul and I cleaned up our breakfast dishes while Dad and Laura got ready for the day. And then, the next thing I knew, I was climbing out of Dad's car and walking the short distance to Death by Java, which appeared as dead as ever from the outside. I paused outside the door, gave the three of them a thumbs-up, then pushed my way inside.

"It was fine when I left yesterday!" Valerie's wail met me the second I was through the door.

"Be that as it may, it doesn't work now. I can't let this slide."

Lyle Carrigan, the health inspector, was back and

was standing behind the counter with Valerie and two of her employees. One of them had been there yesterday, while the other, a tall, pale blonde with a snarky grin, was new to me. They both stood off to the side, watching, as Valerie once again confronted Lyle about problems with the bookstore café, with the employee I recognized looking somewhat nervous by the outburst. Two customers sat in the dining area, watching the show like it was a soap opera, with their mostly full cups sitting in front of them.

"I'm getting it fixed," Valerie said. "I've got someone coming as we speak."

"And yet . . ." Lyle glanced around. "I'm here now and don't see anyone fixing it."

"We just opened!" The frustration was thick in Valerie's voice. "Farrah found the problem like fifteen minutes ago! What do you expect me to do?"

Lyle tapped something into his tablet, then turned off the screen. "Look, I can't help it. The ice machine isn't working. There's water leaking onto the floor. It's a health hazard, so I have to cite you. If it was up to me, I'd give you a pass on this one, but it's not. I need to follow the rules or else it's my job."

Valerie bit her lower lip and stepped closer to Lyle. "Are you sure there's nothing that can be done? We could talk about it, make sure everything gets fixed to your standards. If you have nowhere else to be, we could sit down and hash things out. You know, in the back."

A beat, and then Lyle cleared his throat. When he spoke, there was a decided hitch to his voice. "No, I'm sorry. I'll be back later to make sure everything is in order, but for now . . ." He looked wildly around the room, then spun and all but ran past me and out the door.

"Jerk!" Valerie stomped a foot as she shouted after him, before she herself spun and stormed into the back room.

Show over, the pair of customers rose and left, leaving their coffees on the table. That left me alone up front with Farrah and the other girl—Dee or Nadia, I wasn't sure which. The gum-popping one.

"Can I get you something?" Dee/Nadia asked.

I approached the counter. "Actually, I was hoping to talk to Valerie. I run a bookstore café in Ohio, and she asked for my help."

"Oh yeah," she said. "I remember you now." She popped her gum, didn't make a move to call for Valerie.

"Could you get her for me?" I asked. "Tell her it's Krissy." When she still just stood there, staring at me, I said, "I didn't catch your name."

"I'm Nadia," she said. "That's Farrah." She stared at me blankly.

"So . . ." I looked from Nadia to Farrah. "Could one of you yell back for Valerie for me?"

There was a beat before Nadia said, "Sure. Let me get her."

Nadia spun and *clack*ed her way to the back. Farrah eyed me a moment, then fished a phone out from beneath her pink dress somewhere. She tapped it a few times, her pink nails *clack*ing against the screen in a way that sounded like it might be marking it up.

"I take it the pink is part of the uniform?" I asked, earning a half-smile and a subtle head bob I took for a nod. "Do you like working here?"

"It's all right." That was followed by a not-so-subtle step away from me.

Okay, then. I took the hint and let it go, choosing instead to take a more thorough walk-through of the dining area. Even though it was close to open, there was already trash on the floor, along with a smear of something that looked like chocolate on one seat. A cobweb hung on the bathroom sign, and I noted that one of the doors didn't close all way, leaving a gap that anyone could peek through. I decided not to see how the bathroom stalls looked, at least not yet.

I worked my way back toward the front, picking up and tossing the coffee cups into the trash as I did. Farrah was watching me over the top of her phone with disapproval, but she didn't tell me to stop as I bent over and picked up a balled-up napkin and threw it away.

It took five more minutes before Nadia returned. Valerie floated out right behind her.

"Krissy?" Valerie rounded the counter and joined me. She was wearing flats, and her outfit was a little less showy than the last time I'd seen her, though the jeans were tight and fashionably ripped and her blouse was pure and white as snow, hinting that she didn't plan on working with anything messy. "What are you doing here?"

"Hi, Valerie. I thought about what you said yesterday, and well . . ." I spread my arms. "Here I am."

A scrunching of her nose betrayed her when she

smiled that fake smile of hers, the one that attempted to be polite, but was more condescending than anything. "That's great. It is kind of a bad time, though."

"Your ice machine." At her nod, I said, "I heard you and Lyle talking when I came in."

"I don't know what happened." She made a frustrated sound. "It was fine last night when I left. I even came back after closing because I forgot—" She cut off abruptly and gave me a look like I'd tried to coax her into incriminating herself in some sort of crime. "Well, never mind that. Everything was in tip-top order when I left."

"You checked the ice machine when you were here?"

"Well, not *checked* it. But I was in the back, so I saw it. There was no water on the floor, and I heard it make that racket it does when it's making ice."

I considered that, then asked, "What time did you leave last night?"

"I don't know? Six, maybe? I wasn't keeping track. Why?"

Six was well before Laura and I had gone on our walk. "I walked past just before dark, and I saw a light on in the back room and thought that it might have been you."

"No." Her eyes flickered away, back again. "It was still light out when I left. I don't like being here after dark. It's creepy. You were probably mistaken."

"It was on back there." I pointed toward the door, just in case she somehow didn't get it. "I couldn't be sure, but I thought it might have been a flashlight. Or perhaps a desk light someone walked past? The door was propped open, and the light dimmed at one point and—"

"No one was here," Valerie said, voice going hard. "There was no light on." She turned. "Farrah, was the back-room light on when you got here this morning?"

Farrah's eyes flickered up from her phone. She gave the briefest of head shakes before she was right back to perusing whatever was on her screen.

"See?" Valerie said, turning back to me. "No light. Like I said, you must have been mistaken. Maybe you saw a reflection from next door or something and thought it was a light in here."

I wanted to continue to argue, but why? She clearly wasn't going to believe me, or at least, admit that she might have been here later than she'd said. It made me wonder what Valerie could have possibly been doing that she wouldn't want anyone else to know about?

Perhaps something like sabotaging her own ice machine.

Though why she would do that, I had no idea.

"If that's all . . ." Valerie edged away from me. "I really have a lot to do. I'm waiting for the repairman, and I have . . . *stuff* to manage."

The urge to call Dad and have him come get me was strong, but I knew that if I left now, I'd regret it later. I was here for a reason, and despite Valerie's evasiveness—and attitude—I wanted to get it over with.

"How about I do a thorough walk-through around the place?" I asked. "I'll make a list and give you a few suggestions on how you can improve. You *did* want me to help you attract more customers, right? This is how we can do that."

Valerie made a face, like the thought of me wandering around her bookstore café was enough to make her ill.

Before she could reject the idea, however, the door opened, and a guy who looked like a stripper playing the part of a repairman entered. The top three buttons of his shirt were undone, revealing a bronzed, hairless chest. A belt, with tools that looked as if they'd never been used, hung loosely from his hips. He wore shorts with sandals, and had one of those rope anklets around his left ankle.

"Roman! Thank goodness you're here." Valerie spun and rushed over to him. "I was just about going insane with worry."

"Hey, babe," Roman said with a wide smile, revealing perfectly straight, pearly white teeth. "What appears to be the problem?"

"It's in the back." And together, they walked off.

Abandoned, I decided to go ahead and do my walkthrough, with or without Valerie's permission. Chances were good she wouldn't care what I found. I'm not sure what that said about me, other than "gullible." Both Nadia and Farrah were watching me with disinterest, so I got started.

Using an app on my phone, I took notes about what I saw. I figured that I could send the list to Valerie and if she decided to make changes, great. If not, I'd at least tried. I mentioned the cobweb, along with a note that she might want to consider removing the NO EXCEPTIONS sign since it came off as insensitive and insulting. The bathrooms themselves were surprisingly clean, but one of the toilets in the women's room had a slow leak that someone had stopped up with a wad of paper towels. I assumed Lyle had already pointed that out to Valerie, but I made a note of it anyway.

From there, I headed into the bookstore portion of the store, but before I could peruse the shelves up close, a threatening *hiss*, followed by a deep-throated growl, stopped me in my tracks.

The black and white cat was tucked away in a shadowy corner of the room, which was why I hadn't noticed him—and I could tell it was a him since he wasn't fixed. His fur was grimy, and a dirty, almost black, streak ran across his nose. Hackles raised, he turned sideways and arched his back, making himself look bigger. His eyes narrowed as he growled and hissed again.

"Nice kitty," I said, easing back a step. "Go back to sleep. I'm leaving."

That earned me another hiss and a growl so deep, it seemed to vibrate through the floor. Then, as I backed past the bookshelves, the cat eased back down, tail swishing.

"What was *that*?" I asked Nadia once I was safely at the counter. I pointed in the general direction of where I'd left the cat.

Nadia snapped her gum, craned her neck to get a better look, then leaned back with a smile. "That's Oscar."

"Oscar? Whose cat is he?"

Nadia shrugged one shoulder. "The store's? We just let him hang. Dee takes care of him when she comes in, though she didn't show up today."

"Is he safe?" I asked. "For the customers, I mean."

Nadia gnawed on her gum a moment as she thought about it. "I mean, he's only bit a couple of people.

Don't get too close, and you should be okay." A pause. "So, like, shouldn't you buy something if you want to hang around?"

Bit a couple of people. If Lyle hadn't already seen Oscar, I'm sure he'd love to know that a feral cat was living in the bookstore.

But I didn't want to be the one to turn Oscar in. It wasn't his fault Valerie was letting him stay. He was probably just looking for somewhere comfortable to sleep. It made me wonder if she'd taken care of him in any way at all, gotten him his shots, or even *fed* him. I hadn't seen water or food dishes, let alone a litter box, during my quick peek.

I'd bring it up with Valerie the next time I saw her.

Nadia stepped over to the register, a clear hint to order a drink or leave.

"Sure," I said with a sigh. "Do you have cookies?" A glance at the empty display told me that no, they didn't, but I asked anyway. I could really go for a chocolate-chip cookie soaked in coffee right about then.

"Not right now," Nadia said. "Ice machine's broken."

I opened my mouth to ask what an ice machine had to do with cookie baking, but closed it again and let it go without comment. "A black coffee is fine."

With a put-upon sigh, Nadia turned to get me my coffee, while Farrah continued to stare down at her phone, oblivious to the world around her.

4

Time crept by slower than business at Death by Java, and that was saying something. As I sipped at my coffee, which, to be honest, wasn't as bad as I'd expected, I finished my rounds around the dining area before moving on to the books. I didn't invade Oscar's domain; he was still camped out in his corner, and I didn't want to bother him and become one of the bitten.

I recognized most of the book titles, so that was good. The organization was questionable, with books by the same author being shelved in different places with no rhyme or reason as to why they were separated. As I'd noted before, some books were stacked on top of one another, while others were standing upright. And while there was a counter upstairs where an employee could check out customers, no one was there now, nor had I seen anyone go up there since I'd been there.

It made me wonder what would happen if I wanted to buy a book. Would Farrah help me? Or would I have to take the book downstairs to pay for it? Nadia had left a few minutes ago, though I wasn't sure if she was on break or if she was done for the day. Farrah was all that was left to handle customers since Valerie had yet to emerge from the back.

Of course, there needed to *be* customers first.

I tapped a final note into my phone, glanced at the time, and then, with nothing better to do, I headed for the counter, where Farrah was busily studying the screen of her own device.

"Hi," I said.

Farrah glanced up, raised a single eyebrow in question, and then went right back to staring at her phone without waiting for me to continue.

I tamped down my annoyance. I'd have to add *employee attitudes* to my list of things that needed fixed, but now wasn't the time to bring it up. "I was wondering if I might be able to go into the back and have a look around. Valerie's still back there, right?"

Farrah shrugged. Didn't look up.

"I'm finished up front here, though it would helpful if I could have a peek behind the counter to see how things are organized."

Another shrug. I had a creeping suspicion that Farrah wasn't listening to a word I said.

"Mind if I have a quick look and then head to the back? I won't get in your way." Not that she was doing anything.

"Knock yourself out." Farrah tapped her phone, smiled at something she saw.

I waited a beat and then rounded the counter. I half-expected to find bottles shoved haphazardly onto shelves, coffee bags tipped over, spilling their contents onto the floor. Maybe a puddle of water or two.

Instead, the space behind the counter was clean, and everything was properly sealed and shelved correctly. Lyle's influence? Or was it kept tidy because Valerie and the girls actually had to work back here and they didn't want to slip on spilled beans?

Satisfied, I turned toward the back door, which was closed and didn't have a window. There was no other door in this portion of the store, so unlike Death by Coffee, there was no office immediately evident.

With a glance toward Farrah, who was paying me absolutely no mind, I pushed open the door and stepped through.

Valerie and Roman stood near the ice machine a few feet away, far too close for comfort. Valerie's hand was pressed against Roman's cheek, a coy smile on her lips. Roman was holding a screwdriver loosely in a hand that was resting on Valerie's cocked hip. There was no locking of lips, no grotesque fumbling, yet I felt like I'd just walked in on them in the middle of something far less PG than what was actually going on.

"Uh . . ." Irrational panic flooded my system. I tried to look away, but couldn't. Valerie had a boyfriend, and yet, here she was, seemingly flirting with another man.

"Was there something you needed?" she asked, sounding almost bored, before she stepped out of Roman's grip.

Not sure what else I could say, I held up my phone and blurted, "I have a list."

Roman cleared his throat. "I'll get back to work. I just gotta screw it in a little more, and we're good to go." He winked at me and then turned to the ice machine.

"A list, huh?" Valerie walked over and snatched my phone out of my hand. "What is this?"

"Suggestions," I said, tearing my eyes away from Roman, who'd leaned over the ice machine in a way that was far too suggestive to be real. "To help you draw in more business."

"I see." She frowned. "Can't we just have someone stand outside and tell people to come in?"

"You could, but once inside, you'd also want them to stay and buy something, right? And some of my advice should get Mr. Carrigan off your case."

She gave me a blank look as she handed me back my phone.

"Lyle. The health inspector."

"So, he'd go away?"

"I don't know about that," I said. "But he'd stop citing you." My gaze flickered over to the ice machine, steadfastly refusing to acknowledge Roman's proffered rear end. "What you really need is for someone to come in and go through all the wiring and piping, check all your connections, to make sure nothing is against code."

Valerie glanced back, gaze lingering on Roman, who seemed to notice her attention. He gave a little tush shake, glanced back at us, and winked once more, before tightening whatever screw it was he thought deserved so much of his attention.

"It doesn't look too bad back here," I said, turning away to take in the rest of the room. Like the space behind the counter, everything was where it should be.

The sink was empty of all but a few dishes, which I gave her a pass on considering the ice machine issue. "If you kept the rest of your store like this, it would go a long way toward drawing in customers."

Valerie narrowed her eyes at me. "What do you mean by that?"

Tread carefully, Krissy. "The dining area isn't as clean as it is back here," I said. "I assume Lyle cites you for that more than anything, right?"

Valerie just stared, giving nothing away.

"There's trash on the floor, dust. I didn't look on the underside of the tables, but I bet there's stuff stuck to them. The chairs themselves are filthy."

"That has nothing to do with me."

It was my turn to simply stare.

"The customers do that," Valerie said. "They should respect us enough not to leave their trash lying around. What they do isn't my fault, and I shouldn't be cited for it."

"But it *is* your responsibility."

"Done." Roman straightened and flipped his screwdriver into the air, catching it deftly before sliding it into his tool belt. "It shouldn't give you no more problems." He leaned against the ice machine. "I'll stick around and make sure that it's all running properly, of course. We can work out payment once you have a few minutes."

"Thank you, Roman," Valerie said. She was looking away from me, but I'm pretty sure she winked at him before turning back to me with a frown. "So, you're saying *I* have to clean up after the heathens because they're too lazy to throw their own trash away?"

"You or one of your employees," I said. "It's part of the job."

"I own the place, so that shouldn't be on me," Valerie said, voice going thoughtful. "But I could have my girls do it."

That's a start. "Let me send you the list," I said. "Have them work through it over the coming days, and I'm positive you'll start to see an uptick in business. It might take time, but a little word of mouth should go a long way."

Valerie rattled off her cell phone number and email address. I added both to my contacts and then sent her the list I'd made. Then, I pushed open the door and led the way back to the front, with Valerie dutifully following behind. It was a minor miracle that she was listening to me, so I decided to point out a few of the more pressing issues.

"Now, there is the issue of the cat. I—"

"Krissy Hancock? Is that you?"

I jerked to a halt at the vaguely familiar voice, causing Valerie to bump into me.

"Holy crap, it *is* you. Guys! It's Krissy from school."

Three smiling faces I thought I'd never see again were on the other side of the counter. It took my brain a moment to add the years since high school, but I quickly was able to put names to the faces.

Bray Eckles still had a large mole over his left eye, which hadn't detracted from his good looks when he was in his teens, nor did it now. Tamara Carey once had a supermodel body that had rounded out over the years, though she still dressed like she planned on walking the red carpet at any moment. And Bebe Long was, well, Bebe. She looked exactly the same as she had decades ago. Dark hair. Brown eyes that seeped sultriness. Flawless skin as smooth as glass.

They were, in two words, Valerie's crew.

Instinct from years of verbal abuse had me wanting to flee into the back room. I wasn't sure a single one of them had ever said a nice word to me before. Maybe there'd been a backhanded compliment or two over the years, much like the kind Valerie loved to deliver, but nothing genuine.

"Krissy?" Tamara cocked her head to the side, clearly not recognizing me.

"Yeah. Short Stuff," Bray said. "You remember, right? We joked with her all the time." He turned to me. "Had a barrel of laughs together. Isn't that right, Krissy?"

Joked *with* was *not* what they'd done, but I smiled and nodded. "Sure. I remember."

"Oh yeah," Tamara said, looking me up and down. "You've really filled out over the years, haven't you?"

I bit my lip so hard, I very nearly drew blood. Yes, I'd been far skinnier in my high school days, but so had almost everyone I knew, Tamara included.

"What are you doing back here?" Bray asked. "I thought you moved to Ohio with Vicki Patterson."

"Wait, they were dating?" This from Bebe, who'd barely been paying attention up to that point.

"Nah, she was dating Robert Dunhill when she left," Bray said, surprising me that he remembered since Robert and I met *after* high school. "They're probably married by now."

"Actually—" Before I could tell them that Robert and I had broken up *before* I'd left, or that it was Vicki Lawyer now, the door opened, and Paul walked in.

Seeing him was like a blast of cool, refreshing air. I hurried out from behind the counter and rushed over to him. When I grabbed his hand, I did so like a person desperate for saving, which, quite frankly, I was.

I kissed him on the cheek before asking, "Where are Dad and Laura?"

"They decided to walk back to the house, leaving the car to me." He eyed the trio as he showed me the keys. Valerie, seemingly drawn by Paul's appearance, rounded the counter to join her buddies. "Friends of yours?" he asked.

"Of course, we are. From way back," Bray said, smiling like he actually meant it. "Krissy was a lot of fun when we were younger."

A lot of fun to pick on. "Sorry, guys. I wish I could stay, but Paul and I have somewhere to be."

Both Bebe and Tamara didn't appear to care, but Bray appeared disappointed. *Could he really think we were once friends?* I understood that not everyone was cognizant of their past behavior, but there was no way he could have forgotten the times I'd been close to tears due to their verbal abuse. Could he?

"Ah, man," he said with a shake of his head. "I was hoping we could catch up." His eyes widened. "I know! How about you come to Hooties this Saturday night at like . . ." He looked to the others. When none of them jumped in with a suggestion, he finished with, "Eight-ish. I can let everyone know. We can make it an impromptu class reunion since you've missed all the real ones."

The thought of having a class reunion, impromptu or not, just about gave me hives. "I'm not sure I can make it," I said. "Paul and I have a ton of plans with my dad, and Saturday, we're going to the beach—"

"We should be back by eight, though, right?"

I shot Paul a betrayed glare.

"Sweet," Bray said. "Hooties at eight. My pop still owns the place, so I can reserve it for us. I bet at least fifty will show. Maybe double that."

I doubted it, but at that point, I just wanted to be gone. I tugged on Paul's hand and led him to the door. "We'll see," I said. "It was good seeing you all. Don't forget about that list, Valerie. Bye!"

As soon as we were on the sidewalk, I released Paul's hand and turned on him. "Why would you do that?"

"Do what?" he asked. "You said they were your friends. I thought it would be nice to get to know some of the people you hung out with in school."

"I said nothing of the sort. They're Valerie's friends, not mine." The heat was already fading from my voice as my shoulders sagged. "I'm starving. Do you want to get something to eat?"

Tito's was right there, but I didn't want to stick too close, just in case Bray and company decided to join us. We got into Dad's car, with Paul slipping in behind the wheel. I directed him through traffic, to a quieter part of downtown, where there were still businesses, but the crowds were much thinner and the chances of being spotted at random were fewer.

"There," I said, pointing. "I used to love that place as a kid."

Paul parked in a small lot across the street from a place called the Italian Roll. They specialized in these little pizza rolls that were, when I was a kid, like eating little bites of heaven. I was happy to see that the place was still open, despite being off the beaten path. Metal tables and chairs sat outside the door. I used to love sitting outside, under the sun, sucking down the spicy little balls of lava, but since all the tables were taken now, Paul and I would have to enjoy them inside.

The dim interior was like a slap of nostalgic bliss, as was the heavy scent of marinara and pepperoni that filled my nostrils. Mouth watering, I led Paul to the counter, where I put in an order for a dozen pizza rolls and a pair of Cokes. We then found an empty table and sat down to wait.

"I'm sorry," he said once we were settled. "I didn't mean to put you on the spot back there. I just thought—"

"It's okay," I said, waving off his concern. "Maybe it won't be so bad."

"We don't have to go."

I noted the "we" part of the statement and approved. "No, we don't, but I'd feel bad if everyone showed up and I didn't." I shrugged. "Who knows? It might be fun."

Our order was up a few minutes later. I rose to retrieve it, savoring the smell all the way back to the table.

"Give them a few minutes," I said, depositing the tray in the middle of the table. "Or else you'll scald yourself."

"Hey, Krissy," Paul said, nodding to a point past my

shoulder. "Isn't that the guy we saw arguing with Valerie at Death by Java yesterday?"

I turned and was surprised to see Lyle Carrigan hurrying from the back office, his tablet tucked under his arm. The owner of the Italian Roll, Marco Rossi, followed him out with a frown. He watched Lyle leave and then, with a frustrated shake of his head, headed behind the counter.

"Do you think there's health code violations going on here?" Paul asked, picking up a pizza roll and then quickly dropping it back onto the tray before blowing on his reddening fingers.

"I don't know." A brief war went on inside my head before I stood. "I'll be right back."

"Krissy . . ."

"I know, I know," I said. "But if this Lyle guy is hounding more than one business in town, it might make Valerie feel better." I didn't know why I cared so much, but I did. "Give me five minutes, and then we can eat."

Paul sighed, but nodded. I left him to his burnt fingers and joined Marco at the counter.

"Can I help you?" he asked, barely looking up from the register.

"Hi, Marco. You probably don't remember me. I used to come in here all the time when I was a kid."

He glanced up. There wasn't even an inkling of recognition in his eyes. "I'm happy you've come back. Have you ordered?"

"I have. We're just waiting on it to cool." I smiled, earning myself nothing more than a stare. "I was wondering . . ." I glanced toward the door that Lyle had recently exited. "That was Lyle Carrigan, right? The health inspector?"

A pause. "It was."

"There's nothing wrong here, is there? I love this place and—"

"No, no, it's nothing like that," Marco said. "Lyle and I have known each other a long time."

"I see." I peeked over at Paul. He tried to pick up another pizza roll and dropped it right back onto the tray. "I saw him at Death by Java and Tito's Deli, so I was curious. It seems like he's hanging around a lot."

Marco sighed. "Lyle's doing his job, though not everyone appreciates it. It's sad because I would have loved to move the Italian Roll to that part of town, but I was outbid. Why they can't keep their places up to standards, especially in an area with such potential, I'll never know." He shook his head. "If you'll excuse me, I need to . . ." He gestured toward the register.

Thanking him for his time, I returned to the table.

"Everything good?"

"Looks like it." I glanced back at Marco, who was counting money.

"You don't believe him?"

Did I? Marco hadn't looked happy when Lyle had left, friends or not. It made me wonder if the health inspector *was* hounding him about something. If so, that would make three businesses in town that I was aware of that had a problem with Lyle Carrigan. My guess is that they weren't the only ones.

But it was none of my business what was going on in the Village when it came to Lyle and his job. I turned my attention to Paul and the pizza rolls between us.

"Ready?" I asked Paul, picking up one of the steaming bites. "They're still hot, but they should be edible by now."

Paul picked up his own roll, blew on it. "As ready as I'll ever be."

We dinked them together, and as one, took a bite. Piping-hot marinara and mini-pepperonis shot onto my tongue, instantly scorching any and all tastebuds from it. I gasped, then somehow managed to chew and swallow with my mouth hanging open. Steam billowed with every huffing bite.

Paul, who'd managed to eat his without burning himself, watched me with amusement.

"Hot," I managed, snatching up my Coke and downing half of it in one go.

"But good."

That, they were.

Setting my Coke aside, I took another bite.

5

I went to bed that night feeling pretty good about the prospects for the rest of my vacation. Valerie had the list of fixes she could make to Death by Java to improve business—and to get Lyle off her back. If she decided to ignore my suggestions, that was on her. If she followed through and he *still* hounded her, then she had grounds to complain to his bosses. Either way, I'd done my part, and I was determined to focus on family for the rest of the trip.

The plan was simple. Friday would be dedicated to Dad. We'd go to some of our favorite places, spending father/daughter time together, starting with breakfast at one of Dad's favorite local places, the Scramble, downtown. From there, we'd head back to the house, pick up Laura and Paul, and make a day of it. No Valerie. No Lyle. Just *us*.

"Well, that can't be good."

Strobing red-and-blue lights lit up the early morning

sky as Dad and I pulled to a stop near Death by Java. A small crowd had formed outside, mostly made up of people who were dressed as if they were on their way to work, though a few joggers were thrown into the mix.

"I wonder if the ice machine exploded," I said, eyeing the ambulance parked out front next to a pair of police cruisers. "The guy who fixed it didn't look much like a repairman."

Dad made a noncommittal sound.

"Yeah, I don't believe it either." My heart was doing one of those slow, heavy *thumps* that made it feel as if it were trying to pound its way straight out of my chest. The scene looked all too familiar, and a sense of surrealness flowed through me. "We should probably check it out."

Dad didn't respond. He merely found a place to park, which was far easier this time of morning, and we were soon pushing our way to the front of the crowd gathered before Death by Java. A police officer was standing in front of the door with his arms crossed, attempting to appear imposing, though his scrawny frame made that difficult. He wore large, thick shades, and he had one of those mustaches favored by policemen on old television shows. His name tag read PEEL.

I peered past him, into Death by Java, but there was little to see. A pair of cops were in the dining room, just standing there. They were looking toward the front counter, which, from where I stood, was just out of sight. I assumed that was where the action was taking place.

"What happened?" Dad asked the woman next to him.

"Someone died, I guess." She yawned as if this sort of thing happened all the time. "Can't see a thing."

"'Died'?" I asked, my early dread turning into full-fledged panic. "Do you know who it was? How it happened?"

The woman shrugged. "I just followed the crowd." She glanced at her watch. "And now I'm going to be late for work. Just great." She heaved a sigh, then turned and walked away. A couple of others followed, clearly bored with the lack of visible action.

"I should go inside," I said. "What if it's Valerie?" My stomach clenched at the thought. No, we'd never been friends, but I didn't want to see her dead. I didn't want *anyone* to die.

"How are you going to manage that?" Dad asked, nodding to the cop. "I don't think he's going to let you waltz on in."

From the way Officer Peel glared at anyone who so much as scuffed a shoe in the direction of the bookstore café, I doubted it as well. But I felt I had to do something. If I could generate a distraction or spot an employee, then perhaps I'd be able to slip past the guard and into the store.

But if anyone from Death by Java was inside, they were keeping well out of sight. The only face I recognized was Tito's, from the deli next door. He was wearing a smug grin that morphed into a frown the moment he noticed me looking. He ran his tongue over his teeth as he regarded me, before he turned and headed inside his shop.

"Buttercup."

The tone of Dad's voice had me turning back to Death by Java. Valerie had moved within view, arms and hands in constant motion as she spoke to someone out of sight. She gestured toward the door without looking my way, then threw her hands into the air in what appeared to be frustration.

Could the woman have been wrong? Valerie appeared upset, but that could be because the mustached officer wasn't letting anyone inside, not that somebody had died. And since Valerie was clearly alive and well, a vague hope coursed through me that it was all just a bad rumor, and that it was indeed the ice machine that had caused the fuss.

But I desperately wanted to know for sure.

I made a snap decision and stepped forward.

Officer Peel immediately held up a hand, palm outward. "No one is allowed in. This is a crime scene. This place is closed until further notice."

"I'm not a customer," I said, wincing at the words "crime scene." "I've been helping the owner lately." I nodded toward Valerie, who'd yet to notice me. "If there's something I can do to help—"

"You can help by taking a step back."

"At least tell Valerie I'm here. She's the owner. Valerie Kemp." I flashed him my best smile. "I'm Krissy Hancock. That's my dad, James Hancock."

If I'd hoped name-dropping the local famous author's name would help, I was disappointed. Officer Peel merely adjusted his shades and squared his scrawny shoulders. "No admittance. Step back or else I'll have to take you into custody."

"I heard someone died," I said. "Can you at least tell me if that's true?"

Mustache twitching, Officer Peel crossed his arms. His jaw worked, and while I couldn't see his eyes, I got the impression he was debating whether he should follow through on his threat to arrest me or to simply ignore me.

Before he could make up his mind either way, the door flew open, and a frazzled Valerie Kemp appeared. "Krissy!" She grabbed me by the arm and physically pulled me past the startled Officer Peel. "Tell her that I had nothing to do with it!"

I staggered through the doorway of Death by Java, nearly face-planting on the floor in front of a tall Black woman with crossed arms dressed in slacks and a dark blue shirt. Her hair was pulled back tight from a striking face with high cheekbones and ultra-smooth skin that made her clear brown eyes stand out from the rest of her face. Those eyes were narrowed at me in a way that said she didn't appreciate my sudden appearance.

"Tell Detective McKensie!" Valerie prodded. "Krissy was here yesterday. She saw him leave. He was alive then, and he never came back here, not while we were here. Ask her!"

The woman—the *detective*—didn't ask. She just stared at me.

"Who are we talking about?" I asked. "I don't know what's going on."

A moment passed during which I was sure Detective McKensie was going to toss me right back outside without saying a word. She eyed me like she might a bug in her soup, before heaving a heavy sigh.

"I suppose I should hear what you have to say since you're here," she said. Her voice was buttery smooth, almost sultry. It was the kind of voice that would have most people lapping at her feet if the situation were different. "Krissy, wasn't it?"

I nodded. "Krissy Hancock."

"Do you live around here?"

"I used to. I live in Ohio now. I'm here visiting family."

Her eyes flickered toward Valerie, causing me to nearly laugh.

"No, we're not related. We went to high school together. I'm here with my dad." I pointed at him through the door. He was still standing where I'd left him.

"I see. And you were here yesterday?"

"I was." I shot a glance toward the other cops in the room. They were watching the interaction, faces impassive. No one else was present. "Who died?"

Detective McKensie's lips pressed together at the question. She didn't otherwise respond.

"Krissy was here almost as long as I was," Valerie said.

"Working?" the detective asked, eyes on me.

"No," I said. "Not really. I own a bookstore café in Ohio. Valerie wanted me to have a look around, see where she could improve her store to draw in more business."

"'Improve' is a strong word," Valerie said, earning herself a glare before McKensie turned back to me.

"Did you see anyone else while you were here?"

"Valerie, of course," I said. "Two of her employees, Nadia and Farrah. I don't know their last names."

Detective McKensie nodded, as if I'd merely confirmed what she already knew.

"A repairman showed up while I was working out here. His name's Roman." My eyes widened. "Was he the one who died?"

"Please stop speculating," Detective McKensie said. "Is that the full list of people? Customers? Other employees?"

I started to shake my head, then remembered. "Lyle Carrigan," I said. "He was already here when I got here. Him and two customers. They left their cups on the tables . . ." I trailed off when McKensie's expression darkened. "Lyle was going to cite Valerie for the broken ice machine, which was what Roman came here to fix."

"You saw Mr. Carrigan?"

"I did. He and Valerie were arguing—"

"'Arguing' is a strong word," Valerie said.

McKensie made a zipping motion at Valerie before taking a step closer to me. "When did Mr. Carrigan leave?"

"He's the one who died," I said, not making it a question. At that point, it was obvious based on the questions and Valerie's reaction to them. "He left almost as soon as I got here. I didn't see him at Death by Java again that day."

"But you saw him somewhere else?"

She's observant. "I did. He was at the Italian Roll. He left just when I arrived."

"That seems to happen a lot."

I blinked, not quite sure where she was going with that.

"You show up where Mr. Carrigan is conducting his business, and then he leaves. How well did you know him?"

"Not at all," I said. "The first time I'd ever met him was here."

"Yesterday?"

I shook my head. "The day before. When I first arrived in town, I came here to check the place out. He was here then."

"And he left right after?"

I was torn between indignation and fear. Was the detective really trying to make a connection between Lyle Carrigan and *me*?

"He did," I said. "I never spoke him. Then or later."

"I see." A beat, and then the dreaded question, "Where were you last night, Ms. Hancock?"

"At home. With my family." I took a shaky breath. "Dad's outside. His name is James Hancock. He can confirm my whereabouts. And before that, I was with my boyfriend, who just so happens to be a policeman from Ohio. I could call him if you want me to."

"That won't be necessary."

Beside me, Valerie was chewing on her lip and wringing her hands. I noted that her fingernails were pristine, as was her clothing. She didn't look like a woman who'd just committed a murder. But if she hadn't done it, then who? No other employees were evident. And even if they were, I couldn't imagine any of the girls I'd seen working here killing anyone.

Then again, just because Detective McKensie was treating it like a murder, that didn't mean it was. As far as I knew, Lyle had come in and had a heart attack while pointing out yet another health violation to Valerie.

But if she'd seen him keel over, then why all the questions?

"I don't know what happened," I said. "And I only knew Mr. Carrigan by sight. Yes, he argued with Valerie, but he'd been getting on the bad side of a lot of other business owners in town, too, including Tito."

"Tito Adornetto?"

"I don't know his last name, but I assume that's him. He owns the deli next door."

McKensie shared a look with the other cops in the room before turning back to me. "Did he argue with anyone else? Anyone at all?"

I almost said no, before I remembered. "Mickey. Valerie's boyfriend."

Valerie's mouth opened, and she gave me the most betrayed look I'd ever seen.

"Does this Mickey have a last name?" The detective looked to Valerie for an answer.

"He doesn't have anything to do with this," she said. "All Mickey did was stand up to Lyle when he was harassing me. You know, like a good boyfriend would?"

Detective McKensie simply stared, which appeared to be her go-to move when one of her questions was being avoided.

Valerie did her best to withstand it. She stared at the tops of her fancy shoes for a couple of long seconds before wilting. "Robbins. His name is Mickey Robbins."

There was no satisfaction in Detective McKensie's voice when she said, "Where was Mr. Robbins last night?"

Before Valerie could answer, the door opened, and Officer Peel poked his head inside. "Detective. There's a cop out here. He says he wants to talk to you a moment."

McKensie's eyes never left Valerie when she said, "Send him in."

Peel hesitated, twitching mustache signaling his annoyance, before he vanished back out the door.

"Mickey's innocent," Valerie said. "He was with me all night."

Even *I* didn't believe her, and I wasn't trained to detect lies. Valerie was just really bad at lying. Her eyes darted around the room, and her voice fluctuated in pitch. Maybe they weren't telltale signs of deception, but they sure did make her look like she wasn't telling the truth.

The door opened behind me. I expected another Redwood Village police officer to enter, but instead, Paul Dalton walked through the door, dressed in running shorts and a tank top.

Detective McKensie seemed as surprised as I was when she saw him. "You are?"

"Officer Paul Dalton," he said, brushing a hand against my arm as he stepped forward, a hand extended. "Pine Hills Police Department. I know this isn't my jurisdiction, but I wanted to stop in and see if I could be of any assistance."

"I take it Pine Hills is in Ohio?" McKensie said. "You're the aforementioned boyfriend?"

Once again, I was surprised by how quickly McKensie caught on. "He is."

Paul's smile was as charming as ever. "It is. And I am. Is Krissy in trouble?"

Detective McKensie smiled. "No. She's free to go, though I'd appreciate it if she left her contact information with Officer Peel outside, just in case I have any follow-up questions."

Relief washed over me. "We'll get out of your hair—"

"Actually," McKensie said, cutting me off. "I'd like to talk with Mr. Dalton here for a few minutes." She motioned toward the door. "You can wait for him outside."

An objection was on the tip of my tongue. Paul knew less than what I did. He was only here now because he'd been out on a run and had seen the commotion. He'd probably spotted Dad's car, or Dad himself, and come over to investigate. And then, upon hearing that I was inside, talking to the police, he'd come in make sure I was okay.

Or make sure I wasn't getting myself pulled into a murder investigation.

"Go ahead," Paul said. "This should only take a few minutes."

Still, I hesitated. I wanted to know what Detective McKensie was going to ask Paul, if she was going to verify my story, or if she was going to try to poke holes in it. Paul was right; this wasn't his jurisdiction, so why would she want to talk to him? He couldn't help her. He wasn't a cop here.

Then again, neither was I. I wasn't a cop *anywhere*.

"I'll be with Dad," I said. I took his hand, squeezed, then headed for the door.

Dad was waiting for me in a vastly thinner crowd. "Everything okay?" he asked.

"Not really." I crossed my arms and tapped my foot, too nervous to stand still. I kept my voice low when I asked, "Do you remember that health inspector? The one who was here that first day?"

"I do." A beat, and then, "It was him?"

"Yeah. I don't know what happened, but the detective inside is acting like it was *murder*," I practically whispered the word, but it caught the attention of those nearby, who immediately started gossiping.

Movement from near Tito's caught my attention. I expected to find Tito had come back outside or perhaps one of his employees had stepped out to get a look at the excitement, but it was neither.

It was Mickey Robbins.

"Dad . . ." I whispered, nodding toward where Mickey was standing.

"I see him."

Mickey was craning his neck to see inside Death by Java, but he wasn't moving close enough to where Officer Peel would notice him. In fact, he was doing his best to look inconspicuous to *everyone*, despite his clear nervousness. He was rubbing at his right hand with his left, which, at first, I took for a nervous gesture, but then I quickly realized it was more than that.

A bandage was wrapped around the knuckles of his right hand. And I couldn't be sure, but it appeared as if the fingers of that hand were swollen, as if he'd punched something hard enough to break a bone or two.

Mickey watched the scene for a good minute, maybe two. And then, with a quick look around to make sure no one had seen him, he slipped quietly away.

6

"Are you okay, Buttercup?"

I frowned down into my coffee, irrationally wishing I had the spiced chai tea I'd recently grown accustomed to drinking. The bubbles created by the chocolate-chip cookie I'd placed into my chipped coffee mug before pouring were long gone, and a few soggy crumbs had floated to the top. The chip in the mug, Dad claimed, was symbolic. He said it reflected how in life, even something damaged could still be of use. In reality, he'd always been careless with the dishes and the low-hanging faucet.

"I don't know," I admitted, nudging the mug aside. "I feel like I should be doing something."

Three of us were seated around Dad's table. Dad and me, of course, and Laura, who'd sensed something was wrong the moment we were through the door. Paul was still at Death by Java after Detective McKensie had requested he hang around. He'd claimed she'd requested his presence because he might have a few insights into the crime, though what she expected out of him, I had no idea. It wasn't like he knew Valerie or Lyle or anyone involved in the death, beyond his involvement with me.

But he wanted to help. I couldn't fault him for that.

"It's not your responsibility to do anything," Laura said. "I know you want what's best for your high school friend—"

"She's not my friend." I scowled. "I mean, she wasn't when we went to school together. Now . . ." I shrugged. I was helping Valerie Kemp, sure, but I didn't think I actually *liked* her. Yet I did know her, and she was in trouble, which made me want to defend her. Did it make sense? Not really. But that was me in a nutshell.

"Either way, you're not in Pine Hills," Laura went on. "The police here might not like you snooping around, even with Paul helping them. In fact, they might be harsher on you because you're from out of town."

With my elbows propped onto the table, I folded my hands and leaned my head against them, eyes closed. "I know. It's just . . ." I floundered for an argument, though, against what? I had no clue.

"I understand your predicament," Dad said. "It's the same thing I go through when I write. I want to get my hero or heroine involved in the crime, yet how do I do it and make it believable? If they just show up and start poking their nose into everyone's business, the reader will wonder why the police aren't stopping them."

I cracked open an eye to peer at him. "*I* just show up and start poking my nose into everyone's business. It's kind of what I do."

He grinned. "Don't I know it. When anyone comments about my characters doing something similar, I just talk about you, and that usually shuts them up."

I snorted as I sat back. "I get that I can't go running around, interrogating suspects. While I might have known most of these people when I was a kid, I know almost nothing about them now. But I'm not sure I can sit here and do *nothing*. Even if all I do is help Valerie put things to rights around her café, then I'd at least feel as if I was making a difference."

"Then do that," Dad said, earning him a sharp look from Laura. "What? Why not? You know as well as I do that Krissy takes after me and can be obsessive. If going to Death by Java and trying to figure out how to help Valerie increase business gets her mind off the murder, then I'm all for it."

"You just want to be able to investigate," Laura said. "Turn her into your inside man."

Dad grinned. "Maybe."

"I doubt they'll even be allowed to open, so I'm not sure what I can do," I said. "I already gave Valerie a list of changes she could make, so as long as she follows that, there's little else I can do. And if I show up at her house to talk, she'll probably just kick me out. Or ignore me."

"But if you make the effort, show her that you're available, she might soften her stance on you," Dad said. "I know that Valerie Kemp wasn't your favorite person when you were younger. You tried to hide it, but I saw how she treated you." His lips pressed together briefly before he went on. "But people change. I realize she's difficult now, but there's always a chance that it's a show, a way for her to keep up appearances."

"Appearances as an entitled brat?" Laura asked.

I considered it. I didn't think Valerie had changed all that much, but did it matter? A man was dead. It had happened in her bookstore café.

Someone she knew might be involved.

"Mickey's hand was wrapped," I said. "And he didn't try to get inside to check on Valerie. If he'd done nothing wrong, don't you think he'd have at least *tried* to get past Mr. Mustache to make sure she was okay?"

"'Mr. Mustache'?" Laura asked with a laugh.

"The cop outside. Officer . . ." I frowned.

"Peel," Dad provided. "His name tag said Peel."

"That's it." I drummed my fingers on the table. "Officer Peel was guarding the door, but I was able to get past him." Sure, Valerie yanking me inside had caught him by surprise, but I'd still made it. "Mickey stood out of sight, acting like he didn't want anyone to see him. And his hand was fine when I last saw him." Which just so happened to be the day that he'd all but threatened Lyle Carrigan.

"Do you really think this Mickey guy is the killer?" Dad asked.

"I'm not even sure there *is* a killer," I said. "The detective is working under the assumption that Lyle was murdered, but she didn't come right out and say that he was. It could have been an accident. Maybe Lyle was there illegally and had a heart attack or something. She might have been trying to figure out why he was there."

Of course, based on the questions she was asking, I doubted that was it. Lyle was murdered. Valerie's boyfriend was the prime suspect, at least in my mind. Once

Detective McKensie learned about his injured hand and suspicious behavior, he would be hers as well.

"Assume it *was* murder," Dad said. "What do we know?"

I considered it, and said, "Mickey got into Lyle's face, warned him to leave Valerie alone."

"Death by Java is already struggling at this point," Dad added. "If the health inspector shuts them down, even for a few days, it might hurt them enough that they could have to close permanently."

"The ice machine broke down yesterday," I said. "Lyle insisted on citing Valerie for it, said he'd come back later to check on it."

"Which upsets Mickey, who'd already told Lyle to back off."

"So, he confronts the health inspector, possibly when he came back to follow through on his inspection."

"And, *bam!*" Dad punched his fist against his palm. "He kills him. Maybe it's by accident. Maybe Lyle refuses to back down, and he takes him out before he can file his report."

"But why leave the body in Death by Java?" I asked.

"He could have panicked."

"Or someone came by." I thought it through. "If this happened early in the morning, let's say, just before opening and before the first employees arrived . . ."

"They argue, Mickey kills him, but he doesn't have time to dispose of the health inspector before someone shows up. He slips out the back—"

"I'm not sure there's a back door," I said. "Or, at least, I didn't notice one when I was back there." Then again, I'd been a smidge distracted by Valerie and Roman when I'd gone into the back, so there was always a chance I'd overlooked it.

"Okay, then, perhaps he hides somewhere, waits until the body is found, and then slips out in the confusion," Dad amended. "He comes back later to see what's going on. Kind of like that trope of killers returning to the scene of the crime."

"You two are impossible." Laura shook her head as she rose.

"By which, you mean we are brilliant detectives who are likely on the right track," Dad said with a wink at me.

Laura rolled her eyes. "I'm going to find a lighthearted movie to cleanse my mind of all this talk of murder. Would the two of you care to join me?"

"I'll pop the popcorn," Dad said, rising with a stretch. "I think we could all use the break. What do you think, Buttercup?"

It was a bit early for popcorn and movies, but then again, the day had already been long enough. A few hours of mindless fun sounded like the perfect way to keep myself out of trouble.

"Sure," I said. "A movie would be great."

Dad, true to his word, retrieved a bag of popcorn. "Amish-made," he said, showing me the brown bag before tossing it into the microwave. "It's smaller than what you usually get at the store. A writer friend of mine who lives in Amish country sends it to me every couple of months as payment for some editing I did on one of her Amish mysteries."

The scent of buttery popcorn filled the house, and

we were soon situated in the living room in front of Dad's television. Dad sat in the middle, Laura on his left, me on his right. The couch was just barely big enough for the three of us, but we managed.

I did my best to focus on the movie, which was indeed a lighthearted romp, but I couldn't. I kept wondering where Paul was, if he was helping Detective McKensie subdue a killer, even now. Or had something gone wrong? Could McKensie have decided that Paul was responsible for Lyle's death? He was a stranger in town. It's far easier to believe someone new to town is a killer than someone you've lived beside for years.

We were about halfway through the movie when my phone rang. A quick look at the screen told me it was Paul, which sent all sorts of emotions zinging through me.

I shot to my feet, nearly upending the mostly empty popcorn bowl, and rushed into the dining room to answer.

"Paul?" I tried to keep the desperation out of my voice. Failed. "Is everything okay? Did they catch the killer?" If there *was* a killer.

"No, not yet," he said. He sounded both jazzed and weary at the same time. "There was a lot to process, and the police here were feeling a smidge overwhelmed. We're all done at Death by Java. Gabby was appreciative of my input and asked me to come to the station with her to go over a few more things."

"Gabby?"

"Detective McKensie. She's driving us to the station now." He cleared his throat. "I'm not sure how long this is going to take. I'm sorry." A pause. "I could always tell her to drop me off if you want? I wasn't thinking when I agreed to the ride-along. I kind of got swept up in the moment, I suppose."

I considered it, then said, "No, that's okay. We're watching a movie and figure we might just hang around the house for the rest of the day. Just make sure you're back so we can go to the beach tomorrow."

"Of course. I wouldn't miss it."

"I bought a special bikini, just for you."

He cleared his throat. In the background, Detective McKensie said something, then laughed.

"I'll, uh, keep that in mind," Paul said.

"Good." I grinned. "I'll talk to you when you get here. You'll fill me in?"

"I will. Talk soon."

And then he was gone.

I tapped my phone on my palm, thinking. The police were done at Death by Java. Valerie might still be there. I could ask her about Mickey, about what she knew about the crime.

"Dad?" I called into the living room.

"What do you need, Buttercup?"

"You up for a field trip?"

He stepped into the dining room with a grin. "I thought you'd never ask."

Not only had the police left Death by Java, but so had the crowd. The usual foot traffic passed outside, but not even a possible murder was enough to garner interest for the bookstore café. Valerie truly did have her work cut out for her if she wanted to turn things around.

Speaking of Valerie; she must have seen us coming because by the time Dad and I reached the door, she was already holding it open for us.

"The police have shut us down for the day," she said as we entered. "Probably for a week. I don't know what I'm going to do."

The dining room was empty but for the three of us. Death by Java coffee cups sat on most of the tables. I assumed the police had left them behind because customers sure hadn't. Most of the cups were empty, but three at a nearby table were half full and still steaming.

"Why are you here?" Valerie asked, crossing her arms as she regarded me. "Come to gloat?"

"I wanted to check on you," I said. "See if there was anything I could do to help."

"We're concerned," Dad added.

Valerie blinked, dabbed a finger under her eye. "There's no need to be concerned." Her tone said otherwise.

"Valerie—" I cut off as the bathroom door opened and two men came strolling out.

I recognized Hugh, Valerie's ex, immediately. A mop of blond hair hung down near his freckled nose. He had bronzed skin and a somewhat skinnier build for what Valerie usually went for. I didn't know his last name, only that he'd once dated Valerie and had a hand in helping her do research for Death by Java. And by research, I mean he snuck around Death by Coffee and took pictures and reported on everything I did.

The other man, however, took me a moment to recognize.

I hadn't seen Aaron Middleton, Valerie's ex-husband, in years. In high school, he'd been the jock to her cheerleader. He wasn't as buff as Mickey, never had been, but he was lean and muscled nonetheless. He sported a goatee that had clearly been bleached, considering the light brown hair on his head. Even his eyebrows appeared to have had work done, which, knowing what I did of Aaron, wasn't a surprise.

"Hey, Val, you're out of—" Hugh cut off when he saw Dad and me.

Valerie put on a strained smile. "Hugh, you remember Krissy, right?"

Hugh nodded, seemingly struck speechless by my presence.

Next to him, Aaron scratched at his goatee. "You're the Hancock kid, right? I think I remember you."

I'd be surprised if he did. He hadn't been as outright hostile to me in high school as Valerie had been. In fact, I wasn't sure he'd noticed me, even when I was standing right in front of him. People like Aaron Middleton didn't tend to acknowledge anyone outside their circle.

"I'm James," Dad said, stepping forward and extending a hand. "Krissy's father." The men shook. "I'm sorry to hear about the death. Was it murder?"

Leave it to Dad to get right to the point.

"It looks like it might be," Valerie said.

"Do the police have an idea who did it?" I asked her.

"How should I know what the police think?" She scowled, looked anywhere but at me.

So I asked her point-blank: "What about Mickey?"

"What about him?" Valerie's jaw was tight as she spoke. "He wasn't here, so how would he know who killed Lyle?"

"Valerie . . ." I took a step toward her, lowered my voice. "I saw Mickey outside when the police were here. His hand was bandaged."

"So? He had nothing to do with any of this."

"What happened?" Dad asked. "I assume Lyle died inside Death by Java?"

Valerie hugged herself as she nodded. "In the back." A pause, and then, "I can show you."

I blinked in surprise. "The police didn't close it off?"

She shook her head. "There was no need. They took all the evidence, and it wasn't like there was any blood. They told me not to go back there, but a little look can't hurt anything."

"You two go," Dad said. "I'll stay here." He gave me a meaningful look before a subtle head tilt toward Hugh and Aaron. *He'd talk to them.*

Valerie led the way around the counter to the back door. She paused there briefly, as if second-guessing herself, before she pushed through. She held the door open for me, then flipped on the light. As the door swung closed behind us, she pointed toward another door at the far end of the room, one I hadn't noticed before. "He was found over there."

As she'd said, there was no blood on the floor, no indication that anything untoward had happened at all. "Does the door lead into an alley?" I asked.

She nodded. "It's where we keep the trash bins. I

never go in or out that way, so I assume someone else left the door unlocked, and he came in. Someone probably followed him. A mugger or something."

The question was, of course, why Lyle would come sneaking in through an unlocked alley doorway, even if he was being chased by a thief, but I didn't ask. "Were there signs of a struggle?" I asked instead. The door looked intact and undamaged. There was no splintering that spoke of it being kicked it. No debris on the ground around it.

"He was dead," Valerie said, deadpan. "Doesn't that indicate that there was a struggle?"

I took a deep breath, held it for a count of three, before speaking. "I meant, was there stuff knocked over in the room?" I gestured around at the shelves, which were all as tidy as when I'd last seen them. Nothing was out of place. "Did Lyle fight back?"

"I don't know." Her voice was small, scared. "I don't usually come in first, but . . ." She took a shuddering breath. "I thought he was asleep or something. But when I went over to check." She squeezed her eyes closed, entire body tensing.

I gave her a moment to work through it before asking, "What about evidence? Did the police take anything that might hint at what happened?" *Or at who killed him?* I didn't add.

"Not really. Lyle didn't have his tablet with him, which was strange, but if it was a mugger who did it, then maybe not. All that was on the floor near him was a screwdriver Roman probably dropped when he'd fixed the ice machine."

I almost asked if Lyle had been stabbed, but if he had been, there would have been blood. And while the door didn't appear to be jimmied open, it was possible Lyle—or his killer—had done so without leaving a mark that could be seen from the inside. I'd need to check the alley and see if there were marks there.

But that did raise the question: What was Lyle Carrigan doing at Death by Java when it was closed? And who had been there with him? I found it hard to believe he'd been chased and killed for his tablet.

"This was a mistake," Valerie said, abruptly backing toward the door. "We should go. I shouldn't have let you back here."

I eyed the alleyway door a moment longer, but there was nothing to see. I let my gaze slide around the room until it fell on the ice machine.

And the hinged metal door, which now sported a dent in it the size of a man's meaty fist.

7

Sunlight streamed through the branches of the trees, casting speckled light across the open green of Village Park, which was bursting with life. A pair of squirrels sat atop a half-wall, busily doing squirrely things. A trio of dogs romped together while their owners chatted over coffee. Kids played. Parents looked on. It should have been uplifting. Peaceful.

I stared down at my half-eaten pretzel, hardly seeing it. The large square flecks of salt reminded me of miniature ice cubes, which made me think of the ice machine and the dent. I'd tried to shake thoughts of murder, of bandaged hands and back-room lights, but I couldn't.

"Is there something wrong with your pretzel, Buttercup?" Dad asked, balling up his greasy napkin and brushing away fallen salt particles. "You used to love Walt's."

"No. It's fine." I took a bite as if to prove the point, then chewed and swallowed. "I'm just thinking."

"About Valerie and what happened?"

I took another bite before wrapping up the rest of my meager lunch. "I'd hoped going over there would help, but all I have now are more questions."

"Such as?"

"How did the killer get in?"

Dad shifted on the bench so he could look at me straight on. "Did you see something that might help explain that?"

"No, but I saw the *lack* of something. There were no marks on the door, front or back, that would indicate it being jimmied open."

"That's why you wanted to go into the alley before we left?"

I nodded. "There wasn't so much as a scratch on the door frame, nor around the lock. I'm sure there are other ways to get doors open without keys, but there not being any marks at all makes me wonder if the killer had a key and let him in."

"The door still could have been picked," Dad said. "I could show you how if you want?"

I considered it, shook my head. "No, that's all right." Dad had a set of lockpicks he'd learned to use when he was doing research for one of his books. James Hancock had a lot of talents thanks to his desire to be accurate in his writing, most of which would put him on the wrong side of the law if he were actually to use them. "I believe you. But . . ."

"I get it. We can talk it through if you'd like," he said. "The murder, I mean. I did speak to those two young men while you were in the back with Valerie. Her exes, I suppose they were."

"And?"

"They both claim they know nothing about the murder."

"Which isn't surprising."

"No, it isn't," Dad agreed. "But they *did* insinuate that the Mickey fellow might be involved."

I glanced over at him. "Did they say why they thought that?" Because if Aaron or Hugh wanted Valerie back, blaming her boyfriend for murder was a good way to get rid of him without dirtying their hands.

"Not directly. They both mentioned that he should have been there for Valerie, questioned why he wasn't. They both also talked about his temper, how they saw him yell at the health inspector more than once. The way they were talking, they made it seem like it was only a matter of time before he snapped and killed him."

Which would have meant something if both Hugh and Aaron weren't Valerie's exes. They could be jealous of Mickey and simply wanted him gone.

But his hand *was* bandaged.

"The ice machine was dented," I said. "Lyle's body was found by the door, but that doesn't mean that's where the fight started."

"Are you saying you think there was a struggle?" Dad asked.

"A struggle, or an argument that escalated to the point that someone punched the ice machine. What I can't figure out is why Lyle was there at all."

"Do the police know when he was killed?" Dad asked. "If he showed up at around closing time that night, it's possible it happened then, and not this morning."

"Maybe." I frowned, stared off into the distance. "But I always saw him at Death by Java in the mornings. Early afternoon at the latest. He said he was going to come back to check on the ice machine, but why not wait until his normal time? And there'd be people around at closing. On the street. In the café. I mean, I'm pretty sure they close while it's still light out. Hard to kill someone in broad daylight."

"So, you're thinking he showed up just before opening, when it was still dark, and got into an argument with Mickey—"

"Or whoever opened."

"—and what? They killed him because he still planned on citing them for the ice machine? That hardly seems worth killing over."

No, it didn't. Not unless he was going to take it a step further. But what could a health inspector do besides cite them and possibly have the place shut down?

A couple jogged by. One of the dog owners corralled their pooch and bid the other two *adieu*. The squirrels had left their perch at some point, leaving the half-wall empty of everything but a discarded acorn cap.

"Valerie wouldn't have killed him," I said. "I don't think she would have Mickey do it either."

"But if not him, who?"

Who, indeed?

I thought it over and came up with few ideas. Lyle was found inside Death by Java. He'd gotten in because someone with a key had let him in; I was sure of it.

That meant the killer had to be Valerie, Mickey, or one of her employees, which consisted of a bunch of women in pink dresses and white bows. I knew women could be killers, just like men, but it was hard to imagine someone like Farrah murdering Lyle, even as small as he was, while she was wearing a pink dress.

And there'd been no blood. Could one of the women have strangled him? Bludgeoned him to death? If so, with what? I needed to know the cause of death to even know what to think.

"Someone had to have had a good reason to kill him," Dad said, cutting into my thoughts. "I doubt it had to do with some minor health violation. He might have seen something he wasn't supposed to see. Or perhaps he had enemies beyond Valerie."

A flash. "Marco."

Dad frowned. "Who?"

"The owner of the Italian Roll—Marco Rossi. I saw Lyle with him yesterday. Marco said he and Lyle go way back, though when Lyle left, Marco looked unhappy."

"Like they'd fought?"

"Or something Lyle had said upset him." Now that I thought about it, it was entirely possible that Marco wasn't upset with Lyle like I'd originally thought. "What if Lyle had told Marco about Mickey bullying him?"

"Do you think he would have gone to Death by Java to confront this Mickey guy? And what? Lyle got caught in the crossfire somehow?"

"If there was a fight, perhaps Lyle tried to step in and stop it. He gets knocked down, hits his head, and . . ." It wasn't much of a theory, but it was at least something to go on. "Even if he didn't do anything himself, perhaps Marco knows who might have."

Dad rose, brushed off the bottom of his pants. "Then I suppose we should go talk to him."

I stood, started to follow him, but paused. "Dad?"

"Yeah, Buttercup?"

"Did you tell Paul about the squirrel and the, you know, hole?"

He smiled. "I suppose you'll have to talk to him about it and see." A wink, then he turned and started walking.

Great. Shaking off the thought, I followed after him.

A closed sign hung in the window of the Italian Roll, despite it being early afternoon. I cupped my hands on either side of my face and peered inside.

"See anything?"

"A light is on in the back," I said, squinting into the gloom. The blinds on the windows were pulled closed, meaning it was rather dark inside. "I think. It's hard to be sure with the sun's reflection."

"Let me look."

I stepped back so Dad could have a peek. While he did, I checked the rest of the street. No other shops were closed along this stretch of road, so it wasn't a water-main break or a power outage.

"Someone's back there," Dad said. "I saw a shadow move. And there's trash on the table, like someone's eaten recently."

"Marco?"

"Your guess is as good as mine."

"We should knock and see who answers." If anyone. "If Marco was friends with Lyle and Lyle was killed . . ."

"Then someone might be after Marco as well," Dad finished for me.

I stepped up beside Dad, and using the palm of my hand, I beat on the glass door as hard as I could.

"Marco? Are you in there?" I squinted past the reflection, toward the mostly closed office door, where the light was coming from. I half-expected the light to snap off and a shadowy shape to dart for the back exit, but nothing happened. "Marco!" I pounded harder. "Come out. We only want to talk."

"People are looking," Dad said, nudging me with his elbow. Out of the corner of my eye, I noticed that we were, indeed, drawing stares. After the excitement at Death by Java, it was no wonder.

"At least we'll have witnesses if something happens," I said, knocking again. "Marco!"

The door to the office finally opened, and Marco Rossi stepped out, alive and well, and looking rather annoyed.

Hands on his hips, he regarded me from across the room for a long moment before sighing and walking across the empty restaurant. He unlocked the door and pushed it open just enough to say, "We're closed," through the crack, before he started to close it again.

"We're not here to eat," I said before he could shut it altogether. "We want to talk." A pause. "It's about Lyle Carrigan."

Marco frowned at me through the crack. There was a brief flare of irritation, followed by a drop of the head.

Another sigh, then he opened the door and stepped aside. "Come in. Did they find out who killed him?"

I glanced at Dad as we entered. He was taking in the room, eyes scouring the place like a detective in one of his stories. I decided to take the lead as Marco closed and locked the door behind us. He motioned toward a nearby table, where we all sat before I answered.

"Not yet. It's why I wanted to talk."

"I don't see what I could possibly say that would matter," he said. "I don't know what happened to him, only that he was killed."

I briefly wondered if the police had come out and admitted that it was murder, or if Marco knew something I didn't, before saying, "You and Lyle were friends."

A brief flare of sadness shot through his expression before he stilled his face. "We were," he said. "We had our differences, of course. He was a health inspector, and I own a restaurant, so there were times when he would come in and there'd be friction between us. Stuff like freezer and oven temps and such. Nothing big. Nothing that went beyond a reprimand here or there. And we always got past it. I understood that he was just doing his job, like I was doing mine."

"But not everyone saw it the same way," Dad said.

Marco glanced at him. "No, they didn't. Most people in the Village's food industry hated the man. Lyle did his job, and he did it well. But he didn't like confrontation, and there were some people who took advantage and pushed him around."

"I saw Tito Adornetto shove him out of his deli," I said. "Physically."

Marco pointed at me. "Like that. He'd warn them about cooler settings, the way the meats and cheeses were stored, and there was always pushback. They all knew he was right, but no one likes being told they've screwed up. And when you're cited, it ends up in the reports that anyone can find online, which, if the infraction was bad enough, could cause a drop in customers."

"Did Lyle ever cause someone to have to close because he'd cited them?" I asked. "Or get people fired for it?"

"Not that I'm aware." Marco closed his eyes and rubbed them with calloused fingers. "He did his job, but he also had compassion. He tried to give people the benefit of the doubt. I suppose it's not beyond reason that someone might have gotten let go because of him pointing out *their* violations. It's inevitable. Owners like to have someone to blame, whether they're truly the reason for the citation or not."

It made me wonder if perhaps someone at Death by Java had been fired because of Lyle's complaints. Hadn't Nadia said something about Dee not showing up to work the other day?

"Lyle was here yesterday," I said. "When he left, you didn't look happy."

Marco dropped his hand and leveled me with a hard stare. "Are you accusing me of something, miss?"

"No, but I am curious as to what was wrong. Could it have had something to do with why he was killed?"

Marco stared a moment longer, as if determining whether I was being honest before he answered. "The issue wasn't about me or my place, if that's what you're thinking. Lyle came in and said he was having a hard time with someone. He was worried that if he continued to press the issue, something might happen to him. I told him he was overreacting. He got angry that I wasn't taking it seriously, so he left."

"And then he ended up dead," Dad said.

Marco winced as if he'd been struck. "It's why I closed today. As soon as I heard what happened, I felt like Lyle's death was partially my fault." He took a deep, trembling breath. "I should have listened to him, taken his concerns to heart. I let him walk out of here without even offering to help mediate. I could have called someone, put a word in a few ears. But I didn't. Lyle's dead because I didn't do anything." He slammed a fist down onto the table, causing it—and me—to jump. "Why didn't I listen when I had the chance?"

He shoved away from the table and walked away. He crossed the room and gathered the trash still on the table. After dumping it into the bin, he stood there, facing away from us, for a long moment before he returned, but he didn't sit down. "I'd like to go home now, so if you would . . ." He motioned toward the door.

Dad and I stood. "I have one more question," I said as I pushed in my chair.

Marco's expression tightened, but he motioned for me to go on.

"Who was it that Lyle was afraid of?" I was pretty sure I already knew, but I wanted to hear it from someone else.

Marco walked us to the door, jaw working the entire time, as if he had to chew on the words before he said them out loud. He paused with his hand on the lock before he turned and stared directly into my eyes. The heat in his voice could have peeled paint.

"It was that meathead Valerie Kemp calls a boyfriend," he spat. "Mickey Robbins. He's the one who threatened Lyle, and I'd be surprised if he wasn't the one who killed him."

8

Mickey Robbins. At every turn, his name—and the man himself—seemed to pop up.

The TV was on, but no one was watching it. Dad was sitting with his tablet in hand, pouring over the latest version of the contract his agent had sent him. I couldn't tell if there were sticking points with it, or if his pinched brow and frown was because he still couldn't make sense of the legal jargon.

Laura had been in and out over the last hour, checking in with the both of us, but not prying too much about what we'd discovered. She'd already packed everything for our beach day and had asked us twice if we were still planning on going. We both assured her we were.

I wasn't sure she believed us.

And Paul . . . A quick call after we'd gotten back from the Italian Roll informed me that he was still helping the local police with the case. A promise that he'd be back soon followed, and then he was gone.

So, with nothing else to do, I mentally replayed everything I knew in the hopes of having an epiphany that would solve the case and allow me to enjoy the rest of my vacation, stress-free.

Death by Java was struggling. Lyle Carrigan, the health inspector, had been threatening to cite them for violations. Valerie had thought Lyle was harassing her. Tito thought the same thing with regard to his own business. Mickey didn't like it, and he all but threatened Lyle in front of everyone. Even Marco knew about it.

And then, Lyle was killed, and his body was left at Death by Java. No sign of forced entry. No sign of struggle. Just a screwdriver and a dented ice machine, both of which might not have had anything to do with the murder. Add to that Mickey's hand injury and Tito's seeming glee that Lyle was dead, and I had two prime suspects. Marco believed Mickey was responsible, and honestly, based on what I'd seen thus far, I had to agree with his assessment.

But none of it was proof. Not the injured hand, not the threats, not even Mickey showing up outside Death by Java, looking nervous, after the body was found.

I drummed my fingers on the armrest of the couch, causing Dad to look up from his tablet.

"Everything okay, Buttercup?"

"I—"

My phone buzzed, causing me to jump. Thinking it might be Paul, I snatched it up from the end table and answered without looking at the screen.

"Krissy, I don't know what I'm going to do."

"Lena?" I glanced at Dad, who shrugged before turning back to his tablet. "What's going on?"

Lena sighed heavily into the phone. "This was stupid. I shouldn't have called. You're on vacation. I'm being dumb and worrying over nothing and—"

"Lena, it's okay. I'm just sitting here watching TV at the moment anyway. What's wrong?"

"It's this job." Lena Allison was once a full-time Death by Coffee employee, but she had recently started working with the police in the hopes of becoming an officer of the law and making a difference for those typically—and wrongfully—deemed as trouble. I assumed the call had nothing to do with my bookstore café, where she worked when she had free time, but I couldn't be positive. "I think I'm screwing everything up."

"I'm sure it's not that bad," I said.

She laughed. "Right. You guys leave, and Chief Dalton decides it's time for me to take over some of Paul's caseload. I'm paired with Becca, so it's not that bad." Becca Garrison was one of the local Pine Hills officers. I liked her, and I knew that her presence would have a calming effect on Lena. And Chief Patricia Dalton was Paul's mom, as well as his—and Lena's— boss. "But Detective Buchannan always seems to be lurking around every corner, watching my every move like he expects me to turn into one of the criminals I'm supposed to be chasing."

"No surprise there." John Buchannan and I had a history that often involved him threatening to throw me in jail for poking my nose into his murder investigations. He wouldn't have been the least bit surprised to find out that I was involved in one now, albeit peripherally.

"I'm afraid to do anything. What if I mess it up? I'm not doing much more than handing out parking tickets, but still. Becca's handling all the big stuff, so it's not like a mistake by me would cause a murderer or a thief to go free. It's just making me paranoid, I guess. Like, I expect him to pop out of my closet at any moment."

There was a creak I assumed was Lena opening said closet to be sure Buchannan wasn't lurking inside.

"What does Chief Dalton say?" I asked.

Lena huffed. "She says that I'm doing great. Becca says the same thing. But they could just be being nice. You know, like that teacher who is always telling you you're doing a good job, just before handing back your paper with a big fat D on it. So far, all I've gotten out of Detective Buchannan is a grunt and a watchful eye."

"He could simply be curious about your progress," I said. "You've worked with him quite a bit, haven't you?"

"Yeah." Said grudgingly, as if she knew where this was going.

"Buchannan wants to take the credit for *everything*. And I don't just mean with solving crimes. When you become the success we all know you're going to be, he's going to want to take credit for that too. He'll say that you learned everything from him, will probably expect an award for it."

"I know, but—"

"No buts," I said. "I might not be there to see it with

my own eyes, but I know you're doing great. They wouldn't have put even a fraction of Paul's workload onto you if they didn't think you could handle it."

A long stretch of silence followed while Lena absorbed that. "I suppose you're right." She sounded both relieved and deflated at the same time. "I'm probably just working myself up over nothing."

"There's no 'probably' about it."

A chuckle, then, "How are things going out there? Getting a lot of sun?"

"Beach day is tomorrow," I said. "I fully expect to look like a lobster before the day is out."

"Sounds fun. I wish I was there. I could use some downtime, that's for sure."

"Maybe I'll bring you along the next time Paul and I head this way. We could spend the entire week at the beach and forget all about John Buchannan."

"I'm going to hold you to that. Rita's already planning on tagging along on your next trip. I talked to her yesterday and . . . whew. She's riled up and isn't afraid to let everyone know about it." There was a shuffling sound before she said, "I should let you get back to it. Say hi to your dad for me."

"I'll do that." New thought. "Before you go, how's Death by Coffee doing?"

"The people or the place itself?"

"Both."

"The lights are still on—mostly—and business is about the same as usual. We all miss you, customers included."

The lights are on.

A flash: the shifting light at Death by Java the night before Lyle's murder. A flashlight? Something else? Farrah claimed there was no light on the next day, so whoever was back there had turned it off—or had taken it with them—when they'd left.

Then, twenty-four hours later or so, Lyle Carrigan was found dead in the very same backroom. Coincidence? A clue?

Lena's voice tore me from my thoughts. "I'll see you when you get back, Krissy."

"See you then." I clicked off, mind churning over the possibilities.

Valerie had claimed she didn't know anything about the light. Was she telling the truth? Lying? Had Mickey gone there, dented the ice machine then? When Roman had been fixing it the following day, I hadn't noticed a dent, but I hadn't been looking for one. And since Roman and Valerie were standing in front of it, too close for comfort, I'd kept my focus turned elsewhere, lest I see something that would give me nightmares.

"Everything okay back home?" Dad asked, setting his tablet on his lap. "If you want to talk about it . . ."

"Everything's fine." I stood. "I need to make a call." I hurried out of the room and into my bedroom for privacy. I closed the door behind me, waited a couple of seconds to make sure Dad hadn't followed me back, then I put in the call.

The phone rang four times before a breathless Valerie answered with a curt, "Who's calling?"

"It's me, Krissy."

A beat, and then, "Oh. Krissy." Said like she hadn't heard from me in years. "Was there something you needed? I'm kind of busy right now."

"It's about the light I saw on at Death by Java two nights ago."

An impatient sigh. "Didn't we already talk about this? The light wasn't on when Farrah came in. You were probably mistaken. If that's all—"

"Where was Mickey that night?"

A long stretch of silence followed before she asked, "Why do you ask?"

From her tone, I realized I needed to be careful here. She wanted to protect him, which, since he was her boyfriend, was understandable.

But if he'd killed Lyle, she deserved to know. No one wanted to be dating a murderer. No sane person did, anyway.

"I'm not accusing him of anything," I said. "I'm simply trying to put a timeline for everyone together. Someone was inside Death by Java that night. If it wasn't you, and if it wasn't one of your employees, I'm assuming it had to be Mickey, right? Does anyone else have a key?"

"No . . ." Spoken slowly, almost uncertainly. "I don't see what this has to do with anything."

"Could Mickey have been meeting someone at Death by Java at night?" I pressed. "A friend? You, even?"

"What are you implying?" The heat in her voice told me I'd hit a nerve of some kind.

"I'm not implying anything," I said. "But if Mickey

was there that night, perhaps he was there the follow-ing evening too. He might have seen something that would help the police—"

Valerie cut me off. "Mickey wasn't there. He's not cheating on me. He wouldn't *dare*."

I hesitated. *Cheating?* Where had *that* come from?

Valerie took a deep breath and let it out in a huff. "Look, I'm sorry I snapped at you." She didn't sound it. "It's been a long day, and I'm having a hard time dealing with everything that's happened, so I'm a little short with everyone right now, okay?"

"It's all right. One more question, and then I'll let you go."

Another sigh, this one dramatic enough, she should have won an award. "Sure. Whatever. Go ahead."

"Your ice machine," I said. "I noticed the door was dented earlier today. Do you know when that hap-pened?"

Another long stretch of silence before she said, "I don't know what you mean."

"The ice machine—the one that was broken." As if there was more than one in the back room of Death by Java. "Roman was fixing it when I walked back there, and I'm pretty sure the door was fine then. The next day, when you showed me where Lyle had been found, I noticed the door was dented."

"You must have been mistaken," she said. "I didn't notice anything like that." Said like she *had* noticed, but didn't want to talk about it. Because she—or Mickey—was involved in the murder and realized it was a clue? Or because she hadn't thought of it as im-portant?

Or could she have dented it herself?

I tried to imagine Valerie doing *anything* that would have put a dent that shape and size into a metal door and couldn't do it.

Wait. That wasn't true. I could imagine one thing that could have happened. If it wasn't Mickey who was cheating, but Valerie, and with a certain handyman, possibly late at night where the only light was a flashlight to keep anyone else from noticing . . .

Which led me to another thought.

"You said there was a screwdriver on the floor near where Lyle was found," I said, keeping my tone neutral. "Do you really believe it was Roman's?" She'd claimed he might have dropped it, but was she positive? Or had she merely assumed it was his?

There was a beat of silence before she said, "I don't know. Maybe?" A rustle followed. "I really do need to go. Let's talk later, okay?"

Before I could respond, she was gone.

I lowered my phone with a frown. Valerie was lying. Whether to protect herself or Mickey, it didn't matter. No, I didn't need to know every sordid detail of her and Mickey's relationship with each other—or with anyone else. But if it cleared them of murder, why not at least *try* to explain things away? Being evasive only made her look guilty.

I closed my eyes and imagined the scene. Valerie, at Death by Java, meeting with Roman. Or maybe it was Mickey with one of the bookstore café's employees, let's say Farrah. Either way, they had a flashlight on as they romped around in the back room. Lyle happened by, and, like I did the night before, he saw the light. Maybe he assumed it was the back-room light, left on by accident, and he came up with a way he might be able to cite them for it. Maybe he saw movement and decided to go in and talk about the ice machine. He caught one of them cheating, threatened to cite them . . . because I imagined that hanky-panky in the back room of a café would be a major health violation.

Then what? Mickey—or Roman—killed him because of it? Did that mean Valerie, or whomever Mickey was cheating on her with, had seen the murder happen?

A soft knock at my bedroom door caused me to open my eyes.

"Krissy? You awake?" Paul gently eased open the door.

"Yeah. Just thinking."

"I'm sorry I'm so late," he said, entering the bedroom. "Gabby found out some interesting details on a few of the involved parties and wanted to get my take on it. And you know how slowly police business can go."

"Glacial."

He nodded, dropped heavily onto the bed. "Apparently, Lyle Carrigan had gone to the police about Mickey Robbins and Valerie Kemp about a week and a half ago. He claimed Robbins showed up at his place on Kemp's orders. Robbins didn't do anything but stand outside and stare, but it unnerved him."

"Wow," I said. "That doesn't sound good for Mickey."

"No, it doesn't. You throw in that scene in Death by

Java later and Mickey's current vanishing act, and it doesn't look good for him at all."

I blinked. "Mickey's missing?"

Paul seesawed his hand. "He's not picking up his phone, and he hasn't shown up at home or at Valerie Kemp's place since the body was discovered. I know you know them—"

"I know Valerie," I said. "Mickey is new to me."

He conceded the point. "He's making himself look guilty by avoiding the police. If he doesn't make an appearance soon, he's going to end up being the prime suspect."

If he's not already. I considered telling Paul about what I'd learned, about how Valerie had been evasive about the light and the ice machine, along with my suspicions that one, or both, of them were cheating on the other, but then I decided against it. Paul wasn't on duty. He had no jurisdiction here. And if I told him about it, he'd feel the need to talk to Gabby about it, which would mean another lost day while he helped her with the case instead of going to the beach with me.

"What do you think about us calling it a night and forgetting all about Mickey Robbins and murder?" I asked. "We have a big day tomorrow."

Paul grinned. "You, in a skimpy bikini, on the beach."

I made a face. "Bikini, yes. Skimpy, in your dreams."

He held out a hand, and when I took it, he pulled me down onto the bed next to him. "Have you been spying on my dreams?"

"Do I really need to?" I kissed his temple. "I'm

pretty sure I already know what's going on in that head of yours."

He held on to me for a couple of minutes more, murmuring things I won't repeat here. Let's just say that by the time he was done, I was keen on closing the door because I didn't want Dad or Laura to see me blush. Not for the first time, I wished we had gotten a hotel room somewhere in town, rather than staying with my dad, because there were just some things you didn't—and couldn't—do when visiting your family in their home.

9

"**D**o we have everything?" Dad scanned the pile of beach supplies with a frown. "I feel like we're forgetting something."

"It's all there," Laura said. "I've already triple checked. I even packed extra sunscreen, just in case you don't like the smell of mine, which, knowing you, you won't."

Dad pinched his nose and waved his hand in front of his face before he turned to Paul. "Are you ready for this? The drive should take less than two hours, and that's if I drive. Laura tends to follow all the traffic laws, which means we'll be putt-putting along just under the speed limit. And she hates passing, so if the car in front of us is going twenty miles per hour, then we're going to be going twenty miles per hour."

"Says the man who never drives because he thinks everyone else is a lunatic," Laura said.

"Well, they are!" Dad grinned. "And I'd drive if you'd ever let me. Of course, then all you'd do is squeal every time I come up on another car."

Laura just looked at him, causing him to laugh.

"Okay, maybe my reflexes aren't what they once were, but at least I'd get us there faster."

She rolled her eyes. "If we got there at all." She turned to Paul. "You know those old men who drive like the double yellow line is some sort of rail that they have to ride on?" She jerked a thumb at Dad. "He takes that to heart."

Dad's hand went to his chest, and he staggered back a step. "Are you calling me *old*?"

She raised both hands, palms outward. "I'm just saying that your assessment of our comparative driving skills might be somewhat inaccurate."

"Point conceded," Dad said, bowing his head to her before turning my way. "Buttercup?"

"Don't look at me," I said. "I'm not driving."

"And I have no idea where we're going," Paul said before Dad could look at him.

"Looks like we're putt-putting, then," Dad said with a sigh. "I suppose we'd best get the car loaded so we can get there before dark."

Laura elbowed him good-naturedly, and then we got to it.

Since this was only a beach day and not a full-fledged sightseeing trip, there wasn't much for us to pack. Bags filled with towels, sunscreen, and swimsuits were hoisted and placed in the trunk. A cooler full of drinks— mostly water—was added next to the snack bag, which consisted of carrot sticks, celery, and other freshly chopped veggies.

"I can sit in the back," Dad said once the car was loaded. "If you or Paul wants to ride up front, that is."

"I wouldn't hear of it," Paul said, looking to me.

"Me either," I said. "You can play the role of back-seat driver from up front just as easily, if not more so."

"Ha-ha." Dad smiled as he said it, despite his attempt at sounding offended. "We should get there early enough to snag a good spot. It's going to be busy, so be prepared for that. I was also thinking that on the way back, we could stop at—"

Before he could finish, my phone went off.

We all just stood there, surrounding the car, with everyone looking at me like I'd just belched out loud. Dread welled up in my gut because I *knew* that if I were to answer the phone, if I were to so much as pull it out of my back pocket and look at the screen, our fun little beach day would be ruined.

But what if it's Vicki about Death by Coffee and our electrical problem? Or Jules about Misfit. Or . . .

I made a pained face as I removed my phone from my pocket. A glance at the screen, and I let out a low groan before mouthing, *"Sorry,"* before answering.

"Hi, Valerie. We're about to—"

"Krissy! Thank goodness you answered. I'm at my wits' end here, and I don't know what to do!" Valerie sounded panicked. "My entire life is crumbling right before my eyes."

I took a few steps away from the car. "What's going on, Valerie? Did they arrest someone for Lyle's murder?"

"No!" she wailed. "And that's the problem. I got to thinking about what you said yesterday. The questions. I didn't answer you because I didn't know *how* to answer them. I don't want to believe it, but what else am

I supposed to think? I need you to come over right now. I need to talk this through before I lose my mind."

"Slow down," I said, catching only half of what she'd said. "Tell me exactly what's going on."

She took a deep couple of breaths before she said, "It's about Lyle's murder. That poor man." She tried to inject compassion into her voice, but failed. "I've thought about who could have done it and why anyone would want to kill him, and after serious consideration, I . . . I'm afraid I might be next."

"Did something else happen?" I asked as I imagined Mickey standing outside her house like some horror-movie villain.

"No. If it had, then I might feel better. It's what *hasn't* happened that's got me worried." Her voice dropped and became oddly muffled, as if she was shielding the mic with her hand. "Can you come over? I don't want to discuss it over the phone. Who knows who could be listening? I really do need to talk to you."

The question, *Can't you talk to someone else?* was on the tip of my tongue, but I bit it back. Even if she could, there was no way I could go to the beach and enjoy myself now. Not with an unsolved murder. Not with Valerie sounding as if she was scared for her life. She might be overstating things, might be shooting for overly dramatic so she could get her way, but could I really turn my back on her?

I sighed. "All right. Tell me where you want to meet."

"My place. I feel safe here." She rattled off her address so fast, I had to ask her to repeat it twice before I had it committed to memory. "Thank you so much, Krissy. I know . . ." She coughed, cleared her throat. "I know I haven't treated you the best over the years. The words are always out of my mouth before I realize I'm going to say them, and you know how it is, right? I have an image to keep up, so it's not like I can just apologize where everyone can hear."

"I get it." I didn't like it, but I understood it. To Valerie, her reputation was her life. As a teen, she couldn't be seen being cordial to someone as lowly as me. And she most definitely couldn't be seen as ever being in the wrong. "I'll be there in twenty minutes."

We clicked off, and I just stood there, my back to the others, rubbing at my eyes. A headache was forming, and I had a feeling it was going to be the sort that would last all day.

"That was Valerie Kemp, I take it?" Dad asked.

I nodded, heaved another sigh, then turned around. "Something's come up."

"We heard," Laura said.

"I'm sorry. I can't abandon her." I wished I could, but it just wasn't in me.

"No need to apologize," Paul said. "We understand. If you want, I can—"

"No." I held up a finger, forestalling him. "You three are going to the beach."

The three of them shared a look. It was Dad who answered. "We could always wait for you to finish with—"

I turned my finger toward him. "No. Go. I have no idea how long this is going to take or even what it is she's so scared of." Other than Mickey. I squeezed my phone, was tempted to throw it, before I pocketed it. "If this only takes a few minutes, I'll get an Uber and meet you guys there. Otherwise, I'll see you when you get back."

"I don't—" Paul snapped his lips together when I threatened him with my finger.

"If you're sure . . ." Laura sounded uncertain.

"I'm sure," I said, hating it that I was. "Go to the beach. Have fun. Show Paul all the sights. If I can't make it today, we still have next week."

"Can we at least give you a ride?" Laura asked. "There's no reason for you to have to call an Uber when we're right here."

Worries that Dad or Paul might use it as an excuse to accompany me inside Valerie's almost had me declining, but she was right. "That would be great."

I gave Laura Valerie's address, and then we piled into the car. Dad and Laura sat up front, with Paul and me in the back. As soon as we were strapped in, Paul took my hand and gave me a level look.

"If you change your mind and want me to come in with you, just say the word."

"I'll be okay," I said. "Valerie's probably blowing this whole thing out of proportion. And, hey, if Dad's right and Laura drives too carefully, I might even beat you guys to the beach."

"I heard that," Laura said from the front, while Dad merely chuckled.

"What about tonight?" Paul asked.

I almost asked him what he meant, but then it hit me. "The reunion thing?"

He nodded. "The reunion thing."

"I don't know. If Valerie is scared now, then I doubt she'll want to go. And if she doesn't go, I'm not sure anyone else will."

"I got the impression that *you* were the guest of honor."

I made a face. "I'm not sure how that happened. I wasn't joking when I said Bray and company weren't my friends." But what if some of my old high school friends *were* there? I'd feel bad if they showed up and I didn't. "Let's play it by ear. If everything's settled by tonight, then we can consider going."

"Works for me."

It took less than the promised twenty minutes to arrive at Valerie's place. The small bungalow sat at the end of a quiet, tree-lined street. The yard was barely there, but what little there was of it was well-tended. A short driveway led to a single-car garage. Laura pulled up behind one of those electric cars that looked more like a toy than something anyone would actually drive. I thought it was a strange choice for Valerie; she seemed the type to go for something far showier.

"I'll let you know how it goes," I said as I climbed out of the car.

"Good luck," Paul said with a parting kiss on my cheek.

A moment later, he, along with Dad and Laura, were off to the beach, and I was striding toward the paved walkway that led to the front door of a woman whom I'd once considered my nemesis.

As I rounded the small electric vehicle, I peered

through the window of the garage and was surprised to see another car inside. The silver BMW was far more Valerie's style. And even though it was sitting in a garage, she'd put in one of those window screens that was supposed to keep the sun from heating up the inside. I frowned at it, wondering, if *that* was Valerie's car, then who drove the small, toy-sized car out front?

I had my answer the moment I reached the door.

The bungalow had one of those large windows by the front door that took up a good portion of the frontage. The blinds were raised and the curtains parted, so that as soon as I was in front of it, I could look directly into the living room, where Valerie was seated on the couch, head buried against Hugh's shoulder. Her ex-boyfriend had his arms around her and was gently caressing her back and kissing the top of her head every couple of seconds.

Feeling like a voyeur, I looked away as I knocked on the door.

Valerie answered promptly, eyes red and swollen, as if she had, indeed, been crying, though there were no streaks in her carefully applied makeup. She motioned for me to enter, then led the way to the living room, where Hugh was now seated in a wooden rocking chair by the window, as if he'd been there the entire time. He kept his gaze firmly planted on the tops of his shoes.

"I'm glad you came, Krissy," Valerie said, sitting back down on the couch. "I was beside myself and didn't know who else to call."

"It's all right," I said before turning my attention to

the man who clearly wanted to go unnoticed. "Hi, Hugh. I'm surprised to see you here."

"Krissy." He ran his fingers through his bangs, as if trying to stretch them out so they'd cover his face. "I was in the neighborhood and thought I'd check in to make sure Val was doing okay."

"He showed up right after I called you," Valerie added. "I'm glad he did." She flashed him a smile that was as appreciative as it was inappropriate.

"Do you still want to talk?" I asked. "If not, I—"

"No, I do." Valerie picked up a tissue and tugged at its edges. "You know, I opened Death by Java because I wanted to give something back to the community. I thought the Village could use some high-class coffee. It's why I chose java when it came to my store instead of plain old coffee, like you use. It's just so much better, and I think the customers notice."

I bit the inside of my cheek to keep from saying something I might later regret. Knowing her, she probably believed everything she was saying.

"But look at what's happened!" she went on, tearing a small corner from her tissue. She looked at it as if shocked that it would dare to shred, then she balled the torn corner into the rest of the tissue, so as not to lose it. "Lyle hounded me day and night, threatening to have me closed down over nothing. And now . . . *this!*"

"I knew he was no good," Hugh said. "I told you as much the first day I saw the two of you together."

"But it's . . . it's . . . *Mickey!*" As if that explained everything.

"I feel like I'm missing something here," I said, head reeling from the sudden switch. "I thought we were talking about Lyle. Did something happen with Mickey?"

"He's avoiding me," Valerie said with a petulant stomp of her sandaled foot. "Like I said on the phone, I was thinking about those questions you were asking about Mickey and what he's been up to as of late. It got me thinking, and I realized there were quite a few nights when I had no idea where he was. I'd call him, and he wouldn't answer his phone. Or if he did, he'd be all evasive-like, and he wouldn't tell me where he was. I just assumed he was sleeping with one of his old girlfriends." Spoken as if she couldn't care one way or the other if he did. "But what if that's not what he was doing at all?"

"Where was Mickey the night Lyle died?" I asked.

"I don't know!" she wailed, pressing the balled-up tissue to her mouth. "I don't know where he's been the last few weeks, truth be told. He's assured me it's nothing, but what if it's not? What if he killed Lyle? What if he thinks I know all about it and he's going to come after me next? What if—"

Hugh shot from his chair and rushed over to where Valerie was near hyperventilating. He gathered her into his arms and shot me a glare, as if it was my fault she was panicking. She let him hug her close as they sank back down onto the couch together, resuming the pose I'd noted through the window.

"She's very upset," he explained when her sobs—real or exaggerated—eased. "Mickey meant a lot to her, and now he's doing this. If I wasn't such a gentle soul, I might have a word or two with him myself."

I found that hard to believe. Mickey could easily twist Hugh into a pretzel, and I was pretty sure Hugh knew it.

"Has she talked to the police about any of this?" I asked.

It was like I'd taken an electric prod to her. Valerie jerked upright so fast, the top of her head struck Hugh's chin. His teeth *clack*ed together hard, and he just about fell off the couch when he recoiled. Valerie surged to her feet, then took a quick two steps my way.

"You can't tell them anything about what we talk about here!" she demanded. "They'll arrest Mickey, and what will everyone think about me then? I'll be a laughingstock. I won't be able to show my face around town, and then where would I be?"

Alive, I thought. "If you're afraid he might have killed Lyle and that he's coming for you, don't you think the police *should* know?" I asked. "No one's going to hold it against you if you're the one who turned him in. In fact, they might call you a hero for it. Brave."

Valerie blinked as she thought about it. Yeah, I'd laid it on a bit thick, but honestly, if it made her do the right thing, it would be worth it. "I don't know . . ."

"Listen to her, Val," Hugh said through semi-clenched teeth as he rubbed his jaw. "Better to let them know than to have him show up here in the middle of the night. I could always stay here tonight if it would make you feel better."

Valerie still appeared undecided, so I pulled my phone from my pocket and held it up for her to see. "Let me call them. I'll wait with you for Detective McKensie to show up. You tell her what you told me, give her any other details you might have about Lyle and Mickey's interactions with one another, and then we can go from there."

"I bet you'll feel better if you told them," Hugh added. "It'll be a weight off your shoulders."

And it would give Hugh the in he'd been waiting for. I couldn't help but wonder if Hugh had killed Lyle and had framed Mickey for it. If so, he'd done a pretty poor job of it, considering how little evidence there was, but no one said Hugh was a brilliant man. Even if he wasn't involved, there was no question that he was trying to take advantage of the situation.

"Are you sure about this?" Valerie asked, looking from me to Hugh. "What if I'm wrong? I don't want to do that to Mickey if he's innocent."

"He doesn't have to know that you talked to the police," I said. "He has to realize that they'll want to talk to the both of you. It's not like Detective McKensie would betray your trust when she finally does pin him down, especially if you ask her to leave your name out of it."

Valerie considered it a long moment, lip trapped between her teeth, before she nodded. "All right. Call them." She eased back down onto the couch, though I noted Hugh didn't join her this time. He'd chosen to return to the rocking chair, still rubbing at his jaw, though I could see the calculation in the way he was looking at her.

I stepped out of the room to make the call, which was short and sweet. The officer who answered assured me Detective McKensie would be there within the next fifteen or twenty minutes, then disconnected. That done, I sent Paul a text, telling him I was still at Valerie's and that it might be a little while longer before I could get away. I was still hopeful I'd have time to meet them at the beach, but with how things were going, I wasn't counting on it.

10

Detective McKensie arrived alone. I stood at Valerie's window and watched as she parked and unfurled herself from a car that appeared too small for her long frame. She eyed my car, then Hugh's, before making her way to the front door. She took everything in, right down to the parted curtain, without making it obvious that she was cataloging every sight and sound.

Detective Buchannan would love her, I thought as McKensie knocked on the door. Valerie, who was already waiting, answered promptly and then led the detective into the living room, where Hugh and I were waiting.

"Ms. Hancock," McKensie said, nodding to me. She paused, glanced around the room with a slight frown. "Where's Paul?"

"At the beach with my dad," I said, noting how she'd used his first name, while I was merely a 'Ms.' "After we're done here, I'm hoping to join them."

"I see." Her smile was flat, almost disapproving, before she turned to Hugh. "And you are?"

"I'm Valerie's—"

"Ex-boyfriend," Valerie cut in. "Recently separated. I'm with Mickey now." Her face reddened, and then a flare of panic shot through her eyes as she seemed to recall that she was currently afraid of Mickey Robbins.

Detective McKensie eyed them both before asking Hugh, "Do you have a name?"

"Uh, yeah." A beat before he seemed to realized that she wanted to know it, then, "Hugh. Irwin. Hugh Irwin." He cleared his throat. "Like the crocodile guy."

"The crocodile guy." Not a question, but Hugh answered anyway.

"Yeah, you know the one." A nervous laugh followed. "He used to be on TV a long time ago. And I guess our first names are different, but I meant that our last names are—"

"None of this is about Hugh," Valerie cut in before Hugh could embarrass himself any further. "This is about Mickey."

"I see." McKensie continued to watch Hugh, who was fidgeting and looking like he might be sick. "How about you and I have a chat, while these two wait in another room?" Her eyes flickered to Valerie, then back to Hugh. "I'd like to talk to everyone here before I let you all go."

Hugh paled. "I really should get going."

McKensie's smile was all teeth. "This won't take long."

"You can wait in the bedroom," Valerie said to Hugh. "You know the way."

That caused McKensie's eyebrows to rise. Hugh didn't notice because he had already turned and scurried down the hall. The detective turned expectantly to me.

"I'll wait outside," I said. I had no intention of going into Valerie Kemp's bedroom with her ex-boyfriend. "I need to make a call anyway."

"Don't go anywhere," Detective McKensie warned.

"I won't." I slipped past the two women and out the door into sunlight that felt a little too bright after the tense, gloomy aura hovering around Valerie. I took a moment to close my eyes and let the warmth seep through me before I sent Paul a quick text, letting him know that I hoped to be on the way within the next half hour.

The reply was quick in coming: *Hope to see you there.* It was followed by a kiss emoji that had me smiling.

I debated on sending him one back, but the thought that Dad might see it kept me from going through with it. Funny how no matter how old I got, I still felt like a kid when it came to keeping my personal life away from my dad.

I tapped my phone against my palm as I considered what to do next. I mean, I knew what I *wanted* to do, but I wasn't sure if I should. I didn't want people to think I was a worrywart, but, well, if the shoe fit . . .

I hit the call button and began chewing on my thumbnail as I listened to it ring.

"Krissy? How's California?"

"Hi, Jules. It's been good." Jules Phan was the owner

and operator of Pine Hills's best candy store, Phantastic Candies. He was also my neighbor whom I'd tasked with keeping an eye on my cat while I was gone. "How's Misfit doing?"

Jules laughed. "Spoiled. He's taking over your house to the point that I'm not sure you're going to be able to move back in without his permission."

I smiled. "As expected."

"He tolerates me coming in to feed him, but as soon as that's done, it's like I don't even exist. And if I tell him to get off the counter or try to move him, he becomes more obstinate than Maestro." His white Maltese. "I've never known a cat who could dig his claws into a countertop and make himself feel at least a hundred pounds heavier like your kitty."

"So, he's acting normal, then," I said with a laugh.

"He is. One sec." His voice turned muffled, and there was a *clunk* that I assumed was his cash register. "Okay. Sorry about that."

"No, I shouldn't have called. You're at work."

"It's all right. I could use the break." He groaned, and I imagined him leaning against the counter, crossing legs adorned with one of his colorful outfits. "I'm surprised you called. I figured you'd be out sunning yourself somewhere with Paul."

"I plan on it," I said. "In fact, I'll be heading to the beach with him very soon." I hoped. "It's just . . ."

"I get it. You want to know about Death by Coffee without anyone else finding out that you're not enjoying your vacation because you're too busy worrying about things beyond your control?"

"Something like that."

Jules chuckled. "Vicki has everything under control. I've been stopping in as you requested, and while there have been some fluctuations in the electricity, nothing has gone boom or flat-out shut off for more than a second or two. At least, not while I was there."

"Does she seem okay?" I asked. "Vicki, I mean. I talked to her, but you know how she is." *How I am*, was what I really meant, but he didn't call me out on it.

"She's fine. We're all okay. Really, Krissy, there's no need to worry. The only person who seems upset by your absence—and don't take this personally—is Rita. She's been in here at least four times over the last two days, asking if I've heard from you. She said something about a video chat—"

I groaned. "Yeah. With Dad. They had a nice little conversation the other night on his computer. Has she been trying to reach him again?"

"She has. She thinks you've taken his tablet from him."

"What? I have not!"

"I told her as much when I saw her this morning. She thinks you're punishing her for some reason. Honestly, I think she's just lonely. And we all know how she feels about your father."

Did we ever. Though, while Rita had a thing for my dad, I didn't believe she'd ever act on it. "I'll make sure Dad gives her a call tonight. Paul and I are thinking of going to a class reunion that some old classmates of mine are putting together this evening. Dad should have lots of free time to talk to her then."

"I'll let her know. She'll probably rush straight home and wait with bated breath for the call."

And, knowing Rita, she'd do it with the cardboard cutout of Dad she kept in her bedroom watching over her.

Don't ask.

A car drifted slowly down the road toward Valerie's drive. It lingered half a second before continuing past. I watched as it vanished from sight.

"I'd better let you go," I said, mildly curious. While Detective McKensie *was* at Valerie's, her car wasn't marked, so I didn't think it was some sort of looky-loo. "Tell everyone I said hi."

"Will do. And, Krissy?"

"Yeah?"

"Have fun."

I smiled. "I will. I'll call you in a day or so. And I'll do it at night, when you're not at work. Maybe I can time it for when you're at my place and you can put me on speaker so Misfit can hear my voice."

He laughed. "I'm sure he'd love that."

We said our goodbyes and clicked off just as the slow-moving car returned. This time, instead of passing by, it rolled to a stop behind Detective McKensie's car. It sat there a long moment, engine running, before falling silent, and Aaron Middleton stepped out, a look of confusion on his face.

"What's going on?" he asked. His step was brisk, as if he was afraid something had happened to his ex. "Is Valerie all right?"

"She's fine, just shaken up." I debated on filling him in, but decided it wasn't my place.

He chewed on his lower lip as he looked toward the

front door. "Should I go in?" he asked. "I see that Hugh is here, but . . ." His gaze drifted to McKensie's car.

"Valerie had some concerns she wanted to share with Detective McKensie," I explained, keeping it nice and vague. "They're talking right now. It shouldn't be much longer."

Aaron's brow furrowed as he turned back to me. "Is this about Mickey?"

The question caught me by surprise, but then again, should it have? "Is there a reason she should be worried about him?" I asked, keeping my voice neutral, so as not to give anything away.

He rubbed his hands together as if trying to warm them, despite the sunny day. "Nah. Well, I mean, he's not right for her, so there's that, I suppose. There are days when she clearly needs him at Death by Java, even if only for moral support, and he never shows. Hugh and I have chipped in far more than he has. What kind of guy leaves his girl alone like that?"

"You and Hugh seem to spend a lot of time around Valerie," I said, ignoring the use of the term *girl* for a grown woman. "I'm surprised since you're no longer together. Most people aren't usually interested in hanging around their exes."

Aaron blinked rapidly, then looked away. "Yeah, well, just because we broke up, it doesn't mean I don't still care. And while Hugh is cool and all, he was never right for her. He's best as a friend, and I'm pretty sure he knows it."

Which meant Aaron didn't view him as competition, unlike Mickey.

And while he hadn't said it, it was obvious that

Aaron wanted Valerie back. One look at the way he looked at her, at how he worried about her, and you could see it.

But would his, dare I call it, *obsession* with Valerie Kemp cause him to kill someone like Lyle Carrigan, all to make Mickey Robbins look bad?

I was trying to formulate some sort of question that would answer that for me without making it too obvious what I was thinking when the door opened and Detective McKensie stepped outside. "All done in there," she said. If she was surprised to see Aaron in the driveway, she didn't show it. "Ms. Hancock. A word?"

Aaron took a step toward the door, reconsidered. "May I check on Valerie?" he asked the detective, as polite as could be.

McKensie eyed him a moment before nodding. "She's inside." She watched Aaron as he scurried inside. "That woman has more clingers-on than a Velcro sweater." She turned to me. "Ms. Kemp called you?"

A Velcro sweater? I shook off the thought. "She did."

"She has concerns about her boyfriend, and she calls *you*." The emphasis on the last word was accompanied by an unspoken question. *Why?*

"We've known each other a long time," I said, though *known* was a bit strong of a word. "And since I've been helping around Death by Java over the last few days, I imagine she thought that perhaps I might have a few insights into what's going on."

"About her relationship?" Spoken flat. "From what I gather, you two barely know each other. You don't live around here anymore, isn't that correct?"

"No, I don't," I admitted. "And to tell you the truth, I don't know why Valerie called, other than that I was convenient. Maybe she didn't want to talk to her exes about her current boyfriend since it would be awkward and might hurt a few feelings."

"Then why not call a friend?" McKensie asked. "Someone she sees regularly. You two are practically strangers these days."

I bristled at that, but honestly, she wasn't wrong. "She could have wanted a fresh opinion. I don't know Mickey beyond sight. I have no preconceived notions about him, no past history."

"An outside opinion?"

I nodded. "She's worried Mickey might have been the one to have hurt Lyle. Hugh and Aaron likely would lean toward agreeing with her because of their past relationships. I imagine some of her friends might feel the same way, especially if they have a negative opinion of Mickey."

"Do you?"

"I don't know," I said. "It's not my place to say. I came here, told Valerie that she should tell you everything she knows, and . . ." I gestured toward her, as if saying, *"And now my job is done."*

McKensie eyed me for a long moment before she asked, "What can you tell me about Mr. Carrigan's tablet?"

I hesitated, surprised by the sudden shift. "His tablet? The one with the rubber case?"

"I assume so."

Realization hit, causing my eyes to widen. "It's missing?"

McKensie just stared, neither confirming nor denying it. But if she was asking about the tablet, then chances were good that the police hadn't found it. Valerie *had* mentioned that it wasn't near his body. I'd assumed he'd left it in his car, or perhaps at home, but what if the killer had taken it?

"He was carrying it every time I saw him," I said, thinking it through. "He used it for work, so I don't know whether he ever carried it with him for personal use."

"When did you last see it?"

I thought back. "I suppose it was the last time I saw him."

McKensie's expression turned annoyed. "Which was . . . ?"

"At the Italian Roll," I said, though uncertainty marred the words. "I'm pretty sure that was the last time I saw him."

"'Pretty sure'?"

"Almost positive," I amended. "He was leaving just as I arrived. He had his tablet with him then." I waited a beat, then said, "Valerie told me he didn't have his tablet when she found his body. I take it you didn't find it in his home?"

I might as well have asked a brick wall. "If you recall any other instance when you might have seen Mr. Carrigan, please let me know." She looked at her watch and scowled. "I'd like to discuss Mr. Robbins with you, but I have somewhere else I need to be."

"I'm not sure I can tell you much more than what Valerie has already told you about Mickey," I said. "Like I mentioned before, I barely know him."

"Be that as it may, I'd like to have a little chat. I'll contact Paul, set up a meet." A change came over her face when she said Paul's name. A lightening around the eyes, the bleeding away of tension. It was the sort of reaction I had every time I thought of him, which was normal for *me*. I didn't like seeing it on another woman's face.

"I'm not sure what kind of time we'll have," I said, trying to keep the barbs out of my voice. I wasn't jealous. No, seriously, I wasn't.

Not really.

"I'm sure we'll figure something out." Another look at her watch. "I'll be in touch."

I wanted to argue, but what good would it do? I'd managed to pull myself—and, much to my dismay, Paul—into the murder investigation, all because I couldn't just walk away. If I hadn't insisted on going to Death by Java, if I hadn't taken Valerie's call, I'd be sitting on a beach right now, enjoying the sun with my family and the one man I wanted to spend the rest of my life with.

Instead, it appeared as if we'd be spending a chunk of our time with Detective McKensie, a woman who was clearly smitten with my boyfriend.

I watched as she speed-walked her way to her car. She paused at the door, taking one last speculative look at the cars in the driveway, at the house where Valerie was currently being comforted by a pair of men who were still seeking her love and acceptance, despite the breaking off of their relationships. Then McKensie climbed into her vehicle and drove off, leaving me to stand alone in Valerie's driveway, wishing I was anywhere but.

The good news was, now that she was gone, I *could* be somewhere else.

Putting Detective McKensie out of my mind, I headed inside to find Valerie. She wouldn't like it, but I was going to make her pay me back for our chat by having her drive me to the beach. It was the least she could do.

And yeah, a part of me was annoyed. Mostly at myself, but also at Valerie. If she could just choose one man, could look beyond her own personal wants and needs, then perhaps none of this would have happened. It was a jaded thought, but this was supposed to be my vacation. I wasn't supposed to be there at the house of my high school nemesis, talking about a murdered man with a detective and someone I didn't really even like.

Valerie was in the living room with both Hugh and Aaron. I half-expected them to be locked in some weird, three-person embrace, but they were all seated around the room, with no one touching. There were somber expressions all around, which caused me to feel guilty for my recent unkind thoughts.

"Detective McKensie's gone," I said. "I'm sorry to ask, Valerie, but I was headed to the beach with my family when you called. Do you think you could—"

Valerie surprised me by speaking up before I'd finished. "Yeah, sure. I'll take you. You came here when you didn't have to. I owe you for that at least." She stood. "Give me a few minutes to get ready." She started to leave the room, then paused. "You know, a trip to the beach sounds good right about now. I could use the break from all of this." She waved a hand vaguely around the room.

"I could go with you," Hugh said from the rocking chair. "If you want company, that is."

Aaron rose to his feet. "Me too. I don't have anywhere else I need to be, and I have swim trunks in the car."

They looked like abandoned puppies, desperate for attention.

Valerie smiled at them both. "I think I want to do this one alone, guys. I'll call you later." I noted that her eyes lingered on Aaron when she said the last.

Neither man moved, as if they hoped she'd change her mind.

"Go," she said, making a shooing motion. "It's girl time now."

Hugh and Aaron shared a look, and then, like the aforementioned abandoned puppies, they sulked their way out the door.

"Men," Valerie said with a roll of her eyes. "So, which beach are we going to?"

Before I could answer, Valerie's phone rang. She held up a finger to me and answered the phone with a terse, "What is it?" A moment of silence followed. "Are you sure? You can't—" Another stretch where I could vaguely hear a raised voice that sounded female, but it was hard to tell since it was so faint. "Okay. I'll be there." She clicked off and turned back to me, an apologetic expression on her face.

My heart sank. "You're not taking me to the beach."

"I will!" Her face scrunched up. "But not right away. That was Dee. There's an emergency at Death by Java that needs my attention right away. It can't wait. I prom-

ise that once it's taken care of, I'll drive you to wherever you want to go."

I considered telling her not to worry about it, that I'd
just call an Uber, but the fact that it was an emergency
at Death by Java—which, as far as I knew, was closed
while the investigation was ongoing—had me curious
enough that I thought that I could spare a little more
time. Paul and Dad would understand.

"Sure," I said. "And if there's anything I can do to
help . . ."

Valerie flashed me a smile that was just shy of condescending, then she started down the hall. "Let me
grab my bikini, and then we'll be on our way."

II

It took me a moment to recognize Dee as Valerie and I pulled up in front of Death by Java. She was standing at the doors, wearing jeans and a black T-shirt, and looking the part of a normal, worried woman. There wasn't a pink dress in sight.

"I hope this doesn't take too long," Valerie said as we climbed out of her car. She was wearing loose shorts and a tank top that hung so loose, it didn't hide much. Her bikini was on beneath that, and it might as well have been the only thing she'd worn considering how little the rest of her outfit covered. "I really would like to get to the beach soon."

Dee waited for us by the doors. She was wringing her hands together and kept looking through the glass. As soon as we reached her, she said, "I can't get to Oscar! He's trapped in there and I can't get in, and I don't know what's going to happen to him."

"Calm down, Dee," Valerie said as we joined her. "It's just a cat."

That, of course, didn't sit well with Dee—or me, for that matter. We both shot Valerie a glare that would have sent her scurrying for cover if she hadn't been too busy searching for her keys in her purse to notice.

"I should have been here this morning," Dee said. "I should have at least checked in on him and made sure he was taken care of." She paced away, came right back. "When I realized that no one else would think to feed him, I drove over, and no one was here! What's going on? Did something happen? Did that health inspector close us down?" Panic caused the volume of her voice to rise.

"It's a long story," I said as Valerie finally produced her keys. No sense in scaring Dee with tales of murder. "You take care of the cat?"

Dee nodded. "His name is Oscar. He was a stray, but since Valerie was letting him stay, I figured I could take care of him. I'm not allowed to have a cat at my place. I'm renting, and pets are a no-no, so this felt like the perfect solution."

Valerie unlocked the door and pushed it open. "Go on in and get him," she said. "Just don't go into the back room."

"I'm sorry I dragged you out here," Dee said before she slipped inside, already calling Oscar's name.

Valerie rolled her eyes as she let the door swing closed. "I really hope she hurries. I need at least two hours of good sun to even start to tan." She gave me a smile that was just this side of condescending. "Not that *I* need much in the way of a tan." Her eyes dropped to my legs, then back to my face.

I ignored the implied jab about my glaringly white

complexion and asked, "Are you planning on adopting Oscar and getting him acclimated to people?"

"What?" Valerie made a face. "No. He was living in the alley before he snuck into the shop one day. Smells like an alley cat too." She shuddered in disgust. "But since he was here, and you let a cat live in *your* bookstore, I figured, why not let him stay?"

I could have told her that Trouble, the cat who "lived" in Death by Coffee, was Vicki's cat, and he didn't actually live there. Vicki brought him in when either she or her husband, Mason, were working, often letting him stay until closing time. And, unlike Oscar, he didn't attack the customers. He typically just lounged around somewhere upstairs, usually on a bookshelf, and rarely caused trouble.

"Do you remember seeing Oscar when the police were here?" I asked, because I sure didn't. "You'd think all the commotion would have spooked him."

"I didn't pay attention," Valerie said. She tapped her foot and peered in through the doors. "I'm not sure why Dee is so worried. Oscar can take care of himself. I mean, he gets let out to take care of his business and someone usually lets him back in. Since no one was here, though, he's probably out doing cat things around town."

"What if he's stuck inside?" I asked, trying to keep the annoyance out of my voice. "He would need water and food. And unless you want him to 'take care of his business' all over your floor, he'd need someone here to let him out. Or be given a litter box."

Valerie's nose scrunched. "Ew. Those things stink."

They did, but if you wanted a cat, it was a necessity.

Before I could explain the finer points of cat owner-ship to Valerie, Dee came sprinting out the door. "He's not in there!"

"See?" Valerie said. "There was no need to worry."

"But he hasn't eaten." Dee reached into the pocket of her jeans and removed a small can of cat food, sealed with a rubber lid. "I don't want him eating scraps. He'll get worms!" By the looks of him, I wasn't so sure he didn't have them already.

Exasperation flashed across Valerie's face. "He'll be fine." She turned to me. "Shall we go?"

One look at the desperation on Dee's face, and I knew there was no way I could abandon her here, wor-ried about Oscar.

"Do you want me to help you look for him?" I asked her.

"Really? Yes, please!" Dee practically dropped to her knees thanking me. "He can't be far. He always sticks pretty close when he goes out, but I didn't see him when I showed up, and I looked."

Valerie sighed audibly. "Do we really have time for this?"

"It shouldn't take long," I said, tamping down my annoyance. "If you keep an eye out here, you can text me if Oscar shows up. I have my phone on me."

Another Valerie eye roll before, "Yeah, sure. What-ever. I'll be inside."

And with that, she turned and pushed her way into Death by Java, where I assumed she'd sit at one of the chairs and scroll through her phone until we returned.

"Where do you want to start?" I asked, turning to Dee.

She thought about it a moment, then started walking. "He might be in the alley. He wasn't there earlier, but he could have shown up since. Thanks again for this. I know you don't have to."

"It's my pleasure."

We rounded Death by Java and made our way toward the alley. Dee's head was on a swivel as she looked for Oscar, and she kept fingering the can of cat food, which she'd returned to her pocket. Gone was the pink dress–wearing snob I'd taken her to be. In its place was a woman who seemed genuinely concerned for a cat that most people would dismiss because of how scraggly and mean he appeared. That raised my opinion of her quite a bit.

We reached the alley and had a look around, but no Oscar. Dee frowned, looked both ways, then turned and led the way past Tito's, making those kissing sounds that always seemed to attract cats.

"Do you like working at Death by Java?" I asked as we walked. Trash bins lined the alley. Most were closed and kept relatively clean, while a couple were rusting at the bottom, seeping ick out onto the ground. I hoped Oscar kept well clear of those.

Dee glanced at me, shrugged. "I guess. It's a job. I like Oscar, and I love the smell of coffee in the morning."

Because I sensed it, I asked, "But?"

"But I hate the clothes. I hate having to act like a Valley Girl or some brain-dead cheerleader because that's what Valerie thinks will bring in customers." A pause. "Not that I'm trying to insult cheerleaders or Valley Girls."

"It's okay. I know what you meant."

"And it's not like we're raking in the big bucks, either. I had to buy that stupid dress with my own money. Valerie knows the woman who sells them and had us all order from her. She probably got a kickback for it. And since I bought the thing, I feel like I have to keep working there to justify how much I paid for it. It's not like I can turn around and sell it. Who would wear something like that?"

Not me, that was for sure.

"And then there's Valerie and her endless stream of men," Dee went on, seemingly more than happy to talk about her grievances. "I swear, every time I look up, she's making eyes at every halfway-decent-looking guy who walks through the door. It's getting to the point where I'm not sure if there is a man she hasn't put the moves on at one time or another. It's like she feels as if their attention justifies her existence."

Carefully, so as not to make it seem like I was prying—which I, of course, was—I asked, "Is that all she does? Make eyes at them?"

"Oscar!" Dee called, making more kissing sounds, before answering. "Who knows? I'm always out of there before dark, so thankfully, I'm not there to see what happens at night. Seeing the evidence of it in the morning is bad enough."

"What evidence?"

Out came the can, along with a small silver spoon from her other pocket. She tapped on the side of the can as she said, "Don't get me wrong, it's not like it happens all the time. Usually I just find a few things on the floor in the back, like they were knocked off the shelves by someone doing something they shouldn't be doing." She glanced meaningfully at me. "I haven't found discarded clothing or anything like that, if that's what you're thinking. If I ever do, that'll be it for me."

I couldn't imagine what I'd do if I ever came into Death by Coffee and found someone's boxers lying next to the coffee beans. Fumigate, more than likely.

"Are you sure it's not just the closers being care-less?" I asked.

"No. I asked Farrah about it once, and she told me everything was in order when she'd left. Both Mickey and Valerie were there that night, though, and we sort of put two and two together." She stopped walking and turned to face me. "None of this can get back to Valerie, all right? I know you're her friend—"

"I'm not," I said, cutting her off. "And I won't tell her anything. Promise."

Dee chewed on her lower lip, her eyes scanning the area. This time, I wasn't so sure she was looking for Oscar. "I'm ninety percent sure Valerie is cheating on Mickey," she said. "They might have been there to-gether that night, but there are other nights when I'm running evening errands and I go by and I see her there with other guys, usually one of her exes. She doesn't know I know, so . . ."

I mimed crossing my heart and zipping my lips. "When you say you 'see her with other guys,' what do you mean?"

Dee considered it a moment before answering. "I'm not saying I've seen her kissing someone else or any-thing like that. It's more of a vibe thing. You see two people together, and you just *know* there's something going on between them."

I got it. I got the same vibes from seeing Valerie with Hugh and Aaron, which brought me to my next question. "Who have you seen her with? Other than Hugh and Aaron, I mean?"

Dee studied me a moment, then asked, "What's going on? Why's Death by Java closed?"

I debated on what to tell her, but then opted for the truth. It wasn't like it was a secret. If she were to go home and turn on the news, she'd find out.

I had just opened my mouth to tell her about Lyle's murder when a door opened from the building into the alley, and a guy with a beard that went halfway down his chest exited, carrying a bag of trash. He eyed us distrustfully for a moment before tossing the bag into a trash bin. Another distrustful stare, then he tromped back inside.

"We should probably head back," Dee said with a sigh. "We're not going to find Oscar like this."

I agreed.

We started back toward Death by Java, and since she hadn't pushed the issue, I expected the conversation to be over, but Dee surprised me by speaking up.

"I don't think Valerie wants to hurt Mickey or any of the guys she's cheating on him with," she said. "She just doesn't know how else to act. It's like she thinks her looks are the only thing she has going for her. I'm not sure she understands that she doesn't have to act that way to get people to like her, you know?"

Sadly, I did. The more I got to know Valerie Kemp,

the more I realized that her entire self-worth was wrapped up in how others saw her. She wanted women to be envious; she wanted to attract all the men. She didn't see that she could just be herself, without worrying about what anyone else thought, and *that* would make her a far more attractive person to most people.

Dee fell silent, and I was content to leave it at that. I'd already suspected Valerie was cheating on Mickey, and my conversation with Dee had all but confirmed it. I wasn't positive her infidelity had anything to do with Lyle's murder, but it was a place to start.

What I *did* know was that if she was using Death by Java as a home base for her illicit liaisons, then it was likely that other business owners in the area knew about it.

I need to talk to Tito, I thought. If anyone would know who was going in and out of Death by Java after hours, it would be the deli owner next door.

"Oscar!"

The scruffy, black-and-white cat was sitting near the back door to Death by Java as we approached the bookstore cafe. At the sound of Dee's excited exclamation, he'd risen to all fours and arched his back, but as soon as he saw who it was, his entire demeanor changed. He let out a croaking *meow* and pranced in place, favoring a front paw, as Dee rushed over to him.

"There you are," she said, pulling the can of food from her pocket. "I've been looking all over for you! Are you hurt?"

Oscar made another strangled-sounding *meow*, rubbed up against her shin, and then practically ripped the can from her hand as she popped the lid off and set the food down in front of him. He dove in like he hadn't eaten in days.

"Eat up," she told him. "I don't think Valerie's going to let you in. I'm not sure what to do." She stroked his back, which he allowed. It was clear he trusted her, and I wished that things could be different and she could take him home. He deserved it. They both did.

Oscar shifted his stance so that he wasn't putting as much weight on that front paw of his. It didn't look broken or bloody, so it didn't appear serious. Still . . .

"Has he been to the vet?" I asked.

Dee shook her head and kept petting the cat. "I don't have the money to take him, and Valerie doesn't care. I even bought a cat carrier, just in case, though I've never gotten the chance to use it."

"Where do you keep it?" I asked. "The carrier, I mean?"

"In my car." She glanced back over her shoulder. "Why?"

I hesitated, but there wasn't any real debate on what I was going to do. The cat needed care, and I was in a position to give it to him. No, I didn't have a home for him, but I could at least make sure he got his shots and tests, not to mention having his paw looked at and getting him fixed. The latter should cut down on his wandering some, and that, in turn, would hopefully prevent him from injuring himself again.

"Get it," I said. "If we can get him into it, we can take him to the vet. I'll pay for everything."

Dee rose, eyes widening. "Really? Are you sure?" She glanced down at Oscar, who was still chowing down. "You don't have to do this. I appreciate it, but I—"

"I'm sure," I said, cutting her off. "I'll keep an eye on him while you grab the carrier."

Dee grinned. "Okay. Yeah. I'll be right back."

Moving quickly, but carefully, so as not to startle the cat, Dee hurried back around Death by Java, toward where I assumed she'd parked her car.

As I watched Oscar eat, I wondered who had let him out the night of Lyle's death. Valerie hadn't, nor had Dee. Could one of the other employees have done it? I found it unlikely, considering none of them appeared to have anything to do with the cat.

But if not them, then who?

"Do you know who killed Lyle?" I asked, keeping my voice low so no one else would hear.

Oscar didn't so much as glance up at me. Even if he *could* talk, I wasn't so sure he'd tell me.

12

I grimaced as I applied the last Band-Aid to my forearm, just below the crook in my elbow. To say Oscar
hadn't been happy about being shoved into a cat carrier
and hauled to the vet would be an understatement. The
cat became all claws and teeth and made sounds I'd
never heard come from any animal, let alone a cat. But
between Dee and me, we got him into the carrier with
what I'd consider minimal damage to our persons.

A quick drive to a vet that was open during the weekend, a bit of coaxing to get them to take a stray without
an appointment, and then a decision to let them keep
Oscar for a few days so they could make sure he was in
tip-top shape, made for a long couple of hours. After
that, Dee dropped me off at Dad's. Valerie hadn't been
about to miss her chance to relax on the beach, and so
she'd left long before we'd even finished corralling
Oscar.

I used one of Dad's hand towels to dab at my still-
damp arm. Peroxide was followed by Neosporin, just

in case Oscar's claws were dirtier than they'd appeared. None of the scratches were too deep, but I wasn't going to take any chances, not with how my luck had been going as of late.

Once that was done, I went out into the living room, threw myself down onto the couch, and watched TV while I pouted about missing out on beach day. Dad had sent me periodic updates throughout the day, exclaiming about how nice it was, and how he'd keep an eye on Paul for me because, as he put it, the "eye candy" was rather "spectacular." That was followed by a picture of a bunch of college-age men and women playing volleyball in tiny swimsuits that made Valerie's own look like a poncho.

Time passed. I'm not sure how much. I barely noticed what was playing on the television. I kept thinking about Valerie and Mickey and how they were at the center of Lyle's murder. I was having trouble seeing how they *couldn't* be involved. It had happened in their store. They were both being evasive—with Mickey having dropped completely off the map. They might as well have painted guilty across their foreheads and called it a day.

As much as I hated to admit it, I found myself looking forward to the upcoming reunion. Valerie's friends would be there, as would be people who knew most of the individuals involved with the crime. And since I expected Valerie herself to make an appearance, freshly bronzed from the beach, it would give me yet another opportunity to coax something useful out of her.

It wasn't quite evening when Paul, Dad, and Laura

laughed their way through the front door. Dad's nose was pink, while Laura looked the same as she had when she'd left. Paul, on the other hand, glowed as if he'd become radioactive.

"Forget your sunscreen?" I asked with a wide smile.

"I bathed in the stuff." He stuck a finger into his ear and wiggled it around. "And I have sand everywhere."

"I have a theory that sand is sentient and mobile," Dad said. "It will find a way into every crevice, every device, into every single pore of your body, no matter how hard you try to keep it out."

"Wait until you take a shower," Laura added. "You'll be standing in a sand dune by the time you're done, with no idea where it all came from."

"I think I'm going to go do that now." Paul started down the hall, but he paused when he got a good look at me. "What happened to you?"

"I had a wrestling match with a cat," I said, holding up my Band Aid–adorned arms and hands.

"There's a cat here?" Dad asked, looking around as if one might come darting out from under the table.

"No, but I caught the one that was at Death by Java and got it to the vet. Long story."

"Let me get that shower, and then you can tell me all about it," Paul said, running a hand through his hair. Sand cascaded down onto his shoulders like he had a bad case of dandruff. "Do you still want to go to that reunion tonight? I'm game, but if you aren't, we can stay in."

"I do," I said, brushing the sand from his shoulder. "Now, go shower. Looking at you is making me jealous."

"Wait until I show you the pictures I took of him in the water with those—" Dad flinched when Laura elbowed him. "Okay, okay, I'm kidding."

"James here thinks he's a world-class practical joker," Laura said, leading the way into the kitchen, where she poured herself a glass of water. She downed half of it in one go. "Paul behaved himself. Your dad here was an absolute terror."

Dad held a hand to his chest. "That wounds me deeply, my dear."

Laura rolled her eyes, gave me a crooked grin, and polished off her water without giving me an explanation as to what they were talking about. I was pretty sure I didn't want to know.

"Did everything get sorted with Valerie?" Dad asked.

"Kind of?" I made a face. "It's hard to say, really. She's worried her boyfriend, Mickey, might be the killer. It took some doing, but I coaxed her into talking to the police. Detective McKensie took her aside so I didn't hear what they discussed. I hope Valerie told her everything and didn't leave something out because she was afraid of what it might do to her reputation. Even though she's worried about Mickey, she's still being evasive about a few things."

"That's too bad," Dad said. "I know you two had your issues over the years, but she doesn't deserve this."

"No," I agreed. "No one does."

Paul returned from his shower a short time later, looking much better than he had when he'd arrived. The red glow had dimmed to a more natural shade of pink. He was wearing a nice outfit, but nothing too extravagant since this was merely an impromptu class reunion, not a fancy dinner date.

"*Gabby* asked about you," I told him, making sure to use her first name. "She was disappointed you weren't at Valerie's, and she said she'd like for us to all get together soon and chat about the case."

"I see." Paul cleared his throat. "She was there?"

I quickly explained about Valerie and her reluctant chat with Detective McKensie. "I expect she'll call tomorrow. She seemed keen on seeing you again."

"Making good with the local cops, are we?" Dad asked. "I know a few of them from when I've needed to do research on police methodology."

"I'm going to get ready," I said, glancing at the time. "I'll be out in five."

Dad started talking about one of his visits with the local police as I headed down the hall to my bedroom to get dressed. It took closer to ten minutes than five for me to get ready, thanks to my indecision about what to wear. Hooties wasn't a fancy place, yet I wanted to impress my old classmates. I'm not sure why I cared, but I didn't want to show up just in shorts and a T-shirt.

I eventually settled on a nice blouse with a pair of jeans. I ran a brush through my hair, rechecked my makeup, and then, with a nervous huff, I returned to the kitchen, where Dad was finishing up his story.

"He didn't know what to do," he said with a laugh. "I was afraid that he might arrest me right then and there. Good thing he didn't, because I had no reasonable excuse for why I had the rubber duck in my possession."

"Ready?" I asked, not wanting to know what he was referring to.

"Ready," Paul said, still chuckling from the story.

"You two have fun." Dad handed Paul the keys to his car. "Don't do anything I wouldn't do."

"That's not really saying much," Laura said. "Especially after *that* story."

Everyone but me laughed. No, I *really* didn't want to know what he'd just told them.

Paul and I were soon on the way, with him driving and me staring out the passenger's-side window, a nervous churning in my gut. I'd never so much as considered going to a class reunion before, and while this one was unofficial, people I'd once known *would* be there.

Sure, seeing some old friends might be fun. But I wasn't even sure any of them would show up. This could very well just be a gathering of Valerie and her friends with Paul and me shoehorned in. That would be like a nightmare made manifest.

Think about Lyle, I reminded myself as Paul pulled into the lot at Hooties. The car's screen dimmed as he shut off the engine, leaving us to sit in the glow cast by the obnoxious red and blue hooties sign above the door. A handful of other cars sat in the lot, maybe ten, which didn't bode well for it being a packed house of fifty-plus former classmates like Bray had predicted.

"What should I expect in there?" Paul asked, eyeing the front door and windows, which were tinted to near-black. Nothing could be seen through them. Not even the faintest hint of light or a shape that would tell us what awaited us past those dark barriers.

"Nothing too crazy," I said. "I've only ever been inside once, but it was years ago. Back then, it was all arcade games and greasy food. It was once considered the hip place to hang out for all the cool people in school. It might have changed since then, but I somehow doubt it."

"It's not . . ." He shook his head. "Never mind."

I turned in my seat to face him. "No, tell me. What were you thinking?"

An awkward smile found his face. "I've seen places that look like this before from the outside. And with the name, I just assumed the tint was because anyone inside wouldn't want passersby to see what they were doing."

"Oh." I made a face. "Do you really think I'd take you to a place like that?"

He grinned. "That depends on what you wanted to get out of me afterward."

I smacked him on the arm before we both climbed out of the car. The light banter had done wonders for my nerves, which was probably the point. I took Paul's arm, steeled the last of my nerves, and together we entered Hooties.

It was like walking into the past.

Nothing had changed in the years since I'd last been there. The space was lit up by dozens of arcade machines, each vying for attention with various *clang*s, *ping*s, and *crash*es. Pop-rock music played over speakers spread out around the room. It tried to overpower the noise of the machines, but all it really did was add to the din. Directly across from us was a bar that was relegated to serving Cokes and Sprites since it was frequented by teens, rather than adults.

And there, standing off together in small, clique-like groups, were the attendees of Bray's impromptu class reunion—all twelve of them.

Bray, Tamara, and Bebe were together, of course. No Valerie. No Mickey. A group of men I didn't recognize in the dizzying lights cast by the machines stood nearby. I assumed they were classmates, but if they were, I couldn't recall their names. At the other end of the bar was a group of five women, three of which I recognized as former classmates. The other two were entirely unfamiliar, and I wondered if they were the wives of some of the men.

"You ready for this?" Paul asked.

"Are you?"

Before either of us could answer, Bray noticed us. His entire face lit up, and he waved his hands into the air, as if I couldn't see him in the mostly empty room. "Krissy! Over here!" He turned to the others. "Hey, guys! It's Krissy Hancock. She made it!"

All eyes turned our way as Paul and I crossed the room to where everyone else was waiting. I became suddenly self-conscious about the Band-Aids on my arms, and I wished I could have found some other way to cover the cat scratches that wasn't so obvious. They almost glowed in the lights of the arcade machines.

"Bray," I said as we joined them. "You remember Paul Dalton?" I wasn't even sure I'd officially introduced Paul when we'd met at Death by Java the other day, but Bray acted as if they were old friends, choosing to clasp Paul on the arm with a wide, goofy grin on his face.

"Sure, sure," he said. "I remember. Gene. Guys." He

waved the group of men over. "You remember Krissy, right?"

"Of course." As one of the men stepped over, his name clicked in my head. Gene Rickart. He was, indeed, in my class, but I'd never interacted with him, not even to say "hi" in passing. He reached out and shook my hand, then Paul's, as Bray introduced him. "You're the one who got Mr. Ogletree fired."

"Well, I—"

"Nah, he did that to himself," Bray said, cutting in before turning to Paul. "Krissy here discovered the janitor at the school was smoking in the basement, and she turned him in to the principal. Guy tried to deny it, but the evidence was pretty solid, so out he went."

"She just about got Mrs. Clayborn fired too." I didn't recognize the guy who spoke, though I assumed he was one of Gene's friends.

Gene snorted. "She should have been. Used to hound me about reading. What could a book ever tell me that I don't already know?"

"She *was* a librarian." This from another guy whose name escaped me, though his features were more familiar than Gene's other friend. "Actually, I think she still is the school librarian, if you can believe it."

"She was old when we were in school," Bray said with a laugh. "Has to be ancient now."

Behind him, both Tamara and Bebe, seemingly bored with the topic of conversation, took a step back and put their heads together. My jaded mind assumed they were gossiping about me and how poorly I'd aged since those awkward teenage years when they'd made fun of how I looked back then.

Some things never changed.

"Is Valerie coming?" I asked, looking around. I was ready to talk to her and then get out of there. "I expected her to be here already."

"Nah," Bray said. "She had to cancel. It's cool that you've been hanging out with her recently, though. Almost like old times." He laughed and appeared as if he might try to put an arm around my shoulder, but one look at Paul changed his mind. "You want something to drink? I've got control of the bar, so you can have whatever. It's nothing crazy, though I brought a few bottles of some stronger stuff from home. It's all on the house, of course."

"A Coke is fine," I said.

Paul nodded. "Same here."

"Cool. Coming right up." Bray rounded the bar to grab our drinks, leaving Paul and me standing with Gene and his buds. We eyed each other, but no one spoke. The discomfort was palpable.

I glanced down the bar, toward the group of women, but they appeared to have no interest in talking to me. I decided that once the Cokes were gone, Paul and I would make our excuses and leave.

A part of me would feel guilty for abandoning Bray. He seemed to be genuinely trying to be friends. But he was the only one, and I wasn't about to stand around, feeling uncomfortable, just for Bray's sake.

"You okay?" Paul asked, keeping his voice low so only I could hear.

"Yeah. A little disappointed, I guess."

"If you want to go—"

The door opened, and to my surprise, Mickey Robbins entered. He was dressed as if he was out on a date, and he was even carrying a bouquet of flowers. He stopped just inside the door, took in the small groups, and the otherwise-empty arcade area, then turned and walked right back out.

"Two Cokes," Bray said, sliding them across the bar toward Paul and me. "So, Paul, what is it you do for a living? And how did you meet our Krissy here?"

While I could have stood there and explained how I was *never* "their" Krissy, I had more important things in mind. "I'll be right back," I said. And before Paul, or anyone else, could stop me, I rushed across the room, out the door, and into the night.

Mickey was already halfway across the lot, and he was walking away fast.

"Mickey!" I called. "Wait up a sec."

He glanced over his shoulder at me, and then, with a sigh that caused his big shoulders to heave, he turned and waited for me to jog across the lot to join him.

"Sorry. I'm Krissy Hancock, Valerie's friend." Even coming out of my mouth, it sounded forced, but I didn't know what else to say that wouldn't make him dismiss me and walk away.

"I remember." He looked down at the flowers and then held them out to me. "These are for you, I guess."

I didn't want them, but I took them anyway, making sure to take note of Mickey's hand. It was no longer bandaged, but he had a couple of nasty-looking bruises and scabs on his knuckles. "What happened?" I asked, nodding toward the damage.

Mickey flexed his fingers with a wince. "Got a little too rough during my workout. It's nothing." He folded his hands behind his back. "Was there something you needed?"

"I assume these were meant for Valerie?" I held up the flowers, which were, admittedly, a pretty assortment, though I couldn't name half of them.

Mickey shrugged, looked away. "I suppose they were."

"She's not here."

"I noticed."

This was going great. "She didn't tell you she was skipping out on the reunion?"

"No. We haven't spoken recently."

I absorbed that a moment before asking, "Is everything okay between you two?" I knew that it wasn't, but I was curious as to what he might say.

Mickey ran his tongue over his teeth, kept his eyes averted. "It's been a tough couple of days," he said. "My Val's got a lot on her mind with the whole Lyle thing, and I haven't been doing too hot lately, either. It's messed everything up."

"It's a shame what happened to him," I said. "From what I've seen, you two didn't get along. You and Lyle, I mean."

His eyes narrowed as he turned them on me. "That some sort of accusation?"

"Just an observation," I said. "You aren't the only one, it seems. Tito next door didn't appear to like Lyle, either."

"No one did." Mickey sniffed, then wiped his uninjured hand across his nose as he glanced around the parking lot. It was a move straight out of a tough-guy handbook. "It's a shame he had to die, but I can't say

I'm too broken up about it. He was harassing Val and making a nuisance of himself all over town. It was inevitable, if you ask me."

Inevitable that someone would kill him? I found that hard to believe. "Do you have any idea how he ended up in the back room of Death by Java?" I asked.

Another shrug, sniff, and nose wipe. "No clue. Must've broken in." And then, like that, he dropped the act. "Look, I don't know what happened to the guy. But if you talk to Val, could you tell her to call me? I really want to speak with her so we can clear the air."

About what? I desperately wanted to ask the question, but I held my tongue. I was keenly aware that while there were a dozen people inside Hooties, there was no one in the parking lot with us. If Mickey Robbins was a killer and he thought I was prying too much, who knew what he might do?

"I'll talk to her," I promised. And then, because I was curious, I asked, "Have you tried to call her yourself?"

Mickey looked off into the distance, and for a moment, I wasn't sure he'd respond. "She's not answering," he said, eyes sliding over to me. "Every time I've tried to contact her, I've hit a brick wall. I swear, it's got to do with those two, Aaron and Hugh." His face hardened when he referenced Valerie's exes. "Just . . . tell her to call me, all right?"

And then, without saying goodbye, Mickey turned and climbed into his car. A moment later, he gunned the engine and was gone.

I stood under the parking lot lights for a long time,

just thinking. Valerie had once claimed Mickey was avoiding her, yet he'd just said it was the other way around. One of them was lying. But which one?

I returned to Hooties, mind churning over the possibilities. Could Hugh and Aaron be somehow involved? But if so, how? Could one of them have found a way to block Mickey's number from Valerie's phone, or vice versa? It seemed far-fetched, but it felt like it *was* within the realm of possibility. I didn't think either man was a criminal mastermind, but if they were to put their heads together . . . maybe.

And the big question: If Aaron and Hugh were that intent on coming between Mickey and Valerie, would it be such a stretch to imagine that they might have tried to frame Mickey Robbins for Lyle's murder?

13

I was up bright and early the next morning, with plans to spend every waking moment with Paul, Dad, and Laura. I wanted to go shopping and take Paul around town to show him the sights personally. I wanted to have lunch and dinner at places I'd eaten at when I was younger. Show him my high school. Show him that place in Village Park where I'd seen the squirrel, though I still wasn't sure I was ready to tell him *that* story.

When I climbed into the shower, I had everything laid out.

By the time I was done, my plans were already wrecked.

"Detective McKensie called," Paul said. "She wants us to meet her for breakfast."

A thousand denials were on the tip of my tongue, though I knew they would do little good. You didn't tell a police officer no. "What did you tell her?" I asked.

Paul made a pained face when he said, "I told her we

can do breakfast, but we have plans afterward. I hope that's okay. She made it sound like it was important."

"It's fine." And honestly, it was. If we got our sit-down with McKensie out of the way, told her everything we—and by we, I meant *me*—knew about the case, then we could be done with it. "I'll let Dad know."

Paul nodded, kissed me on the temple, then headed into the bathroom, his clothes for the day tucked under his arm.

Dad and Laura were sitting in the dining room, coffees in hand. One look at me, and my overly observant father already knew what I was going to say.

"Do what you have to do." He raised his mug in salute. "We'll be here whenever you're done."

"Paul already tell you?" I asked.

"It's my psychic superpower at work," Dad said.

Laura merely rolled her eyes.

Paul's shower was quick. Before Dad and Laura were done with their first cup of coffee, the two of us were out the door and headed for our breakfast meeting with Detective McKensie.

She'd chosen a small diner downtown called Juan's. It was nestled between two larger buildings right across the street from the police station, which made it a convenient place for her to conduct the interview. The smell of grease was strong as we entered through the glass front door. McKensie was seated at a booth in the corner, sipping at a coffee. She waved us over with a smile.

"Thanks for coming on such short notice," she said, motioning to the seat across from her. "Coffee's still hot." The pot was sitting at the edge of the table. Two off-white mugs were turned upside down in front of where she'd indicated.

"I'm not sure there's much we can help you with," Paul said as he sat. "Krissy and I are here on vacation and hardly know anyone." He flipped both our mugs upright and then filled them, sadly, sans cookie.

"Understood," McKensie said. "I still would like to go over a few things, if you don't mind. Krissy *has* been in contact with people involved in the case, and I'd love to get her insights." She glanced over at me before turning back to Paul. "And anything you can contribute can only help. I'm not officially on duty yet, so think of this as more of an informal meet."

A grease-stained waiter slouched his way over to our table. We took a moment to put in our orders, and then, without a word, he dragged himself to the back.

"He's not much of a morning person," McKensie said with a chuckle. "Can't get much more than a grunt out of him this early—and I've tried."

Which told me that Juan's was, as expected, one of her regular haunts.

"So," she said after another sip of coffee, "tell me about Ms. Kemp and those men who hang around her like a pack of lonely puppies." She folded her arms on the table as she leveled those cop eyes of hers on me.

"I'm not sure what I can say," I said. "Valerie was married to Aaron, who was her high school sweetheart. They got divorced sometime after I moved out of town. She started dating Hugh after that, then broke up with him. When did they get together? When did they break up? I have no idea. Now she's with Mickey." Or was. With the suspicion of murder squarely on him, I wasn't so sure how long that would last. "That's really all I know."

"See, that's what I don't get," McKensie said. "Divorce. Breakups. And yet, every time I see her, she's with one of these men she's supposedly no longer with."

"It's possible to break up with someone and still be friends," Paul pointed out.

"True, but it feels like more than that."

"Valerie is a flirt," I said. "She used to make Aaron jealous all the time back in high school. They never fought about it, as far as I know, but I can remember him giving a few hard looks to a couple of guys she'd led on because she liked the attention and they were gullible enough to give it."

"I see." McKensie chewed over that a moment. "Other than the big three, are there any other men who have been vying for Ms. Kemp's attention? Recently, I mean. I don't think high school flirtations would have much bearing on what's happened here over the last few days."

I thought about the conversation I'd had with Dee about her suspicions that Valerie was cheating on Mickey. The only people she'd indicated directly were Hugh and Aaron, though she'd hinted that there might be more. "I'm not *positive* she's seeing anyone on the side."

McKensie leaned forward. "But?"

"But there's speculation that Valerie might be cheating on Mickey. I have no proof of it, mind you." I paused. "Though I did see her in a semi-compromising position with a guy named Roman the other day."

"Roman Haines." McKensie's expression darkened. "I know him."

"I don't know if there's anything serious between them," I said, "or if Valerie was just looking for a way to lower the repair bill, but . . ." I shrugged as guilt dried up the words. I hated being a gossip, and that's exactly was what this felt like. It was the sort of thing Rita Jablonski and her friends thrived on. Me? Not so much.

"I'll talk to him." McKensie stirred her coffee with a spoon, though she hadn't added anything to it. "Can you think of anyone else she might have flirted with, even innocently?" A beat, then she met my eye. "Someone like Mr. Carrigan, perhaps?"

Before I could answer, the waiter returned. He deposited our food and left without saying a word. I looked down at my eggs, which had been slathered in butter, and my bacon, which was as flimsy as a wet noodle, with distaste. Neither McKensie nor Paul seemed to mind the grease-fest and started digging in as my stomach roiled.

"Krissy?" McKensie prodded, mouth half-full.

I poked at my egg, watched it jiggle unappealingly. "I'm not sure she was actually *flirting* with Lyle," I said. "He was going to cite her for a broken ice machine, and she was trying to talk him out of it."

"By hitting on him?" McKensie asked.

"Kind of?" I made a face. "I don't think she would have followed through with it. He rejected her, so it's moot, anyway."

"He rejected her?" McKensie gnawed on a slice of floppy bacon, eyes going distant. "Interesting."

Guilt had me lowering my head. I hadn't meant to, but I'd just painted a target on Valerie's back. It didn't take Dad's psychic superpower to know that McKensie was wondering if Valerie had taken exception to Lyle's rejection and had invited him back to Death by Java and killed him for it. Or perhaps Lyle had changed his mind and returned to take her up on the offer, but instead, found himself face-to-face with Mickey or one of Valerie's exes.

Even though my food was as appetizing as soapy water, I started to eat, mostly because I figured that if my mouth was full, then I couldn't say anything else that would incriminate Valerie. I had a feeling she'd be seeing Detective McKensie again very soon.

"I told Ms. Kemp that she could open the café on Monday," she said after a moment. "We've gotten all the evidence we physically could out of the place, so now all that's left is to watch and see if anyone acts strangely."

"If the killer works there, then they might not show up for their shift," Paul said.

"Or they might, and will make mistakes because they're worried someone knows more than they do," McKensie added.

"Nerves can do that."

She winked and pointed the last droopy bacon slice at him. "Sometimes all you've got to do is watch, and the guilty parties make themselves known."

"I saw Mickey last night." The words popped out of my mouth without me knowing I was going to say them.

McKensie wiped her hands on her napkin as she regarded me. "Really? Where was this?"

"At Hooties." I explained my short chat with him, making sure to include the scabs on his hand. Once again, I felt awful, since it felt like more gossip, but it was something the detective needed to know.

"Huh." McKensie thought about it a long moment, then popped to her feet. "I'll look into it. For now, I need to get going. Meals have already been paid for, so no need to worry about that." She met Paul's eye. "Thanks for taking the time to meet with me." She glanced at me briefly. "Both of you."

And then, with a nod to each of us, she left.

I watched her cross the street over to the police station with my gut doing slow, churning flips. I regretted eating the single slice of bacon and two bites of egg I'd managed to force in. Even the coffee was sitting heavily in my stomach.

"Ready to go?" Paul asked.

I pushed my plate away. "Let's get out of here."

We walked back to Dad's car in silence. I desperately wanted to forget about everything we'd just talked about, to go on with my day, spend it like I'd originally planned, but could I really do that when I'd just made Valerie's life even harder by siccing the detective on her? I mean, I was sure Detective McKensie already had Valerie and Mickey in her crosshairs since Lyle had been found dead in Death by Java, but now I felt responsible for whatever happened to them. And it was all thanks to my big mouth.

"Would you mind if we went by Death by Java?" I asked as we climbed into the car. "I want to see if Valerie is there. We can pick Dad and Laura up after that."

"Sure."

He pulled out onto the road and drove the short distance to the bookstore café. Sure enough, through the front window I spotted Valerie moving around inside.

"I'll wait in the car," Paul said as he parked. "I want to call Susie and check in with Kefka and Ziggy." His two Huskies were being watched by his neighbor, who was also his regular dog sitter.

"This should only take a minute," I said, climbing out of the car. I approached the door to Death by Java, mentally going over what I was going to say. Valerie was on her knees, body contorted so she could look up at the underside of a nearby table. She scraped at it, then grimaced as something—gum most likely—fell to the floor.

I knocked, nearly causing her to smack her head on the table when she jumped. She pushed her way to her feet and walked over, peeling off thick yellow rubber gloves as she did.

"Krissy?" she asked, pushing open the door. Her hair was pulled into a messy bun, and sweat and dirt coated her face. She was even wearing a plain white T-shirt and jeans. It was *very* un-Valerie-like. "What are you doing here?"

"Hi, Valerie. I wanted to check in with you." I stepped through the doorway as Valerie moved to make room for me. "I heard you're going to be allowed to open on Monday."

"We can," she said, flopping into a chair. "It's why I'm here now. I got to thinking that it might be a good idea to start working on that list you gave me and see if it makes any sort of difference. I have my doubts, but it's not like I have much else to do at the moment."

I glanced around at the empty bookstore café. "No one else is here?"

She sighed as she tossed her gloves onto the table. "Just me. Aaron and Hugh are busy or else I'd have called them in. And my girls . . ." She shrugged.

"Have you heard from Mickey?" I asked.

A slight tensing of her shoulders was all the reaction Valerie showed. "No, I haven't."

"I saw him last night," I said, watching her face for a reaction. There was none. "He showed up at the reunion. He brought flowers."

A series of rapid blinks. "He did?"

"Gave them to me when he realized you weren't there," I said. "He seemed upset."

Valerie chewed on her lower lip, wouldn't look at me. "So . . . what did he say?"

"Not a lot," I admitted. "He was there for you, and since you weren't there, he left right away. I stopped him, and we talked for a few minutes. He said you two haven't talked recently." I paused, added, "And that you've been avoiding his calls."

Valerie crossed her legs and wagged her foot in clear agitation, but she didn't say a word.

"You made it sound like he was the one avoiding you," I pressed. "Valerie, what's going on?" When she still didn't respond, I continued, "If something is going on between you and Mickey, something more than you being afraid he might be involved in Lyle's death, you need to tell someone. The more you try to hide it, the guiltier you'll look." *Especially after what I said to Detective McKensie*, I didn't add.

Valerie sighed, causing her shoulders to slump. "There's nothing going on between Mickey and me. We're just having a rough patch. It happens."

"You were afraid he might have killed Lyle," I pointed out. "That's more than just a rough patch."

"He didn't do it."

That caught me by surprise. "I thought you hadn't talked to him."

"I haven't." Another sigh, this one annoyed. "But I thought about it some more and realized there was no way Mickey could have done it. I was just upset and jumped to conclusions. I may have seen him and pretended I didn't once. That's all."

"But—"

Valerie abruptly stood and started for the back room. She paused halfway there, looked back at me. "Coming?"

Uncertain as to what was going on, I followed her into the back room, which looked much the same as when I'd last seen it. The dent was still in the ice machine door, but that was the only thing that looked out of place.

"See that?" she asked, spreading her arms to indicate the entire space.

I hesitated, then said, "No?"

"That's right," she said, though I had no idea what she was getting at. "Mickey wouldn't have killed Lyle here. Neither would Aaron or Hugh or any single one of my employees. You might not think too highly of any of us, but we're all smarter than that."

"That's not fair, Valerie. I don't think—"

A hard shake of her head cut me off. "Someone else

came in here and did it. I don't know who, but I realized it wasn't one of my people. It couldn't have been. *You* are a more likely killer than someone I actually care about."

I could have been hurt by the indirect insult, but it was Valerie, so I chose to let it go. "Do you know who let Oscar out that night?" I asked, eyes flickering to the back alleyway door. "Depending on when they did it, there's a chance they might have seen someone hanging around who shouldn't have been here."

"I have no idea," she said. "It wasn't me."

I figured as much. "Someone murdered Lyle Carrigan," I said. "And while you might not believe it, they did it here, which does indicate that it had something to do with Death by Java or someone who works here."

"I disagree. No one here had a reason to hurt him."

"He was going to cite you for health code violations," I pointed out. "And I was told that Mickey went to Lyle's house and stood outside in a threatening manner."

"He does stuff like that," Valerie said with a dismissive wave of her hand. "Mickey hoped it would scare him off."

"And it didn't work. So, what's the next step? Try to scare him off physically?" I softened my tone. "Look, Valerie, just because you don't want to believe that someone you know could have committed murder, the evidence appears to point that way."

She crossed her arms, but I could tell she was wavering.

"Lyle had to have gotten in here somehow," I said. "Maybe someone showed up to let Oscar out, and in doing so, let Lyle in. Maybe Lyle forced the issue, which led to a scuffle. It could have been an accident."

"Or Lyle could have broken in." There was no strength to her argument. She seemed to realize it, because she turned away, changed the subject. "I need to get back to work. I . . ." A cough. "I could use some help if you have a little time."

Her tone was so hurt, so frail, that it hit me like a gut punch. While none of this was my fault, I couldn't help but feel responsible for her. Could I really leave her here alone to wallow in her worry and frustration?

No, no, I couldn't.

"Sure. Let me tell Paul."

Valerie nodded and led the way from the back room. So much for a day with my family.

14

I wiped sweat from my forehead, then stepped back and looked over what I'd just done. The bookshelves were dusted, and the books themselves were upright, aligned, and sorted according to genre. Mostly. There was no way I was going to spend my entire day making sure everything was perfect, but a little organization would help customers find what they were looking for.

If anyone ever came in, that was.

My stomach grumbled, and I glanced at the time. It was just before noon, which meant I'd been there for a couple of hours. There were still things that could be done, but I felt as if I'd done my part. Dad, Laura, and Paul were waiting on a promised call when I was finished, and if I started in on something else, who knew when that would be.

So, I went looking for Valerie and found her in the women's restroom, leaning over the leaky toilet with a perplexed expression on her face. She flushed it, watched as water oozed from the base, then wiped it up with a ball of paper towels.

"You'll have to call someone for that," I said. "It's probably the seal, and it would be better to have a professional look at it."

Valerie stepped back, shot the toilet a disgusted look, and then walked over to the sink to scrub at her hands. "I was hoping it would just stop," she said. "But I suppose I could always call Roman."

Don't, Krissy. I desperately wanted to follow up on that and ask her about her relationship with the repairman, but now wasn't the time.

"I'm done out front," I said instead. "There are a few more things that need to be done, but I figure you can handle them. I'm supposed to meet Dad for lunch."

Valerie's back was to me, but I could see the annoyed expression that crossed her face in the mirror before she said, "Sure. Have fun."

I hesitated, torn. On the one hand, I really wanted to leave and spend the rest of the day with my family. On the other, I still felt guilty for . . . what? I wasn't sure. Maybe I was just a sucker.

"If I get a chance, I might stop back in later," I said, deciding to meet myself halfway. "If you're still here, I'll try to get a few more things done."

Valerie continued scrubbing at her hands and didn't respond. I left her to it.

The breeze felt good on my skin as I stepped outside. Cars rolled down the street, most obeying the speed limit, though a few were pushing it. Pedestrians passed me by at a regular clip. Death by Java *did* sit on a good corner. Business should be booming. Judging by the mostly full tables I could see through the windows at Tito's, the deli was doing just fine. Better. It was doing great.

And yet, Death by Java hardly garnered a glance from passersby. Months of poor service, of questionable cleanliness, had killed any and all interest in the place.

But it felt like there was more to it than that. There were all sorts of places with dirty tables, with less-than-enthusiastic employees, that chugged along perfectly fine despite their shortcomings. Same went for the many businesses that were getting dinged for health violations. Lyle had gone into Tito's, and yeah, he'd been tossed right back out, but I was pretty sure he'd given them bad marks with how Tito had treated him. The customers didn't seem to care.

So why was Death by Java struggling so mightily?

I studied the deli as I called Paul on my cell. My mind was churning slowly over the possibilities, including ones that had Lyle getting killed for playing favorites of some kind. He answered on the second ring.

"Hi, Buttercup."

"Ew. Don't do that," I said, making a face.

Paul laughed. "It didn't come out as naturally as I hoped."

"I don't want it to," I said. "From Dad, I'm used to it. You? I'm perfectly fine with 'Krissy'."

"Noted. Are you all finished up there, *Krissy*?" He purred the name, causing a shiver to run down my spine—the good kind.

"All done," I said as a skateboarder rolled past. Somehow, he didn't run into anyone on the semi-crowded sidewalk. "I was thinking we could have lunch with Dad and Laura at Tito's Deli."

"That's the place next to Death by Java?" he asked.

"It is. Since I'm already here, I could get us a table. I'm beat and really want to sit down."

There was a brief moment of silence when I just *knew* Paul was thinking I had ulterior motives for our lunch, and I supposed he was right. I wanted to ask Tito about Lyle, though I'd need to do so in a way that wouldn't make him suspicious.

Good luck with that.

"Give us fifteen minutes," Paul said. "I'll run it by James and Laura and make sure they don't have other plans. Either way, we'll meet you there."

"Great. I'll be waiting."

I clicked off and then walked the short distance to Tito's Deli. The inside was cool and inviting, if not a smidge cramped, especially at lunchtime. The tables were a little too close together, and since nearly every one of them was full, walking space was nonexistent between the occupied chairs.

I spotted an empty table across the room and was forced to take the long way around to reach it. Mustard was smeared across the top of the table, and a balled-up napkin was sitting next to it. There were only three chairs. The fourth had been nabbed by a group of five dude-bros with backward baseball caps and smarmy grins who were crowded around a nearby table meant for four.

Still, it was all that was left, and I hoped that by the time Paul arrived with Dad and Laura, they'd be gone and I could retrieve the chair.

"Sorry, sorry." A petite teen with corn bread–colored hair rushed over to the table. Freckles covered her face, which only served to accentuate her blush as she wiped down the table. "We're really busy, and I got caught up with the dishes."

"It's fine."

She flashed me a smile, revealing her braces. "This will take just a second."

I waited until she finished cleaning the table before asking, "Is Mr. Adornetto in?"

Panic washed across her face, and her hand went to her name tag, as if she might cover it. *Birdie.* From what little I'd seen of the girl, the name fit.

"I'm not going to complain," I said, giving her a reassuring smile. "This is about something else. Promise."

The look she gave me was uncertain, but she nodded. "He's in the back. Do you want me to get him for you?"

"Please." I sat, still smiling.

Birdie flittered there a moment longer before she hurried toward the back. The next table over, the dudebros burst into a round of laughter and elbowed each other as if one of them had cracked the most amazing joke. It earned them dirty looks from nearly all the other tables, but they didn't deign to notice.

My phone buzzed. I glanced back to make sure Tito wasn't coming before checking the screen. Unknown, but local number. I frowned, and then, with one more glance back, I answered with a curious, "Hello?"

"Krissy?"

The voice was vaguely familiar, but I couldn't place it. "Speaking."

"It's Larissa." A pause, and then, as if the moment she'd spoken her name hadn't hit me like a nostalgic ton of bricks, she added, "Larissa Sweeny."

"Larissa! Hi!" I choked back a sudden tear. Larissa was one of my old high school friends, one of the ones I'd lost contact with long ago and had hoped would be at Bray's reunion. "It's been forever."

"It has." I could hear the smile in her voice. "I got your number from your dad. I hope it's okay."

"Yeah, sure. Of course." I glanced back. Tito still wasn't on the way, which meant I had a moment to talk. "I'm glad you called."

"Me too." There was a smile in her voice. "I can't talk long, but I wanted to check in and see if you might want to get together while you're in town. We heard about the reunion Bray Eckles was throwing and that you'd be there, but we couldn't make it."

The *didn't want to* was implied to take the place of *couldn't*.

I also noted the "we."

"Renee?" I asked, hopefully.

"Renee especially." A laugh. If anyone had hated Bray Eckles in high school, it was Renee Weaver. "We were hoping you might want to meet tomorrow night. Dinner at Redwood Tavern? It'd be just the three of us."

A pause. "Kind of like old times. We'd just be missing Vicki."

A looming presence informed me that Tito had come out from the back and was heading my way. "That sounds great. Yeah, I'd really like that."

"Great! Does eight work?"

"It's perfect."

Tito rounded the table to stand in front of me, arms crossed. He looked like a man who wanted to get back to work. Up close, he looked as intimidating as when I'd seen him throwing Lyle out of his deli. His eyes were dark brown, slightly pinched at the corners, and he had frown lines around his mouth that told me he spent a lot of time scowling.

"I've got to go, Larissa. It was great hearing from you. I'll see you tomorrow night."

"Yeah." A pause. "I'm glad we're doing this." And before I could comment on that, she was gone.

I turned off my screen and set my phone facedown on the table. "I'm sorry to bother you, Mr. Adornetto. I'm Krissy Hancock."

"Call me Tito. Was there something wrong with your service, Ms. Hancock?" He glanced at the clean table, noted the lack of food in front of me. "We are rather busy, so if it's taken longer than usual, I apologize."

"It's not about the service," I said. "This is about something else, if you have a moment." I motioned toward the chair across from me. "Please."

Tito sighed. "Look, I've got a business to run here. And as I mentioned before, we're very busy."

"I understand," I said. And then, quieter, "It's about Lyle Carrigan."

Tito went still, seemed to stop breathing, and then he abruptly sat. "I have five minutes."

Five minutes should be more than enough, though it did mean I'd have to get straight to the point. "As you know, he was murdered."

Tito scowled and made a *get on with it* gesture.

"I've been helping Valerie Kemp over at Death by Java, and while I'm not a cop, I do have an interest in finding out who killed Lyle."

"Good luck with that," Tito said, crossing his arms as he sat back. "Lyle made enemies. Ms. Kemp and her muscle-bound idiot are two of them."

I assumed the "idiot" was Mickey. "You threw Lyle out of your deli a few days ago," I said. "When you did, you said something about him being paid to harass business owners. What did you mean by that?"

Tito laughed. "What do you think I meant? He works at the health department. It's his job to snoop around and find problems with the food industry." A pause, and some of the humor went out of his expression. "*Was* his job, I suppose. I don't know what goes on down there, but I'm sure they have quotas. He needed to meet them. He'd come in, make up some tall tale about machines not working properly or cleaner being stored on the wrong shelf, write up his little citation in that tablet of his, and then he would go collect his bonus or whatever it was that made him do what he did."

"And you didn't like that."

"None of us did. I didn't. Valerie Kemp didn't."

"Marco Rossi?"

"Sure." He leaned forward. "Did you know Marco wanted to move his place over to the corner there?" He pointed toward Death by Java. "I'm pretty sure he had it all lined up too. Money down and everything. Then in comes Ms. Kemp with her perfect hair and body to kill for. One closed-door meeting with the seller, and what do you know? She gets the location. I don't fault her for using her assets like that, but Marco sure didn't like it."

"You think Valerie seduced the seller?" I asked, wishing I could be more skeptical than I was.

Tito shrugged. "You tell me. You're the one helping her out. You see how she is. We all do."

For a brief instant, I wondered if Marco could have resented Valerie's actions and resorted to murder because of it. But why kill Lyle? Valerie, Mickey, or one of her employees would have been a far better target. Remove them, the location becomes open, and he could swoop back in and scoop it up. Kill Lyle, and it might inconvenience her, but it would also remove the thorn in her side, especially since there was no evidence connecting her to the crime. So, how would he benefit?

"What time do you leave here at night, Tito?" I asked, shifting topics.

"When I'm done here," he said with a shrug. "Sometimes that's early. Sometimes late."

"On the night of the murder?"

He looked me up and down, eyes going hard. "Why are you asking? Are you implying that I might have had something to do with Lyle Carrigan's death?"

"No," I said. "But Valerie keeps a cat in her store."

His brow furrowed. "Excuse me?"

"A cat. Black and white. His name is Oscar."

"I've seen him," Tito said. "He gets into my trash and rips open the bags. And if you're not careful, the thing will dart between your feet whenever it's spooked. The thing is a pest. If I was a lesser man, I'd do something about it. I doubt Ms. Kemp is taking much care of it or else it wouldn't be so skittish."

"Oscar was in the store the night Lyle was killed," I said. "Or, at least, that's what everyone at Death by Java believed."

Tito waited a beat, then asked, "And?"

"And someone let him out. I was wondering if you might have seen who that was."

The incredulous look that passed across his face had me blushing in embarrassment. "You think I pay attention to who or what goes in and out of that place next door? We're business neighbors, not friends. I have my own issues to deal with here. I don't care where that cat is, as long as he's not messing with my trash or getting into my place of business." His glance at his watch was so quick, there was zero chance he'd actually read it. "Your five minutes are up. I've got to get back to work." He started to rise.

"Wait. One more question."

Tito hesitated, then settled back down, though he

was tense. His jaw worked, and those dark brown eyes of his looked like deep, black pits.

"It's about Lyle's tablet," I said.

It was as if all the air was sucked from the room. I swear Tito stopped breathing for a full five seconds before he asked in a quiet voice, "What about it?"

"When was the last time you saw it?" I asked, watching him carefully. His reaction wasn't what I'd expected.

Tito's eyes bounced back and forth as he scanned my face, as if searching for some sort of deception. "I assume it was when I last saw him."

"Which was . . . ?"

His blink was slow, measured. "I wager it was when I kicked him out of here."

Assume. Wager. Tito was being awfully careful here. "Did you ever see Lyle *without* his tablet?"

He ran a hand over his scalp. Behind him, the dude-bros rose with a raucous round of laughter and left.

I was about to prod Tito into speaking when he abruptly stood.

"I answered your questions. If you'll excuse me, I'd like to get back to work." His gaze flickered to the empty table. "And please, no loitering. If you aren't going to eat, I would ask you to leave so a paying customer can have your place." He spun away and marched to the back.

I watched him go with a growing concern. Tito had been relatively relaxed when we'd started. I mean, the guy seemed like he was a powder keg of suppressed, angry energy most of the time, but he hadn't appeared too concerned about anything I was asking when I'd first started questioning him about Lyle.

And then I'd brought up the tablet.

The door opened, and Dad, Paul, and Laura entered. They scanned the deli, saw me, and then worked their way around the room, toward my table. I plastered on a smile and greeted them like nothing was wrong.

I knew otherwise.

Someone knew what had happened to Lyle Carrigan's tablet.

And I'm pretty sure Tito Adornetto was that someone.

15

Tito's Deli had once been called the Plain Slice. The change in name coincided with Tito taking over from his father, Carlito, and it heralded an increase in business. Before, there was some confusion, as the old name made people think it was a pizza joint, whereas the newer one made it obvious that it wasn't. There were also countless articles about Tito's ascension to head man, about his more cutthroat nature. Where Daddy Adornetto was kind and generous, Tito was willing to do just about anything to succeed.

And based on the Google Maps view of his house, he'd succeeded just fine.

"What are you looking at?" Dad asked as he entered the dining room. He was dressed in his slippers and robe, clearly ready for a night in after a long day spent running around Redwood Village.

I turned off the screen of my phone and set it aside. "Nothing. Just waiting for you."

His smile said he knew otherwise, but he didn't press. He crossed the room and eased down into a chair with a groan. "Today was fun. I think Paul likes it here." He gave me a meaningful look.

"We *all* like it here," I said. "But Paul and I like it in Pine Hills just as much. I think you do too."

"True." Dad stretched his legs out in front of him with a barely suppressed yawn. "Do you have any big plans for tonight?"

"Not really." My eyes flickered to my phone. "I . . ." I shook my head. "Never mind."

He sat forward. "No, tell me."

I bit my lip and considered what to tell him. On the one hand, talking about it might help me to sort things out in my mind. On the other, it was Dad. Unlike Paul, he wouldn't tell me to sit back and let the police handle it. He'd warn me to be careful, all while urging me to keep looking, to keep digging. In a word, he was an enabler.

And me being me, that was exactly what I was hoping for.

"It's Tito," I said. "Something strikes me as off about him."

"Such as?"

"He's not a very nice guy, for one."

"Being nice isn't a prerequisite for owning a business," Dad said. "Nor does it make him a killer. That's what you're thinking, right? That he killed Lyle Carrigan?"

I scrunched up my face. "Maybe? I honestly don't know what to think. Mickey Robbins is a better suspect, as are Valerie and Hugh and Aaron and countless other people. But when I mentioned Lyle's missing tablet, Tito got all weird on me."

"Weird, huh?" Dad rubbed his chin. "Like he knows where it is?"

"Or that he has it." I leaned forward, pressing hard into the table, as if it was the only thing keeping me from popping to my feet and running out the door. "What if he killed Lyle and took his tablet? What if he still has it?"

"Why would he take it?" Dad asked, before it seemed to dawn on him. "Lyle cited him for something."

"What if the citation was bad enough that it might close Tito's Deli down?"

"Tito wouldn't like that."

"No, he wouldn't. He could have seen Lyle outside Death by Java that night, saw that he had the tablet, and they could have fought over it. He might have killed him by accident, and then, uncertain what to do with the body, he dragged him into the back room of the bookstore café."

"How'd he get in?"

I opened my mouth, then closed it again. How would he have gotten into Death by Java? I was pretty sure Valerie wouldn't have given Tito a key, even for emergencies.

Mickey could have been there. He saw the fight, decided to help Tito by hiding the body. But why in Valerie's place of business and not somewhere else, like a trash bin somewhere down the alley?

Then it hit me. If Mickey thought Valerie was cheating on him, he might have decided to frame her for murder as punishment. It might explain why he was so nervous that morning outside the bookstore café, why he didn't want to be seen.

"Even if he didn't kill him, if there's a chance Tito has the tablet, he might realize that having it makes him look guilty." Dad gave me a pointed look.

"He might destroy it."

Dad nodded. "If we're right, and Lyle was citing him for some major violation, he might think the police could claim it as motive. That's not even mentioning how his possession of the tablet would automatically put him at the top of the police's suspect list."

"I should call Detective McKensie," I said, glancing at my phone. "But what if I'm wrong and he doesn't have it?"

Dad thought about it a long moment before shrugging. "There's not much you can do about that. And, to be honest, I'm not sure there's much the police can do either."

"What do you mean?"

"You can tell them that you think Tito has the tablet," he said. "They'll ask why you think that. You'll say he was acting weird. They'll ask for proof, and you have none."

"Which doesn't give them probable cause," I said.

He nodded. "The detective can go to Tito, ask him about it, but you and I both know he'll likely deny everything. And while I'm not expert, I'm pretty sure that without anything tying Tito to the tablet or to Lyle, the police can't go barging in on him at his house, and they certainly can't search the place."

"Their hands are tied."

"Exactly." It might have been my imagination, but I could feel the *"But yours aren't."*

"Tito's probably just now leaving the deli," I muttered, glancing at the clock.

Dad stood. "I'm going to go check in on Laura and Paul. She has him trapped in my office, going over who knows what." He chuckled. "I expect they'll be at it for a little while longer. And I could always throw in my two cents, keep them occupied for, oh, let's say an extra twenty minutes."

I stood and pocketed my phone. "Could you make it thirty?"

"We'll see. Just . . . don't put yourself at risk, Buttercup." He started out of the room, then paused. "The keys are in the dish on the counter." And then he was gone.

Shooting Dad a silent thanks, I snatched the keys out of the dish, then slipped out the door. I wasn't quite sure what I was planning on doing, but I knew it would involve checking out that fancy house of Tito's, which, if nothing else, was a place to start.

Nerves had me sitting bolt upright as I drove the short distance to Tito's. The house sat at the end of a long, winding road that led to a small neighborhood of houses occupied by the semi-wealthy. Homes of well-to-do business owners were situated next to those of pharmacists and club owners. The yards were of a decent size and the houses were large, but not so big that they required paid help to keep them maintained.

Tito's house was lit up from the inside, and his car was parked in the driveway, just past a pair of full trash cans sitting near the curb. I drove back down the street a little ways and parked near a darkened house that appeared unoccupied, though no for sale sign sat out front. I could see Tito's home in the rearview mirror, but I couldn't make anything out through the parted curtains covering the large front window.

I shut off the engine and sat there for a long moment, listening to it *tick*. I had a couple of options, all of which were risky. I could walk up to the door and knock. If Tito answered, I could ask him point-blank if he'd taken Lyle's tablet.

Downside? If he had, that meant he'd likely killed the health inspector, or at least, had a hand in it. If he'd murdered Lyle, then what would stop him from doing the same thing to me?

No, nix that idea.

I could go to him under the guise of me being apologetic for my earlier questions at Tito's Deli. I could tell him I didn't mean to upset him, that I had a tendency to be overly nosy at times. It was a semi-valid excuse.

The obvious problem with that idea was that it was unlikely that Tito would carry the tablet to the door if he had it. Nor did I believe he'd leave it sitting out where anyone could see it. I'd need him to invite me in, and to leave me unattended in the room where he'd hidden it. The chances of that were less than slim. Tito would be more likely to be annoyed that I'd come all the way out to his home and disturbed him in the middle of the night, when I could have waited until tomorrow and just showed up at his deli.

That left option number three, which was probably the best—and safest—of the bunch.

Stealth.

I climbed out of Dad's car and eased the door closed with a soft *click*. A large tree stood in the front yard of the Adornetto home, near the large window. I figured it would serve as the perfect place to hide so I could have a peek inside. I knew the chances were small that I'd find Tito sitting there with Lyle's rubberized tablet in hand, but it wasn't impossible either.

I walked briskly toward the tree, hands shoved in my pockets, trying my hardest to look like I belonged. No one else was outside, but that didn't mean someone wouldn't glance out their window and spot me. I knew from my earlier research into Tito that he was recently divorced and that his son was an adult, meaning he'd likely be alone.

Tito's car engine was ticking as I passed it by, telling me he must have gotten home minutes before I'd arrived, which was a good sign. If he *did* have Lyle's tablet and planned on getting rid of it, now would be the time. I stepped up behind the tree, glanced down the street to the other houses to make sure no one had noticed me, then looked toward Tito's house and through the parted curtains.

The first thing I noticed was the cat tree in front of the window. The curtains weren't parted because Tito wanted them that way, but because the feline of the house must have been sitting there and had nudged them aside. They'd caught on the sides of the tree so the kitty could look out and survey his or her territory. It didn't leave much in the way of an opening, but it was enough to see that the living room beyond was empty of life. A large, plush couch was flanked on either side by matching recliners. A long coffee table sat in front of the couch, and a steaming mug sat on a coaster there.

"Come on, Tito," I quietly whispered. The mug meant that he planned on returning to the room. I just hoped it would be soon because I felt very exposed standing there, behind the tree. Tito might not be able to see me from his window, but pretty much everyone else in the neighborhood could. And if a car drove by, there'd be nowhere for me to hide.

A shadow moved in a room upstairs. A moment later, a light clicked off. I tensed in anticipation, counting the seconds in my head, and then Tito appeared, dressed casually in loose-fitting exercise pants and a tank top. A fluffy snow-white cat followed at his heel as Tito paced in front of the coffee table in clear agitation.

For a few long minutes, nothing else happened. Tito was running his hands through what was left of his hair and seemed to be grumbling to himself—or, knowing cat owners, being one myself, to his kitty. There was no telltale tablet in his hand, yet I just *knew* that was what he was worried about.

My phone felt heavy in my pocket as I watched him. I could call Detective McKensie now, but what could I tell her? I had no proof that Tito had done anything wrong. She couldn't search his house for the missing tablet at my word, and I seriously doubted Tito would admit to anything if she asked him about it. I needed evidence, even something small, that would give me something more than speculation.

The cat, seemingly bored with following Tito around, hopped up on the cat tree and peered outside. Its large green eyes spotted me immediately, and its ears perked up in interest.

"Shoo," I whispered, motioning for the cat to jump down, though I knew from experience it was a futile exercise. "Go away before you—"

Before I could finish the thought, Tito stopped pacing and crossed the room to the window. I ducked back behind the tree, heart hammering in my chest as my breath locked in my throat. I waited a full minute before hazarding another peek toward the house.

The cat was gone, and the curtains were closed tight.

It was time to go.

I studied the window a few moments more to make sure that Tito, or his cat, wouldn't return, and then I stepped out from behind the tree. Shoulders tense, I crossed the yard, toward his car, and I had just reached it when the rattle of Tito's doorknob had me dropping to my knees, behind the vehicle.

I couldn't make out much from underneath the car, but what I could see had my blood pumping in my ears. Tito, in brown slippers, was walking quickly toward the car behind which I was hiding. My brain registered that he wasn't wearing socks, all while I vainly tried to come up with some reasonable explanation as to why I was lurking in his driveway.

Instead of rounding the vehicle and climbing into the driver's seat like I expected, though, Tito continued past, toward the trash cans at the end of the drive. I re-

mained crouched and eased around the bumper, to the
side of the car, praying he didn't notice the sound of
my sneakers on the paved surface.

I couldn't see what he was doing as he paused at the
trash cans, though I could hear it. There was a *thump* as
he opened the plastic top and let it fall against the side
of the can. A rattle of plastic followed, then what sounded
like a patting of the same plastic surface. A moment
later, there was a new *thump* I took for him closing the
lid, and then the *swish* of Tito's pants legs rubbing together as he hurried back to his house.

As soon as I heard the door close again, I sagged
down against the tire, breathing fast and hard. That was
way too close.

Down the street, a door opened, and a woman with
short hair stepped outside, carrying a bag of trash. She
tossed it in a can sitting just outside her garage, and
then she dragged that to the end of the driveway with a
loud grating sound. She scanned the neighborhood,
eyes seemingly passing right over me where I sat against
Tito's car, before she turned and walked back to her
house. The door closed with a solid *thump* that rever-
berated down the street.

I rose on shaky legs, peering over Tito's car as I did.
The living room light was still on, and the curtain remained closed. My eyes flickered over to the trash can,
curiosity swirling. Tito might have simply tossed a bag
of kitty litter, but I didn't think so. He'd been agitated
when I saw him inside. And I was pretty sure our earlier conversation was the reason why.

Call Detective McKensie!

And tell her what? That I suspected Tito Adornetto had just thrown away Lyle Carrigan's missing tablet? I didn't know the law well enough to know if she could search his trash without a solid reason. I mean, it was garbage, on a curb, where anyone could walk by and root around in it.

And anyone included me.

Steps quick and determined, I hurried over to the trash cans. I wasn't sure which of the two he'd opened, so I started with the nearest. A single black trash bag sat inside. Its drawstring was pulled tight and knotted. I checked around either side of it, saw nothing, so I closed the lid and moved on to the next with a quick glance back at Tito's house. Nothing had changed, yet I could *feel* time slipping away.

I opened the lid, and my heart skipped a beat as I laid eyes on the torn bag. No, a torn trash bag wasn't confirmation of anything, and it was too dark to see what was inside. Gritting my teeth, I shoved my hand through the tear and maneuvered my way past something that felt like a banana peel and a rectangular box that made me think of my favorite brownie mix. I rooted around, scratched the back of my hand on said box, bumped into an aluminum can, a glass bottle, and . . .

Rubber.

I froze, stunned by the fact that I might have been right.

Taking slow, measured breaths, I walked my fingers around the edge until I touched glass. The size was right for it to be Lyle's tablet, but once again, I couldn't be sure without actually looking at it. I gripped the item as best I could and wiggled it free from the rest of the trash surrounding it. The banana peel came up with it, falling to the ground at my feet, but I paid it no mind.

And there it was.

The screen of Lyle's tablet was cracked, as if it had been smashed up against something hard. My mind supplied the image of Tito striking Lyle over the head with it, though I doubted that would have been enough to kill the health inspector. It *could* have stunned him long enough for Tito to grab something else, though, something heavier. Deadlier.

My phone went off, shattering the silence of the night.

I very nearly dropped Lyle's tablet as I scrambled for my phone. In my haste, I *did* drop my phone as I pulled it from my pocket. It clattered to the pavement and kept on ringing. As I reached down for it, Paul's name flashed across the screen. I swiped the red decline button, silencing the sound, just as Tito's front door opened.

"Who's there?" he shouted as I straightened, phone in hand. He spotted me instantly. "Hey, you! Get away from there."

I didn't have time to think. I bolted for Dad's car, heart pounding so loudly that I barely heard Tito's shouted, "Stop! I'm calling the police!" I threw myself into the car, tossed my phone into the passenger's seat, and then, with a gunning of the engine, I sped away.

It wasn't until I was almost back to Dad's that I realized I was still clutching Lyle's tablet in one hand, putting me in possession of what could be the only solid piece of evidence in Lyle Carrigan's murder.

16

"What's on the agenda for today?" Dad asked before he took a sip of his morning coffee.

A chunk of cookie floated to the top of my own mug. I drank, making sure to slurp down the gooey mass, which included a chocolate chip. I avoided eye contact, knowing that if anyone were to ask about my evening escapades, I'd break down and tell them everything. And while no one sitting around the table would turn me in to the police, I didn't want to face Paul's disapproval. Explaining why I hadn't taken his call last night had been hard enough. To tell him that I might have committed a crime, even with good intentions, would be too much.

"I'm up for anything," Laura said. "Whatever Krissy and Paul want to do is fine by me."

"What do you think?" Paul asked, glancing at me. "We could always make up for our lost beach day if you just want to relax."

"You know, I do have a grill," Dad said. "We could

pick some things up and spend the day outside. It's just as relaxing as the beach, but without all of the driving."

I set my mug down, fiddled with the handle. "Whatever you decide," I said, trying to come up with some way to sneak away for a little while without raising suspicions. And I most definitely didn't want Paul anywhere near Dad's car, where Lyle's tablet was currently hidden under the passenger's seat.

Dad snapped his fingers. "I forgot to ask. Did Larissa get ahold of you yesterday?"

"Yes!" I snatched onto the lifeline he'd thrown me. "She wants to meet up with me tonight. Renee too."

"That's great." Dad sounded genuinely happy. "I always liked Larissa and Renee." He turned to Paul. "You should have seen them all together when they were younger. Those four girls—Vicki included—were a handful." He chuckled. "I'm surprised it took so long for my hair to fall out, considering how much stress they caused me."

"We weren't that bad."

"So you think." Dad laughed. "We had to repaint your room, what? Three times in a single year? First it was the nail polish fiasco. Then that time Renee tried to do a backflip off your bed."

"She didn't *try*," I said. "She managed it just fine." Then lost her balance and crashed headfirst into the wall. She came out of it intact. The wall . . . not so much.

"You can still see the indentation where I tried to fix the wall," Dad said. "You should have Krissy show you sometime."

"I might do that," Paul said, though I noted his smile had turned speculative as he regarded me.

I decided to change the subject before he could ask me what was wrong. "I forgot to tell you that Larissa and Renee asked me to dinner tonight. They want to make it the three of us, but I can always ask them if it would be okay to bring you."

"No, that's all right," Paul said. "You go. See your friends."

"We'll keep him out of trouble," Laura added.

I picked up my coffee mug, ran my lips over the rim. "I can't help but feel like I'm ruining this whole trip," I said. "We're supposed to be doing things *together*, and I keep running off on my own."

"It's all right. *Really*." Paul reached over and put a hand on my forearm. "It's good to see you get out. We don't have to spend every waking moment together. We don't back home. I don't see why we have to here."

"And I don't mind having him around," Dad said. "Gives me a chance to tell him stories about you."

"Ugh. Please don't."

Dad merely smiled. Laura was no help.

I sighed, resigned to having my life story told without my input. I had a feeling I'd be trying to set the record straight on the flight home, and likely for days afterward.

"We can always grill out this afternoon," Dad said. "That way, you can still see your friends tonight."

"We'll need to go to the store," Laura said. "We're out of anything grill-able."

"You three can do that," I said. "I'd like to run an errand or two of my own."

"Oh?" Dad asked. "We could always drive you."

"No, that's okay," I said. "Valerie is reopening Death by Java this morning. I want to stop in and make sure everything is running smoothly. It might take five minutes, or it could take an hour if she needs my help. Since I gave her suggestions, I feel kind of responsible for her."

"Understood," Dad said. "That work with everyone?" Nods went around the table. "Perfect. You can take Laura's car and—"

"Actually," I cut in. "I'd like to take yours. I'm more comfortable with it."

"My car has more room for groceries," Laura pointed out.

Dad studied me a long moment, and I just *knew* he was trying to piece together my movements from last night. I gave him my best vacant stare until he polished off his coffee and clapped his hands together. "Well, I suppose it's settled then. We'll meet back here in, let's say, two hours? Gives us time to shop and you time to deal with Valerie."

"Sounds perfect," I said, rising.

Dad and Laura started cleaning up after breakfast, and Paul took me aside.

"You sure you don't want me to come with you?" he asked.

"I'm sure." And to prove it, I kissed him squarely on the lips. "I have to do this."

"I know you do." He gave me a hug, and then a moment later, we were out the door. I took my time getting settled in the car so that the other three were out of sight before I started down the road. Yes, I was going to check in at Death by Java, but that wasn't the real reason why I wanted to go alone. Nor was it the first place I wanted to stop.

My palms sweated all the way to the Redwood Village Police Station, and I could hardly sit still in my seat. Nerves had me adjusting and readjusting my seat belt at least a dozen times. The same went for the rearview mirror. And I couldn't decide whether I was cold from the air-conditioning or hot from the bright morning sun. I eventually rolled down the window and let the cool breeze wash over my flushed skin as a sort of compromise.

I pulled into the parking lot, which was dotted with a handful of cars I assumed were the personal vehicles of the officers. I turned off the engine, then sat there and breathed in and out. I could do this. If I was back home in Pine Hills, I'd think nothing about carrying the tablet inside and handing it over to Detective Buchannan. He'd be annoyed that I'd involved myself in his investigation, and he'd threaten me with a night in a jail cell, but he'd take it and would use it as best he could to nail the bad guy.

But I wasn't in Pine Hills. Detective McKensie might not be as forgiving as Buchannan, which was a strange thing for me to say, considering how *un*forgiving Buchannan could be. I could imagine McKensie snapping the cuffs on me and charging me with theft or contaminating a crime scene or any number of offenses that might or might not have merit.

I'm here. I might as well get it over with.

Huffing out a breath, I slid Lyle's tablet into my purse

and climbed out of the car. The police station was larger than the one in Pine Hills, but it felt strangely similar as I entered through the glass front door. Officer Peel was waiting for me inside.

"I was beginning to wonder if you were going to come in or if you'd sit out there all day," he said, eyeing me like he might a common criminal.

"I'd like to speak with Detective McKensie," I said.

Officer Peel made a sort of snapping, *click*ing sound out of the corner of his mouth. "Would you, now? What is this regarding?"

"It's about the Lyle Carrigan murder." I kept my expression blank and avoided patting or otherwise touching my purse, lest he catch on and want to see what was inside. Explaining it to Detective McKensie was going to be hard enough.

Peel glanced around the room, stroking his mustache. Other officers were busy, or were at least putting on the appearance of being busy. Every so often, eyes strayed to a door across the room, which made me wonder if someone of importance was there.

"Does the detective know you were coming?" Peel asked. "Or is this an impromptu visit?"

"I didn't call ahead." My annoyance flared. "This is important. Is she here or not?"

Another *click*, another stroke of his mustache. "She is. However, she is extremely busy. It would be best if you filled me in on what's so important that you had to come down here this morning." He took a step toward me as he hooked his thumbs into his belt and puffed out his chest. "I'm all you're going to get."

"Dudley. Just send her back."

Red crept up Officer Peel's—Dudley's—neck at the sound of Detective McKensie's voice. He held his puffed-up pose a moment longer before deflating. "Down the hall, first door on your right."

"Thank you," I said, giving Peel my best smile before stepping past him.

McKensie hadn't stepped into view, but I followed Peel's directions and soon found myself in what I took for her office. The detective was seated behind a small, cramped desk cluttered with *stuff*. There was a Los Angeles Angels glass cup–turned–pencil holder. A scratched-up wooden box with a stack of folders on top. A stapler sat beside a wire hanger bent so that it was heart-shaped. More papers. More folders. And, oddly, a brand-new rolling pin was perched precariously on one corner of the desk.

"Have a seat," McKensie said, motioning toward the chair across from her.

I clutched my purse close as I sat. "I'm sorry to drop in on you like this."

McKensie waved me off. "I assume you've learned something about the case or you wouldn't be here. I'd rather you interrupt me than for you to keep whatever it is it to yourself." She crossed her arms, leaned back in her chair. "So . . . spill."

I was surprised by how casual she was being. The softer tone put me at ease, which was probably the point.

"Don't be mad," I said. "But I came across something that you're going to want."

McKensie blinked once, didn't otherwise react.

Quit procrastinating, I told myself before reaching into my purse and removing Lyle's tablet. I handed it over without a word.

Detective McKensie took it with a frown. She turned it over in her hand twice before testing the power button. The screen didn't so much as flicker. Whether it was because it was cracked or because the battery was dead, I had no idea. I hadn't tried it when I'd gotten it, nor had I thought to plug it in before bringing it. She held it up toward me, brow raised in question.

"I found it in Tito Adornetto's trash."

McKensie heaved a sigh, then tossed the tablet onto her desk amid the rest of the clutter. "So, that was you?"

"Pardon?"

"Last night. We got a call about someone sneaking around a well-to-do neighborhood, going through people's trash. That was you."

"I only went through Tito's garbage," I said. "And I only did it because I saw him throw the tablet away. I knew I had to do something."

"You could have called it in," McKensie pointed out.

"I could have, but I wasn't positive that's what he'd tossed. It could have been kitty litter for all I knew. Calling you seemed risky, so I figured I'd check to make sure it was the tablet."

"And when it was, you decided to what? Just run off with it?"

I suppressed a wince. "Tito came back outside. I panicked."

Detective McKensie closed her eyes and rubbed at

her temples. A long stretch of silence followed before she said, "Let me get this straight. You went to Mr. Adornetto's house in the middle of the night to . . . ?"

"Check in on him?" It came out sounding like a question.

She grunted, went on. "You just so happen to see him throw something away and decide to rifle through the garbage. You then find what is evidence against Mr. Adornetto as it pertains to the murder of Mr. Carrigan. Instead of calling me, you decide to take said evidence with you, keep it overnight, and then bring it to me this morning. Am I clear on the chain of events?"

"Pretty much," I said, unable to hide my wince this time. "Sorry."

McKensie mouthed, *"Sorry,"* back at me and then shook her head. "I don't know what to think here."

"I know it doesn't prove that Tito killed Lyle," I said. "But he did have the tablet. I know I should have left it where it was, but like I said, he saw me, and I panicked. If I'd tossed it back into the trash, he would have taken it and hidden it elsewhere, maybe destroyed it. And there might be something on it that might provide a motive for Lyle's death."

McKensie eyed the tablet a long moment before glancing up at me. "You've put me in a precarious position, Ms. Hancock," she said. "I appreciate what you were trying to do, but I do wish you would have called me instead acting on your own."

"It won't happen again."

McKensie still didn't look happy as she stood. "I suppose I need to pay a visit to Mr. Adornetto and see what I can pry out of him. But first . . ." She picked up the tablet, weighed it in her hands. "I'm going to see if I can get this thing working. Hopefully you're right and there's something on here that will make everything else moot." She leveled a finger at me. "You'd better hope this doesn't cost me an arrest. I'd keep yourself busy with your family the rest of the time you're here, if I were you."

I stood. "I plan on it."

When I left the police station, I felt a great sense of relief. Not only was the tablet off my hands, but Detective McKensie hadn't arrested me. She wasn't happy with me, of course, but I could live with that if my contribution ended up putting a killer behind bars.

With my main errand completed, I drove to Death by Java to at least pretend to do what I'd said I was going to do. Tito's Deli next door was open, and I wondered if Tito was inside or if the events of the night had him worried. If he'd killed Lyle, it could go either way. He might want to keep up appearances, since calling off work might seem suspicious. But at the same time, if he was worried that the tablet might lead to his arrest, he might already have packed his bags and be halfway to Mexico by now.

The urge to poke my head inside Tito's to see if he was there was strong, but I resisted it. Everyone would be waiting for me, so I needed to do what I'd come here to do and get back to Dad's. I entered Death by Java, already planning my exit strategy if Valerie tried to talk me into sticking around for more than a few minutes, but I was caught off guard by a loud, excited voice.

"Lordy Lou, I know!" Rita proclaimed. "I can see it just over your shoulder. It's uncanny how similar they are. Look here. You see that? Almost identical!"

Because the dining area was empty of all but one person, I zeroed in on the table at which Dad sat, tablet propped up in front of him. Rita Jablonski's face was on the screen. Behind her, I could just make out the menu board at Death by Coffee and the top of Eugene Dohmer's head, where he was serving a customer.

"Very similar, indeed," Dad said as I crossed the room behind him. "What amazes me is that the two of them didn't get along when they were younger, and yet they both ended up following similar paths. I—" He glanced over as if he'd sensed my presence. "Oh! Buttercup. There you are."

"Dad." I glanced at the tablet. "Rita." I glanced around the room to find that neither Laura nor Paul were in attendance.

"Your father told me you'd be here, dear." Rita *tsk*ed. "I thought we could all have a nice little chat, but when he got here, you were nowhere in sight!"

"I had something else I needed to do," I said before turning to Dad. "What are you doing here? I thought you were going to the grocery?"

"I was planning on it," he said. "But then I got a message from Rita asking if we could chat. So . . ." He shrugged. "I had Laura drop me off."

"Really, dear," Rita said. "I don't know where you've been, but you should sit down and spend some time with your father."

"Did Paul ask why I wasn't here yet?" I asked Dad instead of responding to Rita.

"I saw you lingering outside the car before we left, so I assumed you had something else to do." Dad's eyes twinkled as he said it. "Let's just say you're covered."

I probably didn't want to know, and before I could ask, Valerie appeared from the back. "Krissy! I'm glad you're here. Something's come up, and I'd like to talk to you about it if you have a second."

I sighed, resigned. "I'll be right back." I walked over to where Valerie stood next to a seemingly disinterested Farrah. "What's up?"

Valerie glanced at Farrah and then led me a few steps away. When she spoke, she kept her voice low. "I'm starting to worry," she said. "I think I'm going to lose my employees if things don't change."

"Is it about Lyle's murder?"

"No!" Valerie grabbed my arm, led me another step away. "Not so loud."

"Sorry."

"It's . . ." She shot another worried glance at Farrah. "Dee has called off a few times recently. Now Nadia can't come in. I swear, I'm paying them enough, but what if they're looking for new jobs? It's already hard enough with just the three of them. I don't know what to do!"

"What *are* you paying them?" I asked. I recalled a time when Valerie had called me months ago, asking what I paid my own employees because she wanted to pay her own less than minimum wage.

"That's not really important," Valerie said. "The financials—"

"I'm not the person to ask about something like

that," I said, and I meant it. Vicki was the one who dealt with the money and the business side of things.

"Yes, but . . ." Valerie's voice turned to a buzz as I glanced back at Dad.

"Hold that thought," I said, before marching over to the table. "Rita?"

"Yes, dear?" she replied.

"You're at Death by Coffee." A statement because I could see that she was. "Is Vicki there?"

Rita blinked at me. "Well, I suppose she is. At least, she was a few minutes ago. If you're worried about the lights, they've been on since I got here. No power fluctuations at all, though there was a tiny little dimming when I first came in that I took for my eyes adjusting, so I could be wrong about that."

"Could you get her for me?" I asked, ignoring the bit about the lights. I so didn't need to be worrying about that right now. "Please."

Rita looked stricken, but nodded. "Of course, dear. This won't take long, will it?"

"It shouldn't." I smiled at her. "Thank you."

Rita vanished from view as she stood and walked over to the counter, where Eugene waited.

"What's going on?" Dad asked.

I shook off the question as Vicki appeared on-screen, Rita at her heel.

"Hi, Krissy. Having fun? James."

"Hi, Vicki. It's good to see you," Dad said.

"Can I borrow you for a minute?" I asked. "Valerie has a few questions about finances. I'm not sure how to answer her, and I figure it might be better if you talked to her."

In the background, Rita said, "With *my* tablet?"

"Visuals might help," I said. "You could look her in the eye and see if she's trying to pull one over on you."

"Sure," Vicki said. "I've got a few minutes, if it's okay with everyone else?"

"Fine by me," Dad said. "I'm sure Rita won't mind."

"Of course not, dear. You go right ahead. James and I can finish our conversation later." Though I could tell from her tone, she wasn't happy.

With permission granted, I picked up Dad's tablet and carried it over to Valerie, who took it with a perplexed, "What's this?" just before it registered who was on the screen. "Vicki? Is that you?"

Without bothering to explain myself, I returned to where Dad sat. I slid into the chair across from him. "Sorry about that. She'll bring it back in a few minutes."

"No, it's all right." Dad cupped his chin in his hand and gave me an expectant look. "Now," he said, "mind telling me what happened last night that caused you to rush off to who knows where this morning? And, Buttercup, don't leave anything out."

17

Business at Death by Java continued to be nonexistent during the ten minutes it took for me to go over my night at Tito's house and subsequent morning jaunt to the Redwood Village Police Station to talk to Detective McKensie. Valerie returned just as I was finishing up, and she handed over Dad's tablet with a muttered thanks before stomping off to the back. Apparently, she hadn't come away happy from her conversation with Vicki, which wasn't much of a surprise, considering Valerie's reticence to pay her employees a living wage.

"Rita's not going to be happy," Dad said, waggling his tablet. "I expect to hear from her at any moment."

As if cue, his phone *ding*ed. He checked it, showed me Rita's, *They hung up on me!* text, and then he took a moment to respond. Another *ping* followed. And then another.

"She'll keep texting you until you call her," I said.

"You're probably right." He heaved a resigned sigh.

"Give me a few minutes to smooth things over with her, and then we can head home." He stood and moved to the empty bookstore portion of the café, though he could have made the call sitting in his seat and not disturbed anyone since there was quite literally no one else in the dining area but me and Farrah, who was perusing her phone behind the counter.

I peered at the window toward Tito's Deli, curiosity smoldering just under the surface. I wondered if Tito was inside, and if Detective McKensie had arrived while I'd been talking to Dad. I could go over and have a look around, but what then? If Tito was there and he recognized me as his trash thief, there's no telling what he'd do. Not only that, but Dad was with me. And Paul and Laura were likely on their way back to Dad's by now, if they weren't there already.

The door to Death by Java opened. I glanced back to see Roman Haines walk through the door, tool belt slung low on his hip.

"Hey, babe," he said to Farrah, whose face immediately fell when she saw him. "Could you get the boss lady for me? We've got a little business to work out between the two of us, if you know what I mean?" I couldn't see his face, but I could imagine the smarmy wink that followed.

Farrah pocketed her phone, rolled her eyes, and without a word, retreated to the back, leaving Roman and me alone in the dining room. He turned, hip cocked in a way I assumed he took as fetching, and when he saw me, a grin a mile wide spread across his face.

"Hey there."

"Roman." Noting that Dad was still on the phone

with Rita, I stood and walked over to where the repair-man waited. "Something else break?"

"I don't think so," he said. "I just need to talk to Val-erie."

As subtly as I could, I scanned the tool belt, noted the mismatched screwdriver tucked at his hip. I pointed at it. "I heard Valerie found one of your tools in the back." *Next to a dead body*, I didn't add.

Roman's grin somehow widened further. "Boy, did she ever."

I did well not to groan. "I meant your screwdriver."

He glanced down at his tool belt. "Oh yeah. That thing. It happens."

"Did you leave it here when you fixed the ice ma-chine?" I pressed. "Or did you come back here later that night? You know, to collect payment." I winked, feeling like a complete moron, but I didn't know how else to slither into Roman's good graces.

The ploy appeared to work. The expression that flit-tered across Roman's face made my stomach do very unpleasant things. I could almost taste the slimeball oozing off him.

"You *do* feel me." He bobbed his head in time with whatever music was echoing in his otherwise-empty skull. "We may have had a few minutes to powwow the other night. We didn't quite get physical, but I may have rattled my belt, if you catch my meaning?"

I had an inkling. "Are you and Valerie a thing?" I kept my voice low, even though no one was within ear-shot.

I could see the desire in Roman's eyes. He desperately wanted to brag, to tell me that he and Valerie were doing things that were only ever conceived of in erotic stories told in hushed whispers in the dead of night. Instead, he hitched a shoulder, ceased the endless head bob.

"Not officially as of yet," he said. Then his expression brightened. "But hey, now that this Mickey dude of hers is a suspect in a murder, she might think about giving me a solid chance at hitching a ride on the old Valerie Express. It's most fortuitous."

I was actually surprised he knew such a big word, but I managed to mask my shock as I asked, "How well do you know her boyfriend, Mickey Robbins? Do you think he could have killed Lyle?"

"Guy was a loose cannon," Roman said. "Got all up in my face one day, but he had nothing to say. Was just mad that his girl was making eyes at me. I could have told him that it ain't nothing new. All women look at me that way." He looked me up and down and licked his lips in a way that wasn't just an invitation, but a promise.

Somehow I didn't puke.

"I do feel kind of bad, though," he went on, deflating just a little. "I didn't know the health inspector guy all that well, but I knew his wife some. We kind of hooked up a few years back." The cocky grin was back, but it barely registered on my consciousness.

"His wife?" I asked. "Lyle was married?"

"Sure was," he said. "Name's Leanne. I fixed their water pump about a month ago. Or maybe it was two, three weeks back." His eyes went distant as he thought about it, then he shook his head. "Anyway, thought maybe she might like to hook up again, you know, for old time's sake?"

"Sure," I said. "Was she interested?"

"Nah. She was too upset."

"Upset? Why?"

Roman shrugged. "Beats me. She said something about her husband and his job. I thought maybe he was getting pressure from the top to work harder or something. By then, I was just about done with the job, and since she wasn't keen on getting a little dirty, I was itching to get moving. I had another job lined up, one with far better prospects when it came to the side-benefits department."

Oh boy. This guy was so full of himself that he didn't seem to understand his bragging came off as creepy and sexist.

"Did you talk to her after that?" I asked, somehow keeping the disgust out of my voice. "Or with Lyle?"

Before he could answer, the back door opened, and Valerie rushed out of it with Farrah right behind her. "Roman! Thank goodness you're here. We need to talk."

"Be right there, babe," he said, then turned to me. "You know, if you want to talk about this some more, we could always meet up later. I know this place—"

"No thanks," I said before he could finish. "I've already got plans."

He shrugged, seemed unconcerned by the rejection. "You can find my number online if you change your mind," he said before turning a wide grin on to Valerie.

"I'm all yours," he told her, and she whisked him off to the back.

"He's so gross," Farrah said, before producing her phone and dismissing me without so much a look.

That he was. But for as gross Roman might be, he wasn't entirely useless. Our little chat had produced one important tidbit of information I hadn't had before.

Lyle was married.

Not only that, but his wife had been upset weeks before his murder. Was she upset with Lyle? Mad enough to kill him? Or was it about something else entirely?

There was only one way to find out.

"Whew," Dad said, joining me a moment later. "I wasn't sure I was going to be able to get away. Once Rita gets rolling, she doesn't stop talking, does she?" He paused, studied me. "Did I miss something, Buttercup?"

I considered telling him that it was nothing and that we should go meet Laura and Paul back at home, but I *knew* I wouldn't be able to do that. Besides, it was still early. We had more than enough time to make one more little stop before heading back to Dad's.

"You up for another field trip?" I asked him, dangling his car keys in the air.

Dad snatched them out of my hand with a grin, "Just tell me where you want to go."

Lyle and Leanne Carrigan's address wasn't hard to find online. By the time Dad and I were strapped into his car, Dad had already warned Laura and Paul we might be a few minutes late, and I'd already brought the address up on the navigation screen. Dad followed the directions without asking a single question, though I could feel the curiosity coming off him in waves.

The Carrigans lived in a quiet neighborhood full of modestly sized homes that were a smidge too close together for my liking. No one had a garage—it was on-street parking only, and the street itself was rather full, outside a couple of notable gaps marked by handicap signs. Those houses all had ramps leading up to their front doors.

The Carrigan house had no such ramp. We found a parking spot nearby and made the short walk from the street to the small square of concrete that served as a front stoop. There was no doorbell, so I knocked.

The door opened almost immediately, and a red-eyed woman with light brown hair and a slim build answered. "Yes?" she asked, voice cracking ever so slightly on the word.

"Leanne Carrigan?" At her nod, I continued, "I'm Krissy Hancock. This is my father, James. I knew your husband, Lyle. I was hoping we could talk briefly, if you have the time."

Leanne stepped aside wordlessly. She'd probably had visitors of all sorts over the last few days, so what was a few more? Dad and I entered a dimly lit home full of a lifetime of memories. Books, collectibles, and general *stuff* filled nearly every space. All of it was dusted and kept clean, but it gave the house a lived-in, full-of-life vibe that made my heart ache just a little bit.

Leanne led us into a small dining nook. The table was big enough for two to sit at and eat comfortably, but any more that than would be a challenge. There were only two chairs. Leanne motioned for Dad and me to sit, while she chose to lean up against the door frame, arms crossed defensively, as if she were afraid we were going to tell her something that she didn't want to hear.

"It's nice of you to come," she said once we were settled. "I didn't know many of Lyle's friends, not that he had many. He . . . We . . ." She sucked in a trembling breath. "I'm sorry. This is hard."

"Don't be," I said, already regretting coming. "We won't keep you." I glanced at Dad, who nodded for me to go on. *It's your show*, his expression said. "When I said I knew your husband, I didn't mean to make it sound like we were friends. I'd only met him a few days ago."

Leanne's smile was strained, but there was a fondness to it. "Like I said, Lyle didn't keep many friends, so I assumed as much. His life revolved around work and home. There was no room for anything else. If it wasn't for me, I imagine he would have become a hermit. He would have been perfectly happy that way."

"Did you know much about his work?" I asked.

"Some. He talked about it a little, but he never liked to complain. We spent a lot of time together just watching TV, reading." Her voice hitched. "We enjoyed each other's company, even though we often didn't speak. We didn't need to. Having one another there was enough." She wiped away a tear.

It was clear I needed to keep this brief and let Leanne Carrigan get on with grieving, but I wasn't sure how to ask what I wanted to ask without upsetting her.

"Lyle seemed to focus on work when I saw him," I said. "He never spoke about his family life or what he did outside the job. I didn't even know he was married until I talked to a man named Roman Haines."

A flash of something unkind shot across Leanne's face, replacing her grief for an instant. "I see."

"He claimed that he knew you, but not your husband."

"That would be true," Leanne said. "Mr. Haines prefers to do his business when the man of the house isn't around, if you catch my drift."

"I do. He likes to hit on women." If Dad wasn't there, I would have told her about my own interaction with Roman, but I didn't want to see where *that* conversation might lead.

The laugh that followed was void of humor. "More than that. If you turn him down, he presses the issue. Maybe not right away. And maybe not directly. But eventually, he starts showing up here or there, making comments, pushing you to acknowledge him. It's like he is unable to comprehend the fact that not every woman falls madly in love with him the moment they lay eyes on him."

"He said he fixed your water pump."

"That he did. Lyle was the one who called him, completely by chance, because I wouldn't have. Roman and I . . ." She took a breath, huffed it out. "We have a history."

I glanced at Dad, who asked, "What sort of history?"

Leanne picked at her thumbnail. I noted it was already red and agitated. "It was, I don't know, two years ago? Maybe three. Lyle was off doing some training thing out of town, and I was here alone. I called Roman because the fridge was acting up. He came over and made a move on me. It caught me by surprise, so it took me a moment to react, which he took as an invitation. He kissed me, and I suppose I might not have resisted at first, but then it hit me all at once, and I pushed him away. I told him to leave, but he wouldn't go. I almost had to call the cops. Thankfully, Lyle called right then, and he scurried out the door before I could tell on him."

That wasn't how Roman described their relationship, but I wasn't about to open that can of worms. "Did you tell Lyle about what Roman had done?"

Leanne looked up from her thumbnail and studied us for a long moment. "Even if you only knew Lyle a little bit, you would realize that telling him something like that would have destroyed him. He wouldn't have blamed me, nor would he have gotten angry at Roman. No, instead, Lyle would have questioned his own self-worth. Nothing had happened, yet he'd always think that Roman made his move because he knew how unworthy Lyle was, which couldn't be further from the truth." She took a shuddering breath.

Guilt caused me to rise. "I'm sorry, Leanne. I didn't mean to upset you." I motioned for Dad, who stood. I wanted to ask her what she'd been upset about when Roman had last talked to her, but now didn't feel like the right time. "We should probably go."

She nodded and led us to the front door, but she didn't

open it right away. She stood there, back to us, hand on the knob, unmoving. Unspeaking. It was clear she was working through something, and I let her do it.

"Lyle let people walk all over him," she said after a moment. "His job caused strife between him and the business owners he was forced to cite. He didn't enjoy it, and he often felt guilty about it whenever it happened."

Dad and I shared a look, waited her out.

"But recently, things had gotten so bad, Lyle was starting to worry. I said before that he never complained, but that wasn't quite true. Over the last few weeks, he'd been really upset. I asked him why, and at first, he told me it was nothing. He'd take care of it, he'd said. And then that man showed up outside."

"Mickey Robbins," I said.

She nodded. "Lyle told me a little about him, about why he was angry with him. He said it was about some citations he'd been forced to make, that this Robbins guy was protecting his girlfriend or wife or whatever she was. But I knew there was more to it than just a simple health violation that had the other man worked up. I could hear it in Lyle's voice."

"Did you ever find out what it was about?"

She shook her head. "I called his work, but they didn't know anything. Or at least that's what they said. And Lyle . . . He . . ." A deep trembling breath, then, "This is something I didn't tell the police. I don't know why I didn't say anything. I guess I was scared. Lyle was just—" Her hand tightened on the doorknob. "He died, and I suppose I was afraid that his killer might come for me next if I said something. I thought it was the Robbins guy or maybe Roman because of how I'd rejected him not once, but twice."

She turned, revealing eyes filled with tears. "But I'm not so sure that was it. You see, Mickey Robbins had a reason to be angry with Lyle, though when he showed up outside here, he didn't know it."

She opened the door, stepped aside. Sunlight streamed in, casting a glow upon the dimly lit interior. Dad and I walked past Leanne, into the light. She didn't close the door behind us, but rather, she stood there, tears rolling down reddened cheeks. The hand on the doorknob was clenched into a fist so tight, her knuckles were white.

"Talk to Marco Rossi," she said. "Ask him about Lyle and the deal they made. If anything, *that's* the reason why my husband is dead. And if anyone, he is the man who is responsible."

And then, without another word, she stepped back and closed the door.

18

"Yeah, I'm sorry about this," Dad said, phone to his ear. "Right. Uh-huh." He glanced at me and winked. "It'll probably be an hour at most. Yep. See you then." He clicked off and shoved his phone into his pocket. "I don't think she believes me."

"Of course she doesn't," I said as I opened the car door and slid out. "A flat tire? Really?"

"I didn't know what else to say," Dad said, joining me on the sidewalk. "I didn't want to tell Laura we were off chasing killers like a couple of mopes from one of my novels."

"She knows, Dad. She knows."

We walked the short distance to the Italian Roll side by side. Customers were seated outside, enjoying their pizza rolls, and all those old memories came flooding back once again. But now, knowing there was a chance Marco Rossi could very well be a murderer—or tied to one—I couldn't summon the enthusiasm for those little squares of lava.

You don't know that he's involved. All Leanne had said was that Marco and Lyle had struck a deal and that it might be the reason why her husband was killed. She hadn't said Marco killed him or even knew who did, but it was hard not to wonder. I still thought Mickey was a good bet as Lyle's killer. Even Roman and Tito were better suspects. I hoped that talking to Marco would help me sort it all out.

"Are you ready for this?" Dad asked, hand on the door.

No, I wasn't. "Let's get it over with."

Most of the tables were full as we entered, though orders had died down. No one was behind the counter other than one of the Italian Roll's teenage employees, who was wearing the typical outfit: white shirt, jeans, covered by a white apron with the Italian Roll logo on it. He was leaning against the serving window that led into the kitchen, talking to someone out of sight. A glance toward the open office door showed Marco standing just inside, peering out at us.

"How do you want to do this?" Dad asked.

I strode to the counter by way of answer. "Hi there," I said.

The teen didn't so much as crack a smile at my perky tone. He grunted as he pushed away from the window and moved over to stand behind the register. "What can I get you?"

"We'd like to talk to Marco." I flashed a wide grin to where the man in question stood, scowling. "It's about Lyle Carrigan. I've heard an interesting rumor about how Marco struck a deal with—"

Before I could finish the thought, Marco barked,

"Get in here," and motioned for me to enter his office. Since Dad was standing behind me, he took it as an invite as well, and we both crossed the short distance to where Marco waited. He made room for us to enter, then slammed the door closed behind us.

"What do you think you're doing coming in here talking about Lyle to my employees like that? And loud enough to be heard by my customers? Are you trying to ruin me?" He walked around his desk, but he didn't sit. Instead, he gripped the back of his chair in hands that looked strong enough to strangle both Dad and me at the same time. "Care to explain yourself?"

"I'm sorry about that," I said, going for contrite, but his reaction had piqued my interest. There was, indeed, something to what Leanne had told me. "But I wanted to get your attention. You *did* strike a deal with Lyle Carrigan, didn't you?"

Marco glowered at me for a good long minute before speaking. "Who told you?"

"So, it's true?" Dad asked.

A *crash* came from the kitchen on the other side of the wall. Someone clapped. Marco just stared, jaw working overtime. I imagined his dentist wouldn't be thrilled with him once this was over.

"It could be important," I pressed. "Did you make a deal with Lyle?"

"That's your business, how?"

I didn't have to think about it very hard to know that accusing Marco of killing Lyle would be the wrong tactic here. "He was murdered," I pointed out. "If it was because the two of you were working together . . ." I gave him a meaningful look.

Some of the heat left Marco's expression. "Then the killer might come for me next." His scowl morphed into a thoughtful frown. "Meaning I might be in danger."

"Exactly," I said. "If someone found out about whatever it was that you two were conspiring to do—"

"We weren't 'conspiring'," Marco snapped, but there was little force to it. He released his death grip on the chair and sat down. "We were righting a wrong."

Dad and I shared a look. His subtle nod was permission for me to continue to press the issue. "What happened, Marco?" I asked. "I know you and Lyle were friends. But 'righting a wrong'? What kind of deal are we talking about?"

Marco sighed, rubbed at his face. It took him almost a full minute before he spoke. "There was a time when this part of the Village was the place to be. When I first opened, it was perfect. Business was great, as there was an endless stream of customers."

"But times changed," Dad said.

"They did. It was a slow progression while this end of town became less and less attractive, and on the other end, more visibly accessible locations drew the eye of businesses and tourists alike. Before long, all I had were my old customers, with precious few new ones even knowing I existed."

Marco's eyes flickered up to me, then flashed to Dad, before he planted them back onto the desk in front of him. "Then, when that corner spot opened up, I jumped at the chance to move. I put in my bid, but unfortunately, I lost."

"To Valerie."

He nodded with a barely suppressed scowl. "Death by Java." He said the name of the bookstore café like a curse. "I *know* she cheated her way into it because there's no chance that she outbid me. I'm not going to say how she cheated, but I'm sure you can imagine."

I didn't have to imagine since Tito had all but spelled it out to me. The thought that both men believed the same thing about her didn't bode well for Valerie's innocence in this matter.

Then again, a lot of men hated it when pretty women managed to beat them, whether it was in games or business or whatever it might be. Those same men were often prone to saying some pretty degrading things about the woman who topped them, whether truthful or not.

"That had to get on your nerves," Dad said.

Marco barked a laugh. "You don't say. I tried to talk some sense into anyone who would listen, but the deal was done. Best location in town, and that two-bit—" He clamped his teeth closed, then spoke through them. "That *woman* steals it from me and squanders it. How anyone could fail at that location is beyond me. I probably didn't need to enlist Lyle, but I'm not a patient man. I couldn't wait for her to die a slow death when I could get her kicked out of the place far quicker."

The light bulb went on in my head. "You had Lyle cite her."

"It wasn't like it wasn't already his job," Marco said. "I told him not to do anything illegal or anything immoral. Just go in there, take a good, hard look at the place, and cite her into oblivion. Threw in Tito's Deli for good measure, not because I have anything against Tito, but because I figured it couldn't hurt to add another option in case Valerie withstood the scrutiny. His spot is good too. And it wouldn't make it look like Lyle was targeting only the café if he was also citing other businesses in the area."

"That's what you two were talking about that day he stormed out of here," I said.

Marco's nod was slow, thoughtful. "It was. He said he was worried that things were getting too hot for him to handle. Mickey was pressing him, threatening him." He clenched a fist. "I told him to keep pushing, not to let it bother him. It's my fault that he was killed. If I'd let him back off like he wanted to, then perhaps . . ." He shook his head and fell silent.

Things were starting to make sense. Valerie, using underhanded tactics or not, snatched up prime real estate for her bookstore café. Marco wanted the space, and he wanted to hurry her demise. He had his friend Lyle, who just so happened to be a health inspector, go in and nitpick every violation he could find in an attempt to force her to close. Mickey and Valerie were, unsurprisingly, unhappy about it. So was Tito, who had been tossed into the blender right alongside them. One of them—I wasn't sure which—had gotten fed up and killed Lyle before he could ruin their business.

But which one? And could someone else, be it Hugh or Aaron or even Roman, have stepped in instead?

"Did anyone else know about this?" Dad asked, likely thinking along the same lines as me.

"Of course not," Marco snapped. "Not unless Lyle

told someone, because I sure didn't. Do you know what it would do to me if people found out I was trying to close other businesses in town, even ones that were already failing? I'd be treated like a pariah."

Besides Leanne, I couldn't think of anyone Lyle might have told, other than perhaps someone he worked with. But even then, wouldn't talking to his coworkers about forced citations risk getting him into trouble?

"Wait." Marco's eyes widened. "There might be one other person who knew."

Dad was the one who asked, "Who might that be?"

Marco thought about it, then slowly nodded as he spoke. "I don't know the guy's name. It happened maybe a week ago. Lyle was here, and we were talking. Well, *he* was talking. He'd gotten all worked up and started yelling. This was right about the time he was starting to question our tactics and wanted to stop. Normally, he never used names, just in case someone was listening, but on that day, he did."

He paused, and I just about screamed from the anticipation.

"I recall looking up because the door was hanging open after Lyle had barged in here while I was working at my desk." He patted the desktop in front of him. "That Valerie woman's lover was standing there."

"Mickey?" I asked.

To my surprise, Marco shook his head. "No, not her boyfriend. Her *lover.*" He met my eyes with an intensity that I felt clear across the room. "The repairman. If anyone else knew what was going on between me and Lyle Carrigan, it was him."

* * *

Roman Haines had overheard the plot to ruin Valerie Kemp's business.

I churned it over all the way back to Dad's house. Roman was interested in Valerie. Sure, he appeared interested in almost *all* women, but he did seem awfully smitten with her in particular. If he knew that Lyle was hounding her on Marco's behalf, he could have used that information to get into her good graces, maybe even by holding the information hostage.

For what? A night together in Death by Java's back room? Something more?

And how exactly would that lead to Lyle's murder?

Laura and Paul were waiting at the house. Dad had called ahead, and it had been decided that grilling out would have to wait, so when we arrived, we spent a few minutes freshening up before we all piled into the car and were headed . . . I didn't know where. I'm sure Paul, Laura, and Dad had discussed it at some point, but I hadn't been paying attention.

I kept thinking about everything that had led up to the murder. The deal. The harassment. Lyle getting cold feet. Roman overhearing the conversation between Marco and Lyle. I could see him going to Valerie with the information, thinking himself clever, but then what?

Perhaps Valerie accepted his proposal, spent the night with Roman, and then promptly told Mickey about the deal. Mickey, understandably angry, then killed Lyle, thinking he was doing it for Valerie. Or perhaps Roman decided not to tell Valerie about the deal, but instead opted to kill Lyle as a show of his undying devotion to her.

But in both cases, why leave the body in Death by Java?

Then what about Tito? He'd had Lyle's tablet. He'd been thrown into the mix by Marco, which meant Lyle had been hounding him just as much as he was Valerie. Could she have told Tito what Lyle was doing after she'd learned about it from Roman? In a fit of rage that fit with what I knew of the man, Tito killed Lyle and left his body in Death by Java because he didn't approve of Valerie's methods?

But again, if that was the case, how did he get the body into the bookstore café? I was missing something, and I had no idea what it could be.

"Are you okay?" Paul asked, nudging my shoulder.

"Yeah. Fine. Why wouldn't I be?"

"You have that look on your face."

"What look?"

Paul took my hand. "The one that says your mind is running a million miles an hour. The one that says you're thinking about murder and how you can get yourself tied up into the investigation."

"I'm not—" A building caught my eye, and I yanked my hand out of Paul's own so I could point. "Dad! Pull over."

He didn't question it, pulling up to the curb with a smooth jerk of the wheel. A horn honked behind us, just before a car zipped past, going far faster than they should be.

"Give me five minutes," I said, pushing open the

door and stepping out of the car. "I'll be right back. I promise." Before anyone could respond, I hurried for the building situated smack-dab in the middle of a bunch of other similar, boring-looking buildings downtown.

The Redwood Village Health Department was fronted by a bunch of windows, all covered with long, heavy drapes that made me wonder why they bothered to have windows at all. It was a rectangular box, otherwise. A blast of cold air hit me the moment I was through the front door, and then it was gone as I moved farther into the building. A sign on the wall pointed the way to the food safety department. I followed the arrow, not quite sure why I was there, but my instincts had told me to come in, so here I was.

"Can I help you?" A large woman was sitting at a desk too small for her. She had an enviable head of dark curls that cascaded around broad shoulders hidden behind a knit sweater.

"Hi, sorry to bother you." I scanned the area behind her, but there was no one at the handful of desks clustered together in a series of identical rooms. "Lyle Carrigan worked here, didn't he?"

The woman flinched as if I'd taken a swing at her. "He did. You are?"

"Krissy Hancock. I knew him." I reached across the desk and shook the woman's hand, hoping she didn't catch the hitch in my voice at the stretching of the truth.

"Bailey," the woman said. "Lyle was a dear. I can't believe anyone would want to hurt him." She sighed, then noted my interest in the empty space behind her. "Most everyone is out today. It's just me in here, fielding calls." She motioned toward the phone, which was silent.

"I won't take up too much of your time," I said. "I was curious about Lyle and what he did here. Can you tell me anything about it?"

"Sure." Bailey seemed happy to talk, which wasn't much of a surprise considering how boring sitting there alone must have been. "Lyle was a health inspector, as you know. He focused on food safety, as we all do here. He mostly did random inspections, along with your standard scheduled ones. Not real exciting, but this isn't exactly an exciting profession."

Nothing new there. "You said you handle calls?" I asked. "Do people call in about health violations?"

"Sometimes," she said. "But not too often. Usually, if people don't like something about a place where they are eating, they just don't go back. Or they call the place itself and file a complaint in the hopes of scoring a free meal. Rarely do they come to us about their grievances, but it does happen every so often."

So far, everything was as I expected. "Do you know why Lyle was at Death by Java the night he died?" I asked. I was fishing, but hopeful. Someone had to know *something*. Sometimes all it took was the right question, asked of the right person, and *poof*, everything would fall into place.

Bailey lowered her eyes and made a quick sign of the cross before answering. "I couldn't say for sure why he was there in particular that night, but I will say he'd been spending an inordinate amount of time in that part of town as of late."

"He was filing a lot of citations," I guessed.

Bailey nodded. "Seemed like there was a new one every day. And I *was* getting a lot of calls about the two locations he was frequenting right about then, so I suppose it wasn't much of a surprise."

"Tito's Deli and Death by Java?"

"Those are the ones," she said, pointing at me. "At first, we'd get a call, and Lyle would go in and come back claiming there was nothing to it. Crank calls, I'd guess you'd call them. We get those every now and again. You know how kids can be? Sometimes they can't help themselves."

Footsteps sounded down the hall, then retreated. I leaned in, silently urging Bailey to go on.

"So, one day, the calls up and stopped," she said. "It was like a switch was flipped, yet oddly, that's when other things started happening."

"What do you mean?"

"The calls might have stopped, but then the violations started cropping up."

That's when the deal was struck. "Lyle was the only one to handle these violations?" I asked.

Bailey nodded. "Daily, too." She leaned in closer, as if sharing a deep, dark secret. "I suspect that whoever was making those calls up and decided to cause a little more havoc by actually messing with the places. Two respectable businesses don't just up and start falling apart like that so suddenly. It was all poor Lyle could do to keep up with it."

"Did anyone else go in and confirm the violations?" I asked. "To verify that they were justified?"

Bailey sat back, hand to her chest. "Why would someone need to do that?" Her eyes widened. "You think Lyle was making it up? He wouldn't have done such a thing!" She huffed, then, slowly, her brow furrowed. "No, Lyle wasn't that type of man. If he said there was a health violation, then there was one."

"But do you think someone was sabotaging the businesses?"

Bailey thought about it, then spread her hands. "I suppose we'll see, now, won't we?"

"What do you mean by that?" I asked.

"Like I said, Lyle was a good, honest man. He wouldn't have reported something that wasn't there, meaning there *were* actual violations. But if someone *was* going in and sabotaging these businesses, as you put it, and Lyle found out about it, he would have done something about it. Maybe even confronted the person responsible."

"And you think that whoever it was might have killed him for it?"

Bailey's jaw firmed, then trembled. "They must have. I mean, it makes sense, doesn't it? Someone was causing trouble, and Lyle found out about it. He was too good of a man to want to get anyone into trouble, so he probably said something to them and . . ." She squeezed her eyes closed, and a single tear slid from beneath the lids before she opened them again and fixed me with a hard stare. "Whoever it was made a mistake, though."

"How so?" I asked.

"It's a simple thing, really," she said. "Two businesses were involved in those calls. Two businesses were at the center of Lyle's sudden spike in reported violations." She squared her broad shoulders, then shook a finger at me as she finished. "So, it serves to reason that whoever killed poor Lyle Carrigan had to have access to both of those businesses, because how else could they have sabotaged them if they couldn't get inside?"

19

I groaned as I kicked off my shoes and slouched down onto the couch. Dad, as he'd done countless times before in my youth, wordlessly scooped up my discarded sneakers and moved them out of the way of everyone else.

"I'm going to take a shower," Paul said with a stretch. "Unless you want to go first since you have that thing with your friends tonight?"

"I do," I said. My legs were splayed out before me and refused to obey any sort of mental command to function. "But I don't think I *can*."

"That was a lot of walking," Laura said. "Even I'm kind of pooped."

After the stop at the health department, we'd spent the rest of the day running all over Redwood Village, seeing just about everything there was to see. There'd been no rhyme or reason to where we went. It was very touristy, despite three-fourths of us not being tourists.

And yet, it was perfect.

"Go ahead and get your shower," I said, flapping a hand at him. "I'll hop in when you're done."

Paul nodded and headed for the bathroom, while Dad collapsed into a chair by the window. The last light of the day streamed in through slightly parted curtains, and would soon be gone.

"I'm going to make some lemonade," Laura said. "You two better not go anywhere while I'm busy."

"I don't think you have to worry about that," Dad said.

Laura eyed him a moment and then left. The curiosity was swirling off her, but so far, she hadn't asked what we'd gotten into earlier that day. I hoped she never would.

"So," Dad said when she was gone, "care to share?"

"Share what?" I asked.

Dad kicked off his own shoes, wiggled his stockinged toes. "You went into the health department where Lyle had been working. You're telling me no one there knew anything?"

Oh. *That*. "There was only one person there," I said. "And she didn't have anything concrete." I gave him a quick rundown of my conversation with Bailey.

Dad's brow furrowed. "She thinks it might be someone who has access to both places? Who would that be?"

"Honestly?" I asked. "No one, as far as I know. Separate employees, separate buildings, separate owners."

"Both places would have some crossover in customers," Dad said, thinking out loud. "But customers wouldn't have access to the back rooms."

"And Lyle wasn't killed until after hours."

"A maintenance man?" Before I could answer, Dad shook his head. "No, that doesn't make sense. If it was a mall or something, then perhaps, but not separate buildings owned by different people."

"There's Roman," I said. "He seems to be a popular repairman with the businesses in town. Marco's used him. Valerie uses him. I imagine Tito has, as well. Maybe Roman got hold of the businesses' keys while he worked and copied them. That would give him access any time he wanted."

"But why do that?" Dad asked. "Do you think he planned the murder in advance?"

"Not really." I sighed. "I don't get it. Maybe we're looking at this all wrong, getting distracted by information that doesn't matter."

"What do you mean?"

I thought about it briefly before answering. "Just because Lyle and Marco were working together, it doesn't mean that is why he was killed. It could be as simple as Mickey getting angry with him and killing him because he was citing Death by Java and upsetting Valerie. He could have left him in the back room because he didn't have time to move him."

"Which we've discussed before," Dad pointed out.

"That doesn't make it irrelevant," I said. "But I still can't dismiss the fact that Tito had Lyle's tablet. There's no way that's just a coincidence. But how could Tito have gotten into Death by Java's back room after hours?"

"Could one of Valerie's employees be friends with

him?" Dad asked. "They could have let him in to kill Lyle without realizing that was what they were doing. Maybe he asked them to leave the door unlocked so he could leave a surprise for Valerie, or something like that, and they complied, not realizing they were setting her up for murder?"

Could it really be that simple? I had my doubts, but it wasn't like I was getting anywhere with my own theories. I mean, if what Dad said was true, wouldn't the employee have told someone by now? Or were they afraid Tito would come after them next if they spoke up?

I didn't know. I kept waffling between suspects, each looking just as good as the next. Mickey and Valerie. Tito and Marco. Roman. Even Aaron and Hugh felt like viable suspects under the right circumstances.

But, at the same time, I could come up with just as many reasons why none of them would have done it. Mickey and Valerie wouldn't want to leave a body in their place of business. Marco's plan was actually ruined by Lyle's death, so why kill him? Aaron and Hugh wouldn't want to risk Valerie taking the fall for the murder.

But what about Tito and Roman?

Now, those two . . . I couldn't come up with a good, solid reason for them not to have committed the murder, outside moral and legal reasons. The only problem was, I couldn't see how either of them could have killed him and left him inside Death by Java.

Back to square one we went.

"I suppose it's possible the door *had* been left unlocked," I said.

"What door?" Laura asked, entering the room. She was holding a glass of lemonade. Ice *clink*ed as she swirled it before taking a sip.

Dad and I shared a look, but we were saved from having to admit we were talking about Lyle's murder when Paul entered the room, hair still damp from the shower.

"All done," he said. "Shower's all yours, Krissy."

"Thanks." I popped to my feet, ignoring the burning in my arches and calves. I hurried past Laura to the bathroom, where I took a long, hot shower and tried not to think about murder.

I only partially succeeded.

After the shower, I got dressed and pushed the dire thoughts out of mind. I had other things to worry about, the least of which was dinner with friends I hadn't seen, let alone talked to, in years. Would I even recognize them when I saw them? Would they recognize *me*?

And worst of all, would we have anything in common after all this time?

I found myself standing in my old bedroom, an odd melancholy washing over me. I missed both Larissa and Renee now that I was thinking about them. Over the last few years, I hated to admit that I'd barely thought of them at all. We'd grown apart in both years and distance. All I had were memories—good ones— but memories, nonetheless.

It was strange how it hit me all at once. I'd been back to Redwood Village countless times over the last few years. There was no reason for me not to have looked up my old friends before now, but I hadn't. Did that make me a horrible friend? Or just really bad at keeping in touch?

Stop beating yourself up over this, I scolded myself. People grew apart. It was just a part of life.

Taking a deep, calming breath, I returned to the living room to find everyone else sitting around the TV. A movie was playing at low volume, but no one was watching it. It served as background noise, something Dad had done ever since Mom had passed as a way to keep the loneliness at bay.

"Have fun tonight, Buttercup," Dad said. "Tell Larissa and Renee I said hi."

"Will do." I turned to Paul. "You going to be okay here alone with these two?"

He stifled a yawn. "I'll be fine. I doubt I'll make it much longer anyway."

"We'll keep him busy," Laura promised. "Don't worry about us."

"Take my car," Dad said. "And try to be back by midnight. I don't want to have to wait up all night, worrying about you."

I rolled my eyes, but smiled. Talk about a blast from the past. "Okay, *Daddy*," I said, which caused him to laugh. "I'll call if I'm going to be late." And with a final wave, I headed into the kitchen, where I snatched up Dad's keys, and then I was on my way to Redwood Tavern to reconnect with my past.

The restaurant sat in a well-to-do part of town and was one of those places you went to if you wanted to spend twice as much for a meal than what you'd pay anywhere else. Redwood Tavern's brown wooden exterior gave it a rustic look from the outside. Once through the doors, filtered lights gave a warm, almost fire-like glow to the place. There was no music playing, just the rumble of low conversation, the *clink* of silverware on plates, and the occasional bark of laughter that felt weirdly out of place.

I found Larissa and Renee seated at a corner table, talking quietly to one another. I saw them before they saw me, which gave me a chance to stand back and marvel at how times might have changed, yet at the same time, they didn't. Renee had the same severe look about her that was softened by her brown doe eyes that had always grabbed the attention of anyone who saw her. Larissa's round face had thinned over the years, yet it held the same youthful exuberance that had gotten us into trouble countless times. When she smiled, her entire face lit up in a way that brought a smile to my own face.

Renee was the one who looked up and spotted me. Her eyes went wide, and then she just about leapt out of her chair.

"Krissy! There you are!"

Normally, I'd never stoop to acting like a thirteen-year-old girl in public, but at the sound of my name coming from her mouth, I was transported back in time, and the next thing I knew, I was jumping up and down and squealing and giving out hugs like they were candy. The tears I found myself wiping from my cheeks were of the happy kind, and by the time we sat down, all eyes in the place had turned our way, but none of us cared. In that moment, we were the only three people on the planet.

"How have you been?" I asked Renee once I could speak without sobbing. "It's been far too long."

"It has," she said. "And I've been good. Busy, but good."

"Tell me about it," Larissa said. "Renee is representing half of the Village these days, so getting a spare moment with her is near-impossible."

"Not even close," Renee said, though she seemed pleased. "But I'm doing all right."

"'Representing'?" I asked.

"I'm a lawyer." She made a face like she'd said something dirty. "I handle local conflicts, so it's nothing fancy. You won't be seeing me on TV or hearing about me defending a celebrity or anything like that."

"Wait, wait, wait." I squeezed my eyes shut against what I'd just heard. "You're a *lawyer*? You?"

I remembered how Renee had been the one person in my life whom I thought was most likely to find herself in trouble with the law. Nothing horrible, mind you. But she wasn't above causing a little mischief, and boy, did she ever.

"It's kind of like that guy in that show," Larissa said, snapping her fingers as she tried to come up with a name. Renee provided it right away.

"Saul Goodman," she said with a laugh. "From *Breaking Bad* and *Better Call Saul*. I should be offended, but I'm not. It fits."

Larissa pointed at her with a grin that had me smiling so hard, my face hurt.

"How did that happen?" I asked. "Did someone kidnap you and force you to go to law school?"

"Okay, you're going to love this . . ."

For the next thirty minutes, we spoke of everything under the sun. We ordered, and our food arrived. We talked and laughed. I told them of my life in Pine Hills, of Paul, and how Vicki was doing. Larissa told me of her two marriages, both of which were now in the past and, in her words, "Good riddance." Renee spoke of her life, how she realized that she had no interest in marriage or relationships at all. We talked of life and everything after.

It was one of the best half hours of my life.

Then, as the joy of seeing each other again slowly bled away, the conversation shifted. Not all at once, but slowly, toward the one thing—the one *person*—we all knew was inevitable to bring up.

"I hear you've been hanging around with Valerie Kemp," Renee said, mild disapproval in her voice.

I tried not to take it as an accusation, but with our history with Valerie, I couldn't help it. "I'm not hanging around her because we're friends," I said, before explaining how she'd asked me to help her failing business. "I kind of feel bad for her," I finished. "She's trying, but she's still, well, *Valerie*."

"Tell me about it," Larissa said. "I ran into her about a month ago, and she couldn't help but hit me with one of those insults of hers. You know the kind."

"You mean the insult she *thinks* is a compliment," Renee said with a shake of her head. "I'm pretty sure we've all been the target of those more than enough for one lifetime."

Larissa nodded. "I've tried to get along with her, but it's impossible. You must be a saint to be willing to help her out, of all people. She was really hard on you back in school, Krissy."

I shrugged, somewhat embarrassed. "I try to leave the past in the past," I said. "Though, to be fair," I repeated, "she's trying."

"I heard someone was killed at her place," Renee said.

Before I could confirm it, Larissa said, "Lyle Carrigan."

"You knew him?" I asked.

"Not well," Larissa admitted. "But we crossed paths when I was jumping from job to job. I think it was about a year back that we worked together at the health department. Might have been two years, actually. You know how times flies."

Boy, did I ever. "*You* were a health inspector?" I asked with a laugh. "You used to eat cheese off the floor!"

"Hey!" Larissa said with mock offense. "That piece of cheese fell under the three-second rule. And it was *your* kitchen floor, and I knew for a fact that your dad had mopped it earlier that day because he always cleaned like a maniac when we were coming over to spend the night." She sobered. "But no, I wasn't a health inspector. I answered the phones." She made a face. "Not glamorous, but it was a job."

"I'm sometimes jealous of her," Renee said.

"Right." Larissa rolled her eyes. "You have a solid job, where you get to make your own hours and get paid pretty well, while I bounce from job to job, hoping it sticks for more than a month or two." She waved

Renee off good-naturedly. "But yeah, I knew Lyle. We used to get drinks with one another every now and again. Nothing romantic, mind you. He was married, and at that point, I wasn't looking for husband number three."

"It's sad what happened to him," Renee said. "Lyle, I mean, not lucky number two." She turned to me. "You should have met Cody. You'd wonder if it was possible to have a negative IQ score once he opened his mouth."

Larissa snorted. "He had his moments, that's for sure." She shook her head, moved on. "Lyle was a decent guy. He let people push him around a bit much for my liking, but who am I to talk?" She poked at the remains of her steak. "When I heard he was murdered, I'd like to say I was shocked, but to hear it happened at Valerie's . . ." She *cluck*ed her tongue as Renee nodded.

I looked from her to Renee and back again. "I take it you know something about what happened?" I asked when neither spoke up.

Larissa continued poking at the meat, causing the last of its juices to ooze onto her plate. "I don't *know* anything for certain. But . . ." She glanced at Renee, who motioned for her to go on. "You know Valerie was married to Aaron Middleton, right?"

"I do. And then they divorced."

"He cheated on her, and I'm pretty sure she did the same to him. I don't think any of us were surprised about that."

"Not in the slightest," Renee said.

"She moved on to a guy named Hugh," Larissa went

on. "I've seen him around, seen the two of them to-gether. They broke up too."

"Probably for the same reason," Renee added.

"It's a Valerie thing, right? And now she's with Mickey Robbins."

"Do you know him?" I asked, scooching to the edge of my seat in barely suppressed excitement.

"I don't, but Renee does," Larissa said.

I turned to Renee, who was frowning and staring off into space. There seemed to be some sort of internal battle going on inside of her, one that eventually re-sulted in her speaking slowly and quietly, as if she was afraid someone might overhear.

"Mickey has been in trouble before," she said. "I didn't represent him, but I know of him and his case. You know how people talk?" She scratched at her ear. "Now, don't quote me on this, and don't ask where I heard it, but let's just say the fact that Lyle Carrigan ended up dead somewhere Mickey Robbins frequents doesn't come as a surprise to those of us who know about Mickey's past."

"How so?" I asked. All I knew of Mickey was what people had told me, which mostly consisted of how he interacted with Valerie. His history before her was a complete mystery to me.

The waiter returned and spirited away our mostly empty plates. Renee waited for him to be out of earshot before she responded.

"Like I said, don't quote me on this. And remember that this is hearsay, so there's a chance some of it was exaggerated. Very few people know anything about it since it was kept hush-hush, for reasons I won't get into here." She leaned forward and met my eyes. "But quite a few years ago, back before Valerie met him, a friend of Mickey Robbins turned up dead." A pregnant pause followed, before, "And the way I heard it, Mickey was the one who killed him."

20

That night, I dreamed of my friends, but not in a good way.

We were back in high school, at a football game, walking the track that surrounded the field and ignoring the actual game taking place. Then, in a blink, we were at my house, sitting in my bedroom, talking about boys and movies and everything under the sun.

Yet in every window, standing in every doorway, and following us wherever we went, was Mickey Robbins.

Sometimes he'd have a knife. Sometimes he'd have a rope pulled taut between his meaty hands. It was like those horror movies where the killer would walk slowly toward the victim, and no matter how fast they ran, they couldn't get away from the inevitable—yet we seemed oblivious to his presence. I saw him, but I couldn't tell anyone, could only watch as he moved ever closer.

When I woke up, I was tired, yet determined. I

wasn't going to let thoughts of what Mickey might do—or might have done—ruin my vacation.

"Good morning, Buttercup," Dad said through a yawn as he poured coffee. "Care for a cup?"

"Only if you've got a cookie for it."

"Of course." He retrieved another mug, dropped in a chocolate-chip cookie, then poured coffee atop it. He handed it over with another yawn.

"Long night?" I asked, injecting as much calm into my voice as I could manage.

He glanced at me over the top of his mug and winked. "Very." I decided I didn't want to know what *that* meant.

"Morning," Paul said, shuffling over. "That coffee?"

"It is!" Dad produced another mug and poured without having to be asked. "I was thinking—"

Paul's phone rang, causing us all to start. He glanced at the screen, then quickly answered. "Paul Dalton speaking." He listened, eyes flickering over to me, then to Dad. "I can." He checked the time on the microwave. "Give me twenty minutes." He clicked off.

"Who was that?" I asked.

He took a long drink from his coffee, then set the mug aside. "It's no big deal. I'll fill you in when I get back." He hurried away, presumably to get dressed.

I watched him go with a frown. "He didn't answer my question."

"It's probably nothing," Dad said, before gesturing at me with his mug. "I bet it's that detective. You know? About the case."

"Hmm." My frown deepened. It seemed awfully early for Detective McKensie to call, especially since Paul actually had nothing to do with her investigation. And if it *was* her, why wouldn't he just tell me?

Paul appeared a moment later, dressed for the day. He hadn't dressed up, nor did he look any different than usual, so there were no clues there. He gave me a quick kiss on the cheek, took Dad's proffered keys, and then rushed out the door like he was on fire.

I sipped my coffee, still frowning. It wasn't that I didn't trust Paul; I did. But I knew how McKensie looked at him. Knew that Paul didn't know anyone else in town. Where could he possibly go that he couldn't take me or tell me about?

"Do you have plans for the day?" Dad asked, seemingly far less concerned about Paul's sudden flight than I was.

I took another sip, then set my mug down beside Paul's. "You know, I think I might go have a chat with Valerie." If anyone would know something about Mickey's past, it would be her. And if she didn't . . . Well, her boyfriend being a suspect in an old murder investigation was something she *should* know about.

"Want some company?" Dad asked. "Laura's got a thing today, so she's not going to be around much."

"A 'thing'?"

Dad shrugged. "No clue. She told me about it last night, but I was distracted at the time."

"You weren't listening."

"I was." He grinned. "Just not closely."

"Uh-huh." I looked down at my pajamas. "I'm going to get ready and go. This shouldn't take long, so there's no need for me to drag you along." And then, because I didn't want him to worry like I was worrying about

Paul, "It has to do with something Renee and Larissa told me last night. You know, girl talk."

"Oh." He made a face. "I probably don't want to hear it, then."

I gave him a quick kiss on the cheek and said, "Probably not," though I knew the opposite to be true. "I'll give you the CliffsNotes version of it when I'm back."

"You do that."

I went about my morning routine in record time and was out of the house within twenty minutes of Paul leaving. Since Paul had Dad's car and Laura had her *thing*, I chose to walk to Death by Java, hoping Valerie would be in and that this wouldn't be a wasted trip.

The walk was invigorating, though by the time I'd reached downtown, I was sweating far more than I would have liked. There was little in the way of a breeze, and the air felt almost heavy with impending rain, despite there being only a handful of white fluffy clouds in the sky. Maybe it was my mood more than any actual incoming inclement weather.

Death by Java was unsurprisingly slow. At least there were a few customers in the dining area, sipping at their coffees, which was an upgrade to how it had been as of late. No one was behind the counter when I entered, though I did spot Dee, dressed in the hated pink dress, kneeling on the floor beside a bookshelf. I joined her, but I kept my distance when I saw she wasn't alone.

"Hi, Ms. Hancock!" Dee said, popping to her feet. Oscar was curled up in a new cat bed, looking as grouchy as ever.

"Dee," I said. "Oscar is back from the vet, I see."

"He is." She grinned. "He's all checked out and passed with mostly flying colors. I have some medication to give him, but I can crumble it into his food and he doesn't seem to notice. He wolfs it down no matter what."

"That's good to hear." The cat looked better too. He looked as if he'd been given a bath and had his nails trimmed. Another couple days of pampering, and he might look like any other house cat. "His paw okay?"

"Yep. The vet said he probably got underfoot and was stepped on or that he could have leapt from too tall a height. He was walking normally before I picked him up." Dee bit her lower lip, and some of the joy left her. "I really wish my landlord would allow me to keep pets. I was only scheduled to work four days this week, and I can't keep an eye on him when I'm not here. If he'd had somewhere else to go, maybe he wouldn't have gotten hurt."

"The landlord won't make an exception?" I asked. "Where is it that you live?"

"An apartment over on Sutcliffe." Dee shrugged. "It's not great, but it's decent. And I've tried to talk to him, but . . ." Another shrug. Something in it made me wonder if she was afraid to ask for too much, lest she be booted from her home for being a pest.

I filed the information away to consider later, then moved on to the real reason I was there. "Is Valerie in today? I'd like to talk to her for a few minutes."

"She's in the back." Dee knelt back down beside Oscar. The cat lifted his head enough for a few strokes, before laying it back down again. "She's been back there practically all day."

"Thanks." I started to leave, paused. "I'm glad Oscar is doing okay. He's lucky to have you." And then I left her and the cat to it.

I made my way around the counter to the back, figuring that Valerie wouldn't mind. I wondered who was supposed to be working the front, then put that in the back of my mind when I saw Valerie standing there, staring at the dent in the door of the ice machine. I didn't think she'd noticed me until she spoke in a slow, almost-deadened voice.

"Do you ever look back on your life and realize that you've made more mistakes than correct choices?"

I wasn't sure how to answer that, so I didn't. "Are you okay, Valerie?"

She glanced over at me and gave me a smile that was more frightening than comforting. "Why wouldn't I be? My business is floundering. Employees keep calling off. My life is in shambles. A man was found dead in my shop, and I don't know if someone I care about did it." Her eyes slid back to the dent. "And *you*, of all people, have come to bail me out. I'm pretty sure the universe hates me."

I took a step toward her. "Did something else happen?"

She stared at the dent a moment longer before she suddenly seemed to snap out of whatever dark place she'd been in. "No. Everything's fine." This time, her smile was more natural, though there was still a dark cloud hovering around her. "Is there something I can do for you, Krissy?"

I wasn't buying her sudden shift. "Valerie," I said,

taking another step toward her, "if Mickey did something—"

"What? No. Mickey didn't do anything. Other than not answer when I call. Or call me back. Or show up at my place when I'm sitting there all alone, with no one to make sure I don't fall into . . ." She took a deep breath, plastered on that fake smile of hers. "It's nothing."

It sure didn't sound like nothing. "Talk to me," I said, spreading my hands invitingly. "Just because we didn't get along when we were younger, doesn't mean we can't now."

A flurry of emotions flashed across her face. There was the expected disgust and annoyance, followed by what I took for a genuine desire for someone to actually *listen* to her. Aaron and Hugh would, but they'd only do so because they were trying to get back into her good graces. And I was pretty sure the both of them would only tell her what she wanted to hear, which I'm positive she realized. She might be shallow, but she wasn't stupid.

And while having someone stand there, agreeing to whatever they thought she wanted them to agree to, could be nice, that wasn't what Valerie Kemp needed right then. What she needed was a friend.

Sadly, I was as close as she was going to get to one.

"Mickey did that," she said, motioning toward the dent. "He hauled off and punched it because he didn't like the fact that I was here alone with someone else."

"That night. When I saw the light?"

Valerie was wearing tight pants with no pockets. She

ran her hands around her hips, where pockets should be, like she was desperate to shove her hands into them, but couldn't. "For a little while, yeah."

"Was it Roman?"

She made a face. "Not even." The disgust morphed, but it didn't go away. "It was Hugh. We didn't *do* anything," she hurriedly added. "We just talked. But Mickey didn't believe me. He knew about my past and refused to believe that I've changed." She met my eyes, and I noticed they were wet, near to spilling over. "I have. I really have."

In that moment, I believed her. "Aaron and Hugh both still care for you, despite whatever you've done."

"I know," she said, with the ghost of a smile. "And I like having them around. You might not understand, but I *need* them to want to be around me. I've focused so long on what *I* want, I kind of forgot about my friends and the people I care about so much so that they hardly care about me anymore."

"Bray and the others—"

She scoffed, cutting me off. "They came here that day for you, not me. They pretend that we're all still best friends, but we're not. Bray honestly wants to make amends for how he acted when he was younger, especially toward people like you." Another scoff, this time for another reason. "Like it would change anything."

I felt we were getting off the topic of what was important, so I veered the conversation back to where I believed it should be. "Mickey punched the ice machine," I said. "Do you think he killed Lyle?"

"Of course not!" Valerie sounded genuinely appalled that I'd even consider the notion, even though she'd thought along those same lines recently. "He doesn't have that sort of violence in him."

Considering the ice machine, I wasn't so sure. "I heard a rumor that he was connected to another death a few years ago. A friend of his died, and there are rumors Mickey might have killed him."

Valerie waved away the idea. "That's ridiculous. Mickey would have told me if he'd *killed* someone."

I almost pointed out that no, killers didn't often confess their crimes to anyone, let alone someone they were in a relationship with, but I let it go. It sounded like Valerie knew nothing about what had happened, so asking her about it was pointless. Hopefully, she'd at least consider what I'd said, just in case it turned out to be true.

"I understand your concerns, Krissy, I really do," she said before I could come up with something else to say. "But there's nothing you can do to help me anymore. Lyle died. I was mad at Mickey for getting mad at me, so we fought, and I started thinking that maybe he killed Lyle just to spite me. He didn't. But now we're all screwed up, and I don't know if we're ever going to be able to mend our relationship." Her lower lip pouted. "It's not fair!"

No, it wasn't. And something felt off about how she and Mickey were suddenly having troubles. Sure, Lyle was dead, but you'd think that would have brought them closer together. Valerie wanted comfort. Mickey could have provided it.

And yet, he hadn't. She claimed he was avoiding her, but was he? He'd shown up at Bray's impromptu reunion at Hooties, looking for her. When I'd confronted him, he'd claimed she was avoiding *his* calls. Something wasn't adding up, and I was beginning to wonder if perhaps there was more to it than two adults giving each other the silent treatment.

"Let me see your phone," I said, an idea forming.

"What? Why?"

"Just . . ." I made a "gimme" motion with my hand.

Valerie narrowed her eyes, but she retrieved her phone from a small purse I hadn't noticed sitting on a nearby shelf. She held the device tightly a moment before handing it over.

I shouldn't have been surprised, but the screen wasn't locked, so I was able to access her data without a password or fingerprint. I went to her recent calls list and immediately saw the problem.

"Valerie . . ." I turned the phone toward her.

She stared at it blankly. "What am I supposed to be seeing?"

"Mickey's number." I tapped the screen next to it. "That symbol. He's been blocked."

"On my phone?" She scrunched up her nose. "That doesn't make sense."

"Well, he is." And I had an inkling as to who might have done it. "Here." I went ahead and unblocked his number. "Try him now." I handed over the phone.

Valerie gave me a skeptical look, then tried. "Straight to voicemail," she said. She sounded exasperated. "I told you—he's avoiding me!"

"Or your number is blocked on his phone, too," I said. "I bet he didn't do it either."

"I don't get it. You think it was an accident?"

Valerie might not "get it," but I thought I was starting to understand. And, no, I didn't believe it was an accident that they'd both managed to block one another without realizing it. "I'm going to talk to someone," I said. "After I do that, I'm going to contact Mickey and get this whole thing sorted out. You should expect a call from him sometime later today, tonight at the latest."

"I guess, but—"

I started for the door. "Everything is going to work out, Valerie. Just sit tight."

And then I left. I might not know who killed Lyle Carrigan, but I was starting to understand how Valerie's life had suddenly started to crumble around her, seemingly through no fault of her own. And despite our differences, if I could help her pick up the pieces, I was going to do just that.

21

I didn't have a car.

The realization hit me the moment I stepped outside Death by Java. I desperately wanted to talk to Aaron, Hugh, and yes, even Mickey, but not over the phone. I wanted to sit down with them face-to-face and put an end to all the speculation swirling around them about their relationships with Valerie. And, perhaps, find a way to help her love life finally sort itself out.

No, doing so wouldn't solve Lyle's murder, but that wasn't what I was going for.

"*You!*"

I jumped at the sound of the angry voice coming from my right.

Tito was walking my way, finger leveled at me. "It was you."

"Tito." I took a step away from him, which caused him to jerk to a stop as if he suddenly realized how intimidating he was being. "I don't know—"

"Don't try to deny it," he said. I could almost see the

steam flaring from his nostrils. "As soon as the police showed up at my place yesterday, I knew you were the reason why." I started to object further, but he held up a hand, took a couple of deep, calming breaths, and then said, "I don't blame you. And as frustrated as I am by your methods, I'm glad you did it."

I blinked at him, surprised. "You're glad?"

Tito started to respond, but he seemed to realize we were standing out in the open, where passersby could hear us. He motioned for me to follow him and headed for the back alley. I hesitated a heartbeat, not quite sure I should follow him where there would be painfully few witnesses in case he decided to attack me.

Curiosity, however, won out.

I followed Tito into the shaded alley, yet it felt oddly hotter back there than when we were standing out under the sun. Tito's Deli blocked off most of the breeze, and I suppose my jumping nerves also had something to do with why my palms were damp with sweat.

"Okay," I said once we were out back. "I'm here." And then, because I didn't want to belabor the point, "You had Lyle Carrigan's tablet."

Tito's jaw worked as he ran his hand over his head. "I did."

When nothing else appeared forthcoming, I prodded him. "Why?"

"I didn't kill him, if that's what you are thinking." His stare dared me to contradict him. "I didn't know he was dead when I took it. I found the tablet over there." He motioned toward the far end of the alley. "It was just lying there, out in the open. I recognized it immediately because of that rubber shell Lyle kept on it."

"So, you just up and took it? You didn't think to tell anyone about it?"

"I said it was just lying there," he snapped. "It didn't turn on when I found it, so I took it inside, where I have a charger. I know I should have called the health department since it's likely their property, but . . ." He paced away and fell silent. He was clearly agitated.

"But Lyle was dead."

"No." He shot me a scowl. "I mean, yes, he was, but I didn't know that then. At that point, all I was thinking about was all the false claims Lyle was making against my place of business. I wanted to have a look at what was on the device and see if he was fabricating any others."

"Was he?"

"I don't know. I couldn't get in because it was password protected. Then I find out the man is dead, and I'm standing there with his property in my possession. I didn't know what to do. If I took it to the police, they would have thought I killed him."

"You could have told them where you found it," I pointed out.

"That wouldn't have proven anything. They'd still take a closer look at me, and where would the scrutiny get me? I was already dealing with fallout from Lyle's claims. I even had to fire someone because of them, though I suppose that was for the best."

"Wait. You fired someone? Why didn't you tell me that before?"

Tito sighed, some of the fight going out of him. "Why would I? It's none of your business."

True. "But you did fire someone?"

"I had to. I realized that every time this person—and no, I'm not going to name him—worked the closing shift, Lyle would be in the next morning and would find something left out in the open or a freezer would be set to the incorrect temperature. It only happened when the person in question worked, so I did what any other business owner would do and had a talk with him. When that didn't change anything, I fired him. The violations stopped almost immediately."

My mind was racing. "He was sabotaging the deli."

"Or he was extraordinarily inept," Tito said. "Either way, once he was gone, things calmed down, though Lyle kept coming back. I'd had enough of him, so I kicked him out whenever I saw him." He leaned his head back, looked up to the sky. "I didn't have anything to do with his death, but I can't say it upset me. He was making my life miserable. And even after his death, he haunted me. That tablet." He spat on the ground. "If I hadn't found it, then perhaps the police would have, and then they'd have already discovered who killed him. And then we could have all moved on with our lives without Lyle Carrigan."

"Why didn't you give the tablet to the police anonymously?" I asked.

"And how would you propose I do that? Mail it to them? Sneak up on one of them and slip it into their car?" He scoffed. "There was no way to get it to them without someone finding out that I was the one who'd had it."

"So, instead of looking for a solution, you just threw it away?" I tried not to sound incredulous, but I couldn't help it. "It's evidence in a crime!"

"I know that," he snarled. "I didn't know what to do. I was weighing my options when you showed up and started asking questions. I realized that it was either get rid of the tablet, or have the police come breathing down my neck. It was stupid, I realize, but what else was I going to do? If I became a suspect in a murder, what you do think it would do to my business? I'm short-handed already. People would quit. Customers would stop coming in. I would be ruined just as readily as if I'd let Lyle keep hounding me."

All of it was true. As much as I might not like what Tito had done, it made sense. No one wanted the police sniffing around them, even if they had nothing to hide.

"Look, lady," Tito said, putting as much disdain into his voice as he could. "I never asked for any of this. I tried to protect myself, and instead, I screwed every-thing up. I saw you that night—knew even then that it was probably you—digging around in my trash. And when I realized the tablet was taken, I knew I was cooked."

"You're not under arrest," I pointed out.

"I'm not, no. The detective was surprisingly under-standing. I don't know if she ever got into the damn thing, but I wouldn't be surprised if there's some sort of evidence of malfeasance on Lyle Carrigan's part some-where on it. Will it point to his killer?" He shrugged. "I have no idea. But I'm counting on it proving that my deli wasn't as bad as that man tried to make it seem. I only hope that information becomes public. It's the least they could do."

I searched his face for deception, but I couldn't find

any. "The screen," I said. "It was cracked. Was it like that when you found it?"

Tito rubbed at the back of his head and looked away. "I might have done that once I realized I couldn't bypass the password. Had one of those—what do you call them?—psychotic episodes, where I thought that maybe if I physically battered the thing, it would suddenly let me in. It was dumb, but I was at my wits' end." He sighed. "I've got to get back inside. I just wanted to let you know that I know it was you snooping around my place that night, and that I'd appreciate it if you stay far, far away from me and my place of business." A pause. "*And* my home."

With that, he turned and entered Tito's Deli through the back door, leaving me alone in the alley.

I stood there for at least five more minutes, thinking. If Tito was telling the truth, it sounded like the fired employee was responsible for the recent spate of violations that had taken place within the deli. Was he, as Tito said, inept? Or was it something more sinister? There were the calls to the health department, followed by the sudden increase in violations. I was truly beginning to wonder if that employee had been working with Lyle. I wished I had a name so I could talk to him.

But how did a saboteur at Tito's Deli tie in to Death by Java? Tito implied his fired employee was male. Everyone who worked at Valerie's bookstore café was female. Was someone there working against her? Or was I trying too hard to make abnormal pieces fit into a standardized puzzle?

I decided to let my subconscious work on it as I

pulled out my phone and did a quick search. A moment later, I was actually on the phone, waiting for an answer.

It came after only the second ring. "Yeah? Who's this?"

"Hugh?" I asked, though I recognized his voice. "It's Krissy Hancock. Valerie's friend." I winced. Every time I said it, it came out sounding wrong.

"Okay?"

"We need to talk." I paused. "It's about her phone and a certain blocked number."

A long stretch of silence followed. I expected him to play dumb and ask, *"What number?"* but instead, when he finally did speak, he sounded resigned. "Where are you?"

"Outside Death by Java." Or I would be once I left the alley, but close enough.

"I'm in the area. Give me five minutes." Another pause. "Don't go inside. I don't want Val to see us talking. And . . . don't tell her anything, all right? Let's talk first." He clicked off before I could answer.

I pocketed my phone and then walked to the front sidewalk. I'd just barely settled in to wait when a horn honked. Hugh was sitting across the street in his tiny electric car, motioning frantically for me. I checked both ways, then crossed over to where he was parked.

He opened the window a crack. "Get in," he said before rolling it up again.

A brief flash of worry flared through me, though I dismissed it. If Hugh tried to drive off with me in the passenger seat, I was pretty sure I could overpower him. Or at least make it hard enough for him to drive that we wouldn't make it far before crashing into a light pole. Not ideal, but it would be better than getting whisked away someplace I'd never be found.

I didn't think Hugh had any ill intent toward me, so I rounded the car and got in.

Hugh had both hands on the wheel and was staring straight ahead. He looked nervous, which I suppose shouldn't have been a surprise, considering. The fact that he wanted to talk to me so badly about the blocked numbers told me that I'd been right and he was responsible, at least partly.

"Does she know?" he asked with a side-eyed glance my way.

"About Mickey's number being blocked? Yes. About who did it? Not yet."

Hugh's shoulders sagged as he leaned back in his seat. "Okay. All right. Good."

"No, Hugh, it's not good," I said. "You blocked Mickey's number from her phone, and I assume you blocked hers from Mickey's."

He winced, didn't otherwise respond.

"Why?" I asked, before shaking my head. "No, never mind. I know why. You still care about her."

He closed his eyes, nodded. "It wasn't my idea."

Of course it wasn't. "Aaron?"

"Aaron," he agreed before he took a deep, trembling breath. "None of this can get back to Val, okay? I'll tell you everything, but you have to promise me that you won't say a word to her."

"Hugh—"

"*Please.*" He all but sobbed the word. "If you tell her, she'll never talk to me again. Or Aaron. Neither of us could handle that. Mickey is all wrong for her, so it's not like what we did is *bad* for her. If she stays with him, it will ruin her entire life. You know it as much as I do."

Sadly, from what I'd seen of Mickey and Valerie together, I tended to agree. But I also wasn't so sure that either Aaron or Hugh was right for her either. I left my thoughts unsaid as I motioned for him to go on.

Hugh studied me, then must have decided that my silence was as good as a promise, because he started speaking.

"So, the day that . . ." He cleared his throat. "That night . . ."

"After Lyle was killed," I supplied.

"Yeah. That." He shuddered. "You came in that day. Val and Aaron and I were there."

"I remember."

"After you left, the three of us were sitting at the table, talking about everything. She mentioned a few things about Mickey that rankled me a bit. Aaron too. Well, eventually Val got up to use the restroom. She left her phone sitting there, which is when Mickey tried to call. Aaron and I let it go to voicemail because, why wouldn't we?" He rubbed his hands across the steering wheel. "That's when Aaron got the idea."

"To block Mickey's calls?"

"We knew they were having it rough, and with the murder, things were going to get even tougher. We didn't know if he'd come around, but we figured it couldn't hurt to minimize their contact. Like I said, Aaron's the one who had the idea. I knew Val's passcode. It was simple, really. A few swipes and done."

"And Mickey's phone?"

"That was all Aaron," he said. "I don't know how he did it, but he managed to get ahold of it and block her. Mickey's so dim, Aaron probably asked to make a call or something and he handed the phone right over."

I frowned. Mickey had been making himself scarce, yet Aaron had found him? Interacted with him, even? All while even the police were having a hard time locating him? "Do you know when he did it?"

"No clue. That night, maybe?" Hugh shrugged. "Does it really matter? Once the numbers were blocked, both Aaron and I did our best to make ourselves available to Val. We both wanted to be there for her, to make sure she understood that no matter what, we'd do what was right for her. We'd let her decide who between us she thought was best."

"Like a competition?" I asked, unable to keep the mild disgust out of my voice. They'd treated her like a prize to be won.

Hugh heaved a sigh, laughed, seemingly oblivious to my disdain. "I suppose it was. We figured that once Mickey was out of the way, Val would choose one of us to replace him. We were both there for her. She'd been with each of us once before, so why not try again? It made sense."

"What about Roman?" I asked. "Couldn't she have chosen him instead?"

Hugh snorted. "Roman? The repairman? No, she wouldn't have chosen him, even if he was the last guy on earth. She has no interest in him. He can't be trusted."

Like you can? "Do you really think she'd choose you?" I asked, genuinely curious.

"Of course." Hugh squared his shoulders, tried to look regal. "I'm the one who knows her best. I can give her everything she wants without having to stoop to underhanded tactics."

I wanted to point out that blocking Mickey's number *was* an underhanded tactic, but I let it go. "You were with her the night before the murder," I said instead. "She said that the two of you only talked."

"We do that," he said with a sharp nod. "That's what gives me the advantage. Val can talk to me. Aaron and Mickey and all the others? They're just muscle. They don't have the brains." He tapped the side of his head. "We talked that night like we have so many other nights. We even went back to her place together to continue our conversation, since she never likes staying at Death by Java past closing. It was almost romantic." He smiled in a way that said more than words how much it had meant to him.

I started to ask another question, but then I realized what he'd just said. "You left at closing time? You didn't stay late? Spend time in the back with the backroom light on?"

Hugh shook his head. "I told you—she doesn't like being there after dark. Once the last customer left, we stayed for maybe ten minutes more, and then we left. It was still light out. I don't know who was there that night after we left, but I can tell you for sure, it wasn't us."

22

I drummed my fingers on the table, a cold cup of coffee sitting forgotten in front of me. I was back at Dad's, and after assuring him that everything was all right, I left him in his office so he could make a few calls to his agent, likely about that contract of his. Paul wasn't back, and neither was Laura, which gave me time to think.

The problem was, I didn't know *what* to think. Hugh had said he and Valerie had left Death by Java by closing time on the night I'd seen the light on in the back. Later on, Valerie had implied it was only a few minutes before that, but she had said much the same as Hugh when I'd *first* asked her about it days ago. Had she gone back to the café sometime after she and Hugh had parted for the evening? Or had someone else been there, someone she was trying to protect?

That made me think of Mickey. She'd been flip-flopping on him as of late, but she always seemed to want to protect him, even when she'd claimed she was afraid he might have killed Lyle. It would make sense for her to lie about being there that night if she knew— or even suspected—it was Mickey who'd been at Death by Java after closing.

But if it *was* him, why was he there that late? Why was Lyle?

That brought me to what Tito had said about the employee he'd fired. Could Lyle—and possibly, by extension, Marco—be responsible for that? Lyle and Marco struck a deal to have Lyle cite both Death by Java and Tito's Deli so that one of them would be forced to close and Marco could swoop in and move the Italian Roll to a better location. Perhaps Lyle, needing help so that his citations couldn't easily be dismissed, bribed one of the employees at Tito's, who sabotaged the place, allowing for the health inspector to come in and cite them for the manufactured violations.

If Lyle had done that at Tito's, then wouldn't it stand to reason he'd likely do the same at Death by Java?

That's who was there, I thought, still drumming my fingers. Someone who worked at the bookstore café had been working with Lyle. Mickey wasn't staying late, cheating on Valerie with someone else. Valerie wasn't fooling around—or just talking, as she claimed—with Hugh in the back room. One of the girls, who were clearly disgruntled by the low pay and unflattering work attire, must have agreed to help Lyle.

But which one?

My phone buzzed, causing me to jump. *Vicki*. Heart thumping, I answered.

"Please tell me that Death by Coffee didn't explode," I said by way of answer.

Vicki laughed. "No, we're still here. Trouble's currently lounging on one of the shelves upstairs, holding court over the books, while I'm sitting here in a bright and shiny dining area, in a very good mood."

I sat up straighter. "The power issue?"

"Taken care of." I could hear the relief in her voice. "Our friendly neighborhood electrician *finally* showed up. He was here for all of five minutes before he had it fixed. Apparently, my husband isn't as well-versed in electrical work as he thinks he is."

A very faint, "I heard that!" caused her to laugh, and me to smile.

"Thank goodness," I said, blowing out a breath as I sagged back in my chair. "I was worried that something major was wrong and that . . . I don't know. That we'd lose power long-term and all our customers would stop coming in and that we'd never be able to get them back."

"That's why I called," Vicki said. "I knew you wouldn't be able to relax for as long as everything was in limbo here. Now there's nothing left for you to worry about. So, have fun already!"

Nothing to worry about other than a murder, Valerie's collapsing business, and Paul's sudden flight out the door, likely to meet with a police detective who was clearly smitten with him.

I decided Vicki didn't need to hear about all that, so instead I asked, "Have you seen Lena?" If there was any other pain point left in Pine Hills, it was with how she was doing. "She called a few days ago. She was worried about how things were going with her training."

"She was here earlier today, actually," Vicki said. A pregnant pause followed before she added, "There's good news and bad news."

Uh-oh. "Did Buchannan do something to upset her?"

"Quite the opposite. It looks like Lena will be joining the Pine Hills Police Department as a full-time officer of the law. From the way I hear it, she'll be partnered up with Becca Garrison, which, if you ask me, is a perfect fit."

I suppressed a squeal before asking, "What's the bad news?"

"The bad news isn't really *bad* news, per se. Lena was here because she had to put in her notice. Hard to work at a bookstore café when you're spending most of your time patrolling the streets, hunting for criminals."

"True." I let myself feel sad for a couple of seconds before shaking it off. "I'm going to miss having her working behind the counter, but she's doing what she wants, and that's what matters. Besides, she'll probably be in daily for coffee. It'll be like she never left."

"I agree." Vicki huffed out a sigh, and I imagined her pushing her way to her feet. "I should get going. I just wanted to let you know that everything's good here. You should get back to enjoying your vacation."

"I'll do that." Or, at least, I would as soon as I stopped worrying about things I couldn't control.

"I'll talk to you when you get back, Krissy," Vicki said. "And then you can tell me all about what's going on in the Village."

"Oh, I will. You're not going to believe the half of it."

"Knowing you, you're probably right."

We both laughed as we disconnected. Before I could set my phone down, the door opened, and Paul walked through, hands shoved deep into his pockets. He looked like a man who'd just been caught coming in after a late night at a bar. As soon as he saw me, his face flushed red.

"Hey," he said, eyes flickering past me, toward the empty living room. "Where's James?"

"In his office." I stood. "Have a good time?"

He shrugged, looked even more chagrined. "It was okay. Glad to be back." He removed Dad's keys and set them on the table before returning his hand to his pocket.

I narrowed my eyes at him. Something was up. "How's Detective McKensie?" I was fishing, but what else could it be?

Another shrug. "Dunno. Haven't seen her. Ah!" Relief washed over him as Dad exited his office and headed our way. "I need to borrow your dad for a moment," he told me before, "James, can we talk?"

"Of course," Dad said with a flourish and a bow. "Please, step into my office."

"Don't mind me," I said. "You can talk out here. I'm done with my calls, so you won't bother me."

"That's all right." Paul kissed me on the temple before crossing the room to where Dad waited. "This will take just a minute."

I opened my mouth to argue, but my phone buzzed in my hand.

"Go ahead and take that," Dad said. "Then we can

all find a nice place to eat and maybe catch a movie or something. Or we can grill out. We have everything for it now, so why not?"

"I could go for a burger," Paul said.

"Perfect," Dad said, then the two of them headed back to Dad's office to talk.

Without me.

With a frustrated sigh, I answered the call. "This is Krissy."

No response.

"Hello?" I glanced at the screen, noted the local number, and then put the phone back to my ear. "Is anyone there?"

More silence. I was about to hang up when there was a heavy sigh from the other end, followed by a groaned, "Yeah."

I know that voice. My senses immediately went on high alert. "Mickey?"

Another, "Yeah."

I waited a beat, then prodded him. "You called?"

I expected another "Yeah," but got a sigh instead.

I could have been annoyed, but I wasn't. Mickey Robbins calling me was a good sign. It meant he had something to say. About the murder? About Valerie? I had no idea, but I figured it had to be about one of those topics. Maybe both. His reluctance to speak, despite being the one who'd called, told me that whatever he had to say was a big deal.

"We should talk," he said after a couple of excruciatingly long seconds. "Face-to-face."

I glanced toward where Paul and Dad had gone. "When?"

"Now, if you can manage it."

Dad's keys were sitting on the table. I could be gone before anyone was the wiser.

Is that such a good idea, Krissy?

No, it wasn't. But I desperately wanted to know what Mickey had to say, and if I told Dad or Paul where I was going, they'd insist on coming. And if they came with me, chances were good that Mickey wouldn't talk. He'd called *me* for a reason.

"Where?" I asked.

"Do you know Village Park?"

"I do."

"I'll be there in five minutes, sitting on one of the benches." A pause, and then the all-too-dramatic, "Come alone," before he clicked off.

I didn't hesitate. I snatched up Dad's car keys and all but sprinted out the door.

As promised, Mickey Robbins was seated on one of the numerous benches in Village Park, picking at a pretzel from Walt's and tossing the chunks into the grass, though there were no squirrels or birds there to eat it. Another wrapped pretzel sat on the bench beside him. I assumed it was for me.

"Mickey," I said as I approached. I didn't sit right away. He appeared harmless with the pretzel in his hands, but he *was* a big guy. He could tear me up and toss me to the birds just as easily as he was doing to the baked dough.

"Hey." He scooted over even though there was more

than enough room for me. "I got you one. You don't have to eat it if you don't want to."

"Thank you." I picked up the pretzel and sat. "I'll save it."

He shrugged, kept his eyes forward. "Up to you."

"You wanted to talk?" I prodded after a few moments of watching him tear tiny pieces of the pretzel off. The ground was littered with chunks, telling me he'd been at it for a while—and he'd likely gone through more than one pretzel in the process.

"I talked to Valerie," he said, glancing at me side-eyed. "From what I gather, I have you to thank for that."

"It was no big deal," I said.

"Sure. Right." He sniffed, ran a hand across his nose. "It was good to hear her voice, but I realized . . ." He shook his head, brow furrowing. "She asked me about my past. That's another thing I have you to thank for."

"I wasn't trying to—"

He waved me off with one big hand before going back to destroying the pretzel. "It's fine. It was good to get it off my chest." He huffed, tossed what was left of the pretzel into the grass. "But I did want to clear the air with you. Don't know why, but I do."

"Okay?" I said, making it a question.

Mickey stared off into the distance for a long moment before he spoke. His voice was slow and measured, like a man reliving something he didn't want to. "I was just a kid. Maybe nineteen. Twenty. Hard to recall since I really don't want to remember it, if you get me?"

I nodded, let him continue.

"I was just getting into lifting, though I'd always been pretty big without it. Strong. You know, genetics." He chuckled. "Met a few guys about my age who were into the same thing. They had other interests I wasn't too keen on, but when you're young, you can overlook stuff like that. It's nice to have someone you can do things with, you know?"

I did. "I take it that it was one of those guys who died?"

His nod was slow, almost sad. "I don't know what happened, really. We were out at an hour when most smart people were tucked away in bed. But we were young and dumb." His jaw firmed. "I guess I still am."

"Mickey . . ."

He waved that big hand of his at me again. It took me a moment to realize it was the same one he'd injured punching the ice machine. "When you're that age, you take chances. You think you're invincible. I was that way back then, though I tended to be the quieter one of the crew." He laughed. "Imagine that, right?"

The sound of a skateboarder rolling by somewhere behind us caused him to fall silent until the sound of the wheels on the pavement faded away. Only then did he continue.

"We were messing around on top of some building. Well, the guys were, anyway. I'd gotten into a scuffle with one of them, a guy we called Scrat. I can't even remember how he got the name." He gazed off into the distance. When he continued, he was no longer speaking to me. "Scrat was all wiry. Could lift more than you'd expect for his size. Won a few bets at the gym because of it." He sighed. "Anyway, Scrat held his own against me when we fought, bloodied my nose and blackened my eye while I only managed to scrape his knuckle with my tooth."

"Then he ended up dead," I said, putting it together quickly. "And the police blamed you because of the fight."

"Yeah. He fell. I don't know how it happened, or if anyone was responsible for it. I was there, but I wasn't, if you know what I mean? I suppose I was pouting while the rest of them were having the time of their lives." Another sigh, this one heavier than the last. "One minute, Scrat was there, the next . . ." He snapped his fingers. "Gone."

I couldn't imagine, but I could take a guess about how he'd felt. "You didn't do it, but you felt responsible," I said.

"Yeah." Mickey sniffed, wiped his injured hand across his nose. "It never left me. I put up a wall, I guess, so that no one could see how badly it affected me. Never let it down, not until Valerie."

A squirrel finally took notice of the pretzel pieces and rushed over. It looked around the park, as if wondering how it had gotten so lucky, and started stuffing its cheeks.

"I screwed up," Mickey said, watching it. "With Valerie. With, well, everything. I tried hard to protect her, used my size and reputation to intimidate. It's the only way I know how to be." He tipped his head from side to side, cracking it. "But I didn't kill Lyle Carrigan. I want to make that clear. I didn't much like the guy, and I can't say I'm too broken up about his death, considering how he'd been treating my Val, but I didn't kill him."

"Do you know who did?" I asked.

Mickey flexed his fingers, as if wishing he still had a pretzel to tear into. "I don't know anything for sure," he said. "And because of my past, I don't want to talk to the police about it. They already think I got away with one murder, so what's to stop them from pinning me with this one? You know, make up for not nailing me for the last."

I doubted Detective McKensie would do such a thing, but telling him that wouldn't matter. "You could tell me," I said. "And I can talk to the police in your stead. I don't even have to use your name. I could tell them I'd heard it anonymously. And even if you don't know anything for sure, a rumor, even a *feeling*, could help." Though facts would be far more valuable to the police.

Mickey thought about it for a long time, fingers still flexing. Then he leaned toward me, face so close to mine, I could feel his breath on my cheek when he spoke.

"I think I saw who did it."

My heart did one of those little jumps. I wasn't sure what I'd expected him to say, but that wasn't it. "You saw it happen?"

Mickey cracked his neck again, did one of those shoulder rolls big guys always did in the movies. "No, but I saw someone outside Death by Java that night."

My mind was racing. "Lyle?"

Mickey shook his head. "I never saw him, which is

probably why I didn't say anything. That, and, well, you know."

"You didn't want to talk to the police," I said. "But why not tell Valerie who you saw? Or leave an anonymous message for the detective?"

He opened his mouth to respond, then closed it again. He did that a few times before making a frustrated sound. "I don't know," he admitted. "I suppose I was trying to protect Val."

"*Valerie* was there?" I just about bounced from the park bench.

"No, it wasn't Val. I thought it was at first, since who else would be hanging around outside Death by Java in the middle of the night? It was too late for her, anyway. It was too late for *me*, to be honest. I'm not as young as I once was."

None of us were. "Mickey," I said. The anticipation was killing me. "Who did you see that night?"

Both of his hands bunched into tight fists. When he spoke, he did so through clenched teeth. "Aaron," he said. "Valerie's ex-husband. He was standing outside Death by Java that night. And by the look of things, he was waiting for someone."

23

My phone rang as I was about to climb back into Dad's car.

"Hi, Dad," I said by way of answer. "Sorry I took off on you like that. Something came up."

"Where did you go?" There was a faint twinge of worry in his voice. "Paul and I came out of the office, and you were gone. *With* my car, I might add."

I debated on making up some story about needing to run to the store, but I changed my mind. I needed to talk to Aaron Middleton, and I didn't want to do it alone.

"Mickey Robbins called," I said. "He wanted me to meet him at Village Park."

A short pause before, "And you went alone?"

"It's a public place. He bought me a pretzel." As if that made my risky vanishing act okay. "He wanted to set the record straight about some rumors going around about him."

"Did he?"

I considered it. Mickey could easily have lied about his past, his involvement in his friend's death, but I didn't think so. "He did. And I don't think he killed Lyle Carrigan."

"Oh?" Genuine curiosity filled Dad's voice. "Then who did?"

I glanced at the pretzel I'd carried back to the car. It was resting in the passenger's seat, uneaten. It would be poor backup if and when I confronted Aaron about what Mickey had said about him.

But Dad . . .

"Is Paul still there?" I asked. "As in, within hearing distance?"

There was a faint *click* I took for a door closing. "He's in the living room. I told him I would call you and see where you'd run off to. I'm in my office now." A beat, and then, "What do you need me to do?"

"First off, don't tell Paul where I went."

"I won't," Dad agreed. "But *you* should when you see him next."

"I know. I will. But not yet." My mind was racing with possibilities. "Make up some story about why you need to leave. Your car broke down, and you need to meet me so we can wait for a tow truck, perhaps."

"He'll want to come," Dad said. "And it doesn't make much sense for me to meet you on foot if the car broke down."

"I don't know. Make up whatever you want," I said. "Just . . . don't let him come." I winced as I said it. I didn't think Paul would interfere with my plan to talk to Aaron, but he wouldn't be happy about it. And, just like with Mickey, I doubted Aaron would talk if a police officer, even one who didn't have jurisdiction in the Village, was listening to what he had to say.

No, this was something I needed to do, not quite alone, but without official backup.

"I'll come up with something," Dad said. "Where are we going?"

I almost told him, but I caught myself. I didn't think Dad would spill the beans, but telling him meant he'd be forced to lie to Paul's face when he was inevitably asked where we were headed. He was already stretching the truth as it was. No reason to make it worse.

"I'll tell you when I pick you up. I'll be waiting for you outside the Kemp house down the street in about five minutes."

"It might take me longer than that to wiggle my way out of here without raising suspicions."

"That's okay. I can wait."

I clicked off, mind whirling. I felt like I was getting close to learning who had killed Lyle, and the thrill of the chase was starting to take over. Yes, I knew what I was doing was risky. Yes, I knew I should simply call Detective McKensie and tell her everything Mickey had told me and let her handle it.

But if I was wrong, then I'd be wasting her valuable time, which, in turn, might allow the killer to escape. And it wasn't like I was going to go up to Aaron and demand he admit to killing Lyle. A few questions never hurt anyone, especially if I could couch them in questions about his relationship with Valerie.

I started the car and drove the short distance to Valerie's parents' house. I pulled up to the side of the road and parked, but I left the engine running. Dad wasn't there yet, so I sat back and chewed on the pretzel Mickey had bought me as I worked through what I knew.

Lyle was working with Marco, who wanted to move his place of business. He used someone at Tito's Deli to help sabotage the business, to create health violations he could then cite. The assumption was that he'd done the same at Death by Java. Somehow Lyle ended up dead. Because his coconspirator had turned on him? Because their plan was discovered? I didn't know.

But Aaron was waiting outside Death by Java on the night of the murder. That put him at the murder scene near the time of death. Even if he didn't kill Lyle, there was a chance that Aaron saw who did, even if he didn't realize it.

By the time Dad came speed-walking down the sidewalk, I was just about bouncing from my seat in anticipation of the conversation to come. I double-checked Aaron's address online, and then, as soon as Dad was strapped in, we were on the way.

"Okay, where are we going?" Dad asked.

"Aaron Middleton's," I said before explaining what Mickey had told me, along with my thought process afterward. "If he was waiting for Lyle, as Mickey believes, that means he might have killed him. If he was waiting for someone else, that person might be the killer. Either way, whatever Aaron has to say could tell us everything we need to know."

"What if whoever he was waiting for had nothing to do with it?" Dad asked.

"Then we might be able to dismiss them as a suspect," I said. "We'll just have to see what Aaron has to say for himself."

There were no cars in Aaron's driveway when we arrived, and the house looked empty. It wasn't until we pulled all the way up in front of the house that I saw a garage tucked under a low-hanging branch of a tree that looked like it was about to fall over. The garage door was up, revealing Aaron's car parked inside. It made me think that he'd either just gotten home, or he was about to leave. I parked behind his car in a way that effectively trapped him in, just in case he decided to make a run for it.

"What's the plan?" Dad asked before we got out.

"We're just going to have a casual conversation," I said. "I'll do the talking. You can be my backup."

"I'm the muscle, huh?" He lifted his upper lip, and then half-mumbled his words Rambo-like. "I can do that."

"I hope it doesn't come to a fight," I said, hiding my smile. "Or we're screwed."

"Very funny." His voice—and lip—returned to normal. "My strength lies in my wit."

I rolled my eyes as I climbed out of the car. "That'll help when Aaron's bench-pressing you with one hand."

"If he's laughing, it will."

The banter dried up as we approached Aaron's front door. The house was older, but well-maintained. I realized as I stepped up to the door that this could very well be the same house Valerie had lived in back when she and Aaron were married. It felt strange to be there, like I was treading upon her past, uninvited. It was possible he'd moved since they'd divorced, but it felt right for him to have remained in the same house, especially since he refused to let his love for her go. What better way to hold her close than to remain where her memory was the strongest?

I pressed the doorbell and stood back to wait. Dad stood sentry right behind me, arms folded behind his back, playing the part as my bodyguard. All that was missing were the sunglasses and black suit.

Aaron answered the door with a perplexed expression on his face. "Krissy?" He looked from me to Dad, and his confusion deepened. "What's going on?"

"Hi, Aaron. I'm sorry to barge in on you like this, but I'd like to talk."

He frowned. "I've got to leave for work in like"—he glanced at his watch—"ten minutes. Can it wait?"

"It's about Valerie," I said. And then, just to pique his curiosity, I added, "I've already talked to Hugh about what I found on her phone."

Aaron ran a hand over his mouth, eyes flickering between us, before he stepped aside. "I can spare fifteen minutes max, then I really need to go."

Dad and I entered the house. I wasn't sure what I'd expected, but I was surprised to find his home clean and moderately well-furnished. I wondered if the paintings on the walls and the semi-fancy furniture spread around the rooms was Valerie's doing, or if Aaron had more depth, more taste, than I gave him credit for.

He led us into an eat-in kitchen and motioned for us to sit. Without asking, he grabbed a trio of Cokes from the fridge and handed them out before he, too, sat, though he perched at the edge of his chair like he might up and bolt at any moment.

"What did Hugh say?" he asked. He tried to make it casual, but it came out strained, worried.

"You blocked Mickey's number on Valerie's phone," I said. "And vice versa."

He cracked open his can and took a drink before responding. "He told you all that?"

"I'd already found the number blocked on Valerie's phone," I said. "I pressed him about it, so don't blame him."

Aaron's nod was slow. "And he ratted on me."

It wasn't a question, but I spread my hands, as if saying, *I'm here, aren't I?* anyway.

Aaron eyed me for a long time, then seemed to make up his mind about something because he shrugged dismissively. "We had the opportunity, so we took it. No crime in that. You know how close Valerie and I used to be. Mickey's got her all tied up, and she doesn't realize what he's doing to her. Hugh and I just wanted to speed their downfall along, that's all."

"And then, once their relationship was over, the two of you would swoop in," I said.

Aaron's smile was chagrined. "Or at least try. You gotta understand, I made a mistake when I was younger. I'm still paying for it. But I've changed, I really have. Once Valerie sees it, she'll practically beg me to take her back. I won't have to force her or even convince her. I just have to be there for her when she needs me."

"But there's Hugh," I pointed out. "He cares for her

just as much as you do, and, like you, he's already been in a relationship with her."

"Yeah, but he was"—he gestured vaguely in the air— "a fling. Something different. You know, like you eat Rocky Road ice cream all the time, then you want to try plain old vanilla and see how it tastes. It's fine for a little while, but it's not what you really crave. Before long, you're back to your chunky, chocolaty comfort."

"What does that make Mickey?" Dad asked. When I glanced at him, he gave me a subtle shrug.

Aaron sighed, set aside his can. "Mickey's off-brand. He looks good when you see him in the store, sitting next to your old favorite, but he can't compete with the real thing."

I decided to move on from ice-cream terms and pushed in another direction. "Do you think Mickey killed Lyle?"

Aaron met my eyes. His gaze didn't waver when he said, "I do."

"Did you know Hugh and Valerie were there late the night before? They left a little after closing time."

"They do that," Aaron said, seemingly unbothered by the fact that his "competition" was spending late nights alone with his ex-wife.

"Do you know if they were there the night Lyle died?"

"How would I know that?" he asked. "I suppose they might have been. It's not like I'm keeping tabs on her."

"I don't know," I said, playing it cool. "Since you were there that night, I assumed you might have seen her or Hugh around."

His blink was slow and measured. "Where'd you hear that?" He reached for his Coke, then pulled his hand back without grabbing it. His leg started jigging up and down beneath the table. When neither Dad nor I answered, he said, "There's nothing wrong with being there. It's not like I know anything."

"So, you *were* there?" I asked.

He reached out again, this time picking up his Coke. When he took a drink, I noted his hand was shaking.

"Aaron," I said, "if you saw something that night, you should tell someone. Even if you don't think it's important, it might be. And if you and Lyle got into a fight—"

"We didn't," he said, cutting in with a sharp shake of his head. "I never saw Lyle, didn't know he was going to be there. I . . ." He squeezed his eyes closed, his entire body tensing. "Don't tell Valerie." When he opened his eyes, he looked worried. "Please. I'll explain everything. Just . . . don't tell her, okay?"

I mimed crossing my heart, but I didn't verbally agree. If Aaron's actions had somehow caused Lyle's death, the police would need to know, which would mean Valerie would eventually find out, no matter what I promised him.

Aaron swallowed hard, causing his Adam's apple to bob. He considered me, then Dad, then seemed to come to some sort of decision because his entire body sagged.

"I was looking for someone else that night."

"Who?"

"A girl. Doesn't matter who. We've been seeing each other off and on for about three months now. Nothing serious. She was supposed to stop by here late that night, but she called off at the last minute. Said she had something she needed to do. I kept pressing her since, like, what could she possibly have to do so late at night? She let slip she had to stop by Death by Java. I decided to wait for her there in the hopes I could, you know, change her mind about stopping by my place."

I glanced over at Dad, who was keeping his face carefully blank.

"Look," Aaron said, scooting even farther to the edge of his chair. "Valerie and me aren't together. There's nothing wrong with having a little fun on the side while I wait for her to see reason."

"You don't think that it might upset her to find out you were seeing someone else behind her back?" I asked.

Aaron scowled. "It would, which is why I didn't tell her. And since it hits so close to home, it would make it worse for everyone."

Hit close to home? At first, I had the wild thought that he was running around with Valerie's *mother* behind her back. And then realization dawned.

"She works at Death by Java."

He winced as if I'd struck him. It was all the answer I needed.

Aaron was sleeping with one of Valerie's employees without Valerie's knowledge. And as if that wasn't bad enough, I had the feeling that this same employee was the person Lyle had enlisted to help him sabotage Death by Java. Why else would she have "something to do" at the bookstore café so late at night when no one else would be there?

"Who is she?" I asked.

"I'm not going to tell you that," Aaron said. "That's between us. And if Valerie *does* find out about us, she'll fire her." He frowned. "Or she will if she hasn't already."

"What do you mean?"

Aaron stood up, paced away. "I'm sorry. I need to get to work. You should go."

Dad and I rose. I didn't want to leave, but what choice did I have?

Aaron walked us to the door, looking for all the world like someone torn between talking and keeping his secrets. His brow was furrowed in thought, and his fists kept clenching and unclenching. He held the door open for us, but he didn't close it in our faces the moment we were outside, which gave me a chance to ask him one last time.

"Why do you think Valerie might have already fired someone?"

Aaron wordlessly stepped outside and locked the front door. He removed his car keys from his pocket and urged Dad and me along beside him as he walked toward his garage. We were halfway there when he finally spoke.

"I'm probably worried for no reason," he said. "We've all been under a lot of stress lately, so it's understandable why she might want to take a few days off." He tried on a smile that didn't reach his eyes. "Forget I said anything. Now, if you would move your car, I really do need to get going."

Dad started for the passenger's seat, but I handed him his keys and took it instead. I was too distracted to drive. I was mentally going over the list of employees at Death by Java and when I'd last seen them. Farrah was there most days, so she wasn't Aaron's girlfriend or fling or whatever you wanted to call her. Dee had called off a few times recently, but she'd been there earlier that very day, fussing over Oscar.

But Nadia . . .

Thinking back, I realized I hadn't seen her since Lyle's murder.

Nadia was the mole.

If she'd been working with Lyle Carrigan to sabotage Death by Java, she might know why he was murdered. And I suspected, due to her sudden disappearing act, she might also know who was the one who had done it.

24

The phone rang and went to voicemail.

"Come on, Valerie," I muttered, dialing again. Once more, it went straight to voicemail. It made me wonder if Hugh had gotten ahold of Valerie's phone and blocked me in retaliation for my interference with his plan to break her and Mickey up.

I'd tried to find Nadia's address online, but it was kind of hard to do when all I had was a first name and place of employment. Same went for a phone number. But Valerie would know. If I could ever reach her.

"Death by Java?" Dad asked, though we were already heading that way. I'd tried to call there first, but, like with Valerie's cell, no one had answered.

I gave him a sharp nod, and we were soon parking out front of the bookstore café. "I'll be right back," I said as I got out. "Keep the car running."

I was anxious to talk to Nadia, so much so I was half-convinced that if I didn't talk to her *right now*, someone else might die or the killer would escape.

I barreled my way through the front door, noted the handful of people scattered around the room sipping coffee, and went straight to the counter, where Valerie was standing, talking to a man with his back to me. I didn't so much as pay him a glance as I stepped up beside him.

"I need Nadia's address," I blurted before realizing I was being rude. "Sorry to butt in like this, but it's import—" My eyes widened. "Marco?"

He didn't quite sneer at me, but it was close. "Go right ahead. Say what you have to say. I think I'm done here anyway." He shot Valerie a dirty look before he turned and walked out the door.

"What was that about?" I asked her.

Valerie stared after him a couple seconds more before saying, "He tried to buy me out." She shook her head. "I can't believe he thought I was trying to sell. Although . . ." Her expression turned thoughtful.

"You might sell Death by Java?"

She shrugged. "It's not like it's been going great. Maybe things will turn around. But if they don't, I might as well keep my options open." She turned her focus fully on me. "Now, what's this about Nadia?"

"I need to see her," I said. "And as soon as possible."

Valerie pulled a face, like she couldn't fathom why I'd want to talk to one of her employees. "Why are you looking for Nadia?"

"She hasn't been at work for the last few days."

"You think I haven't noticed that?" Followed by a patented Valerie eye roll. "She's kind of left me hanging. Right in the middle of a crisis, no less."

"I know. And I think I know why she's called off."

Valerie's hands went to her hips. "Care to share?"

"I . . ." Did I want to tell her? If I was wrong and Nadia had nothing to do with what had happened with Lyle, I could be getting her into trouble for nothing. Her relationship with Aaron was beside the point, though I did think it was something Valerie should know about if she was considering going back to Aaron. Things could get messy real fast.

I was saved from having to come up with an excuse when, "I know where she lives," came from behind me.

I turned to find Dee standing by one of the bookshelves, Oscar lying on the floor next to her. The cat was eyeing me distrustfully, though he was making biscuits in the air near Dee's heel, telling me he was in a good mood, despite what his face implied.

"Sorry," I told Valerie as I started Dee's way. "I'll fill you in later."

Valerie huffed and muttered, "Whatever," before vanishing into the back.

I joined Dee, careful not to disturb—or get too close to—Oscar. "Thanks. I really do need to talk to Nadia."

"Is she in trouble?" Dee asked.

Was she? I had no idea how to answer that. "I'm not sure," I said. "That's why I need to see her."

Dee considered that a moment and then seemed to come to a decision. "It's probably better if I don't know the details, especially with everything that's happened lately." She rattled off Nadia's address. "I don't have her number, or I'd give you that too. I only know where she lives because I gave her a ride home once when her car broke down. We're not close."

"It's all right," I said, repeating the address over and over in my head so I wouldn't forget it. "Thank you so much, Dee."

"No problem. You've helped Oscar and me, so I felt like I should return the favor."

I hurried back to the car. Dad was waiting right where I'd left him, and by the time I was seated and strapped in, he was already pulling out onto the road. I told him the address, and then sat back, shaking ever so slightly from the exhilaration of it all.

"Should we call the police?" Dad asked once we were moving in the right direction.

"Probably," I admitted. "But not yet. I want to see what Nadia has to say before we call." I didn't think Nadia had killed Lyle, so I wasn't worried about her coming after me. But I did think she had information, and I didn't want to spook her by having the police show up on her doorstep unannounced.

I was a nervous ball of energy by the time we pulled up in front of a complex of two-story apartments with outdoor entrances. From the outside, they weren't terribly appealing. Most of the rooftops had an aged look to them that warned of impending leaks. And they all were a beige color that made them appear dirtier than they actually were.

"She's in that one," I said, pointing.

Dad parked in front of the indicated building. "I've heard questionable things about the ownership here," he said. "*This* is the sort of place a health inspector should frequent."

From what I'd seen thus far, I tended to agree. "Maybe you should wait—"

He shut off the engine and popped open his door. "Not a chance."

I didn't argue. I got out of the car and took the lead as we headed for the set of stairs that led up to Nadia's apartment. They were old, made of questionably sturdy wood, and looked like they were a good stomp away from collapse. Still, I pounded up them like my life depended on it, reached the small, deck-like structure that served as Nadia's stoop, and knocked.

When no one answered, I knocked again, this time adding my voice. "Nadia. It's Krissy Hancock. Valerie's friend." It still didn't roll right off my tongue the way I'd intended, but I let it go. "I just want to talk to you for a few minutes, and then I'll go away."

"Maybe she's not home," Dad said.

A creak from inside said otherwise, so I knocked harder. "Nadia, please."

"All right, all right. Don't beat the door down. Sheesh." The door opened, and there she was, looking, to be frank, awful. Gone was the gum-popping, pink-dressed girl from Death by Java. In her place was a woman wearing gray sweats and a torn T-shirt that hung loosely from one bare shoulder. It might have been cute if it wasn't for her matching gray pallor. "Come on in, I guess." She started to step aside, but stopped. "Who's that?"

"That's my dad," I said. "Ignore him."

"Howdy." Dad gave her an aw-shucks wave and smile.

Nadia pulled the tattered sleeve of her shirt up onto her shoulder, but there was nothing to keep it from sliding right back down. She let me and Dad in her apartment before hastily closing the door behind us.

"I don't know why you're here," she said. "But if it's because Ms. Kemp sent you, you can tell her that I'm getting better and I'll be back to work soon."

"You're sick?" I asked, glancing around the apartment. The furnishings were sparse, but nice enough. The TV was on and muted. A box of Kleenex sat on the coffee table, with a balled-up tissue sitting beside that.

There was a slight hesitation to Nadia's response. "Yeah. Sure." Nadia walked past me and resumed her place on the couch. She picked up the tissue and dabbed at a nose that looked dry, though her eyes were red-rimmed and worried.

"Nadia," I said, motioning for Dad to follow me into the living room, where she was seated. "I talked to Aaron."

She blinked at me. "Okay, so?"

"He said you two were . . ." I didn't know how to finish without sounding rude, so I just waved my hand vaguely toward her.

That earned me a massive eye roll. "Banging? People do that sort of thing."

Dad snorted from behind me.

I ignored him. "You know he used to be married to Valerie, right?"

"Duh." Another eye roll. "I'm not stupid, you know. But they aren't together now, and it's not like I plan on moving in with him or anything." She seemed to relax. "If that's what this is about, you can go. I don't have to talk about my relationships with you."

"No, you don't, but—"

"You know"—Nadia stood—"I think you *should* go. I shouldn't have let you in."

"Aaron—"

"Is none of your business." She crossed her arms and tapped a bare foot. "I asked you to leave. Don't make me call the super."

I imagined a man with sparse, slicked-back hair, with a thick golden chain around his neck hanging down into an open shirt sprouting with chest hair, then dismissed the thought. "I—"

"May I use your restroom?" Dad asked, cutting in. "I really do hate to impose on you like this, but . . ." He rested a hand on his belly. "I am lactose intolerant, and I made the mistake of grabbing a milkshake before we came over. The bloating is killing me, and if I don't relieve it soon . . ."

"Okay, ew." Nadia's already-pale complexion tinged green. "First door on your left. Make it quick. And, like, use the spray when you're done. It's sitting on the back of the toilet."

"Thank you." Dad shot me a wink that only I could see before waddling down the hall like he was, indeed, about to explode.

We both watched him go before turning to face one another.

"Nadia," I said, putting on my kindest, gentlest voice, "I didn't come here about Aaron."

She blinked at me. "Okay?"

"You were at Death by Java on the night of Lyle Carrigan's death."

Nadia sucked in a breath, hand going to her chest. "I . . . I don't know what you're talking about."

"Lyle and Marco Rossi were working together," I said. "They were trying to get Death by Java and Tito's

Deli closed so that Marco could move the Italian Roll to the new, better location."

"Why are you telling me this?" she asked, though by the way her eyes darted around the room, I could tell that she knew exactly why I was saying it.

I pressed on. "Tito told me he had to fire one of his employees because health violations kept cropping up every time that employee worked a shift. Once the employee was gone, the violations stopped."

Nadia took a step back. "Really. I don't know—"

"You were working with Lyle," I said, cutting her off. "You were sabotaging Death by Java for him."

I expected another denial, but Nadia's expression hardened. "So? It's not like I'd be missing much if the place closed. Look at this place." She flung a hand toward her sparse furnishings. "I can hardly afford a pizza with what Ms. Kemp is paying me."

"What happened?" I asked, keeping my voice steady despite how my nerves were jumping. "That night. You told Aaron you had something to do at Death by Java, which is why he was waiting for you there."

She sighed. "I was dumb. I didn't mean to let it slip."

"But you did. Did he catch you meeting with Lyle?"

"What? No. Aaron left before Lyle showed up, I made sure of it." Her look of defiance started to waver. "But when Lyle did get there, he was . . . different."

"Different how?"

Down the hall, the door cracked open ever so slightly, telling me that Dad was listening to everything we were saying. Good.

"He . . ." She frowned. "He didn't want to do it. I

never sabotaged anything. All I was supposed to do was unlock the door and let Lyle in when he showed up. He'd do his thing, I would lock up, and that would be that. I mean, the night before he died, he was fine."

A light bulb clicked on in my head. The night when Laura and I had seen the light on in the back, Lyle was sabotaging the ice machine so he could show up the next morning and cite Valerie for it.

"He promised no one would get hurt," Nadia went on. "And that I wouldn't get into trouble because no one else would know about it. Then, when Death by Java closed, Marco would give me a job at a higher wage than what Ms. Kemp was paying me. I could move out of this apartment, get a real place, and stop having to scrape by."

"What happened that night, Nadia?" I asked. "When Lyle died?"

"I don't know!" she all but wailed. "He showed up, and I unlocked the alleyway door for him like I always did. He was already acting weird when he got there, and as soon as the door was open, he changed his mind about the whole thing. He told me to go home, that he'd take care of everything. He apologized to me, said that he was sorry he'd dragged me into it. I wasn't sure what to think, so I just left him there. I didn't know someone would come in and *kill* him!" Tears formed in her eyes.

"Did you see anyone else there that night, other than Aaron?" I asked. "Tito from next door? Valerie? Mickey? *Anyone?*"

She shook her head. "It was just the two of us." A

pause. "Wait. When I was leaving, I heard him making a call." Her eyes met mine. "He called Marco."

Before I could press her about that, the front door of Nadia's apartment opened, and Marco Rossi entered. "I think that's enough, Nadia," he said, closing the door behind him with a *click*. He then turned the dead bolt before flashing a smile void of humor onto me. "You are a very annoying pest, aren't you?"

"Marco, I—"

"No, no. No more talk. Move over there, please." He motioned toward the couch, where Nadia had already retreated to. When I didn't move, the smile vanished. "Now."

There was such menace in his voice, I complied.

Marco stepped farther into the room, took a moment to look around. "Just us, then?" When neither Nadia nor I responded, he nodded. "Good. I really wish it hadn't come to this, but here we are. I'd hoped that this whole thing would blow over, and it would have, but *you*"—his eyes met mine—"just had to keep asking questions." He sighed, moved his hand to the small of his back, where I assumed he had a gun.

My mind was racing. It took every ounce of will-power not to look down the hall toward the bathroom, where Dad had gone. If there was any way out of this situation, it was going to be through him.

But I needed to buy time. The best way to do that? With my mouth.

"You killed Lyle Carrigan," I said. "Why? He was working for you, helping you."

Marco's face contorted, and for a moment, I thought

he might whip out the gun and shoot me right then and there. After a moment, his features eased, though his smile didn't return. "He was, but then he got cold feet, thanks to Tito firing his other assistant. Lyle was afraid Tito had discovered what was happening and that he'd tell someone. He was afraid he'd lose his job, his reputation." He scoffed. "Coward."

"But why kill him?" I pressed. "If he was so afraid of getting caught, you could have let him go, found someone else."

"Who?" Marco asked. "No one else at the health department would have helped me. And if the citations stopped, then what would force Valerie Kemp's hand?" He shook his head. "I had to. When Lyle called that night, he told me that he was done, that he couldn't do it anymore. I couldn't let that stand, not when we were so close. I convinced him to wait for me so we could talk about it. He agreed. But when I got there, he refused to see reason, went so far as to say he was thinking about turning himself in. Can you imagine? Ruining his life, for what? Morals?" Marco all but spat the words.

Nadia sank down onto the couch, trembling so hard, she appeared close to falling apart.

"So you killed him," I said.

"What else was I supposed to do?" Marco said. "If he turned himself in, it would implicate me in his crimes. He'd only lose his job. I'd lose my business. I couldn't let that happen." He took a trembling breath. "I tried to make him understand that he couldn't walk away, that if he did, it would ruin both our lives, but he wouldn't listen. I grabbed him, tried to shake some

sense into him. And then . . ." He met my eyes. "I didn't
do it on purpose. I let him go, but he was off balance.
He fell. I don't know what happened. Maybe it was
shock. Maybe he hit his head just right. I don't know,
but whatever it was, the next thing I knew, he was lying
there, dead, in the horrible back room of that bookstore
café."

"You could have called an ambulance," I said. "They
might have been able to save him."

Marco laughed. "Why would I do that? They save
him and then he tells everyone what happened? I'd be
even worse off than before." He paced one way, then
the next. "I realized that I could take advantage of the
situation, so I left him there, figuring that the police
would have to shut the place down. I grabbed his
tablet, since I didn't know what he kept on it, and went
to leave." His expression darkened. "And I very nearly
ended up like Lyle because of that beast they let wan-
der the store."

"Oscar?" I asked.

"It came out of nowhere. Darted right between my
feet, and I nearly fell. I dropped Lyle's tablet, and it
bounced off somewhere in the dark. I would have looked
for it, but I had made enough noise, I was afraid someone had heard, so I left it before I was caught."

I could feel the shift as much as see it. A sort of
calm washed over Marco as he leveled his gaze on
Nadia and me. "I would have let everything play out as
it would, but when you showed up, asking about Nadia,
I knew I had to get rid of her before you had a chance
to talk to her. It took me longer than I liked to find out

where she lived, so here we are." His hand moved from the small of his back. In it, he held the gun that moments before had only been speculation. "Sit."

"Marco—"

"*Sit!*" His hand jerked up. "No more talk."

I started to ease down onto the couch, just as the world exploded with the sound of a machine gun.

I dropped flat to the floor, thinking that Marco had opened fire, though how that little gun of his could have made such a racket, I had no idea. Beside me, Nadia was screaming, hands covering her head. Across the room, Marco had likewise dropped to the floor, cursing up a storm.

And down the hall, running toward us like a half-mad bull, was Dad.

I missed most of what happened. There was the sound of the machine gun, *rat-a-tatt*ing throughout Nadia's apartment. Nadia's screams and the subsequent ringing in my ears as I tried to make sense of what was going on.

Dad flew down the hall and collided with Marco, who'd just started to rise from where he'd fallen. There was the sound of a scuffle, then a meaty *thump*. My heart lurched, and I scrambled to my feet, thinking I'd help Dad, but the fight was already over.

Dad had Marco pinned face down on the floor, arms bent behind his back in a way that had to hurt. A welt was growing on the side of Marco's head, and he had a dazed look in his eye, telling me he'd been struck pretty hard. There were no bullet holes anywhere.

Dad had his cell phone held high over his head. He

thumbed a button, and the machine gun sounds ceased before he brought the device to his ear. "Sorry about the noise, Detective. Suspect is subdued. We'll be waiting for your arrival." He clicked off and tightened his grip on Marco's wrists before glancing at me. "You should unlock the door, Buttercup. Detective McKensie should be here any moment."

25

The *clink* of forks on plates and the low murmur of voices filled the room. I sat across the table from Dad, with Laura to one side of me, Paul on the other. The place where we were eating was expensive and a vastly different experience from anywhere we'd been since Paul and I had arrived in Redwood Village.

But that was okay. It was a nice change, considering what I'd been through.

Marco Rossi was behind bars. The Italian Roll was closed. Death by Java and Tito's Deli were still open, though I wasn't sure how much longer the former would remain so. Last I'd heard, Valerie was still struggling to generate business and was considering selling to the highest bidder.

It was kind of ironic to think that if Marco had just been patient, he could have purchased the place and been moved in by the end of next month, not that I would have seen it. Paul and I were due to return to Pine Hills tomorrow. I would miss Dad and Laura, but

I was anxious to get back home. I longed to see Misfit. Rita. Death by Coffee. Jules and Lance and Vicki and everyone and everything else.

Our impending flight seemed to be weighing on everyone around the table, Paul included. There wasn't a lot of chatter, just light talk here and there as we ate. Every few minutes, Dad looked over at Laura, who smiled at him before glancing at me. Paul kept his eyes on his plate, seemingly preoccupied. I couldn't help but wonder if he was sad about leaving or if he was still mad at me for chasing after a killer and very nearly getting myself shot. To say he was upset when I'd first told him was an understatement of gargantuan proportions.

"This is nice," I said, hoping to break the tension.

"It is," Dad agreed.

Paul flashed a smile, went back to his food.

"Didn't you already talk to the detective?" Laura asked, her voice dropping to a near-whisper.

"I did." I noted her frown, sat up straighter. "Why?"

She didn't have to answer because a moment later, a shadow fell over me, and there she was, Detective Gabby McKensie, dressed in her usual attire, though she appeared somewhat rumpled around the edges, like she hadn't been getting much sleep.

"I'm sorry to interrupt," she said.

"No, no, please, pull up a seat." Dad motioned toward an empty chair at a nearby table.

"That's all right. I'm not staying." McKensie turned to me. "I was passing by and saw you through the window." Was that a lie I detected in her voice? Hard to say, but we *were* close to the windows, so it was possible. "I thought you'd like to know that he confessed."

"Marco?" I asked, though who else could she be talking about?

She nodded with a tight smile. "He didn't try to deny anything. Considering I'd already heard most of it when your father called me, faint as it was, there wasn't much *to* deny." She looked to Dad. "Smart thinking, by the way."

"I have my moments."

She grunted, turned back to me. "It also helped that I had Ms. Pearson's statement. When confronted with that, Mr. Rossi folded without much of a whimper."

It took me a moment to realize Ms. Pearson was Nadia.

McKensie rubbed at the back of her neck with a frown. "This whole mess might have been avoided if people would just *talk*. Even after the murder, if just one of the people involved had come forward, we could have had Marco locked away days ago." She sighed. "I spent days thinking that handyman—"

"Roman," I supplied.

"—was involved because of that screwdriver we found at the scene, but nope, he had nothing to do with it. He said he'd been with Ms. Kemp and had dropped it, though from what everyone else has said, that appears to be mostly a lie." Frustration tinged her tone.

I wasn't surprised. If Nadia had come forward right away, McKensie could have zeroed in on Marco, and I could have enjoyed my vacation. I wouldn't have rocked the boat when it came to Valerie and Mickey and Aaron and Hugh, though I suppose that ended up for the best.

The truth was out, and the lot of them could work things out on their own.

But still . . .

"What about Nadia?" Dad asked. "Ms. Pearson. Is she in trouble?"

McKensie thought about it a moment before answering. "She's out of a job, but she didn't do anything that would get her into trouble with the law. I mean, I'm sure we could charge her with something, but we won't. I expect it will take time for her to repair her reputation and find a new job, but she'll pull through eventually."

That was good to hear. As much as I didn't approve of what she'd done, Nadia didn't deserve to be thrown in jail for it. Or turned into a social pariah, for that matter.

"Was there anything useful on Lyle's tablet?" I asked, curious more than anything. "More than just his usual work notes and reports?"

McKensie nodded. "There was. I'm not at liberty to say what, but let's just say that even if Marco hadn't confessed, there was enough there to put him in a bad way. Let's call it the icing on the cake."

That was good, though, once again, it served as a point of frustration. If Tito had turned in the tablet the moment he'd found it, then, once again, the detective could have been talking to Marco right away instead of chasing other, false leads.

"Anyway, that's all I came in here to say." Detective McKensie clapped her hands together, drawing a few curious eyes. "I hope you don't take it the wrong way, but I hope to never see you again." The smile on her face said otherwise.

"I'm pretty sure we all feel the same," Dad said.

And then, with a farewell wave and a final, lingering glance at Paul, Detective McKensie walked away.

"That was nice to hear," Dad said when she was gone. "I'd like to point out that she didn't yell at us for our part in what happened."

"The two of you are lucky you didn't get yourselves hurt—or killed," Laura said. "The next time Krissy is in town, I'm not going to let either of you out of my sight."

"That might help," Dad said. "We could always use a lookout. Isn't that right, Buttercup?"

Laura nudged him with an elbow, but I barely noticed. I was focused on Paul, who checked his watch as if impatient to be gone before he resumed silently staring at his food.

"I'm all right," I said, reaching out and touching his hand. He didn't pull away, but he did flinch, as if I'd startled him. "I should have told you what I was going to do, but you know how I am."

"I do," he said with the ghost of a smile. "Impulsive."

"And reckless," I added. "I didn't mean to scare you." Our eyes met briefly before he went back to his meal. I decided to let it go and changed the subject. "I forgot to tell you, but Oscar found his forever home."

"That's the cat, right?" Dad asked.

"The one at Death by Java, yeah. Dee was taking care of him as best as she could, but it was hard to do with him living at the bookstore café."

"That was nice of her," Laura said. "Not everyone is willing to do that."

No, they weren't. "I called her landlord the other day," I said. "They normally don't allow pets in the apartments, but after a little convincing on my part, he changed his mind." I grinned. "Oscar is now living with Dee."

"That's great!" Dad said. "Good for you. And her. *And* the kitty."

It was. It had taken some doing, too. The landlord had argued against it, but when offered an extra deposit for any prospective damages, he acquiesced. Dee didn't know about that part, and if I had my way, she never would.

Paul checked his watch again, then cleared his throat loud enough that I could have heard him from across the room.

"I've got to hit the restroom," Dad said, abruptly standing. "No fictional gastrointestinal distress this time, but I think my teeth are about to float away."

"Really?" Laura said, rising to her feet beside him. "You could have kept that last part to yourself."

"Where's the fun in that?" Dad winked at me. "I'll be back soon." He took Laura's arm. "Unless Laura has other uses for me while we're back there, that is."

"Stop it," she said with a laugh, but she didn't release his arm as they walked away, toward the restrooms in the corner.

I watched them go with a frown. "That was weird. I really hope the two of them don't—" Whatever I'd been about to say was obliterated from my head as I turned around. Paul was no longer seated next to me. He wasn't standing, either.

"Krissy Hancock," he said from where he knelt next to my chair, eyes glittering in the overhead lights. My entire universe narrowed down to the small black box he was holding in his hand. With a smooth movement, he opened the lid, revealing a ring that sparkled even brighter than his eyes. "Will you marry me?"

Time stopped. Everything made so much sense now. His nervousness. His sudden departures over the last few days. The secrecy. My heart didn't beat; no air passed through my lungs. I couldn't speak, couldn't even think. It was as if that one single second took an eon to complete.

And when it did, it ended with a single, resounding word.

"Yes."

Visit our website at
KensingtonBooks.com
to sign up for our newsletters, read
more from your favorite authors, see
books by series, view reading group
guides, and more!

Become a Part of Our
Between the Chapters Book Club
Community and Join the Conversation